INDEPENDENCE DAY
RESURGENCE

P9-CSV-930

DON'T MISS A SINGLE PART OF THE
INDEPENDENCE DAY SAGA

The Complete Independence Day Omnibus
by Dean Devlin & Roland Emmerich,
and Steven Molstad

Independence Day: Crucible
by Greg Keyes

Independence Day Resurgence by Alex Irvine

The Art & Making Of Independence Day Resurgence

Independence Day: Dark Fathom
graphic novel by Victor Gischler and Steve Scott, Rodney
Ramos, Alex Shibao, and Tazio Bettin

Independence Day: The Original Movie Adaptation
graphic novel

OTHER NOVELS BY ALEX IRVINE

Dawn Of The Planet Of The Apes
Pacific Rim
Batman: Arkham Knight – The Riddler's Gambit
Iron Man: Virus
Transformers: Exiles

INDEPENDENCE DAY
RESURGENCE

NOVELIZATION BY ALEX IRVINE

BASED ON THE SCREENPLAY BY
NICOLAS WRIGHT & JAMES A. WOODS
AND DEAN DEVLIN & ROLAND EMMERICH
AND JAMES VANDERBILT AND THE STORY BY
DEAN DEVLIN & ROLAND EMMERICH AND
NICOLAS WRIGHT & JAMES A. WOODS,
BASED ON CHARACTERS CREATED BY
DEAN DEVLIN & ROLAND EMMERICH

TITAN BOOKS

Independence Day Resurgence™ – The Official Movie Novelization
Print edition ISBN: 9781785651311
E-book edition ISBN: 9781785651366

Published by Titan Books
A division of Titan Publishing Group Ltd
144 Southwark Street, London SE1 0UP

First edition: June 2016
10 9 8 7 6 5 4 3 2 1

This is a work of fiction. Names, characters, places, and incidents either
are the product of the author's imagination or are used fictitiously,
and any resemblance to actual persons, living or dead, business
establishments, events, or locales is entirely coincidental. The publisher
does not have any control over and does not assume any responsibility
for author or third-party web sites or their content.

TM & © 2016 Twentieth Century Fox Film Corporation.
All rights reserved.

No part of this publication may be reproduced, stored in a retrieval
system, or transmitted, in any form or by any means without prior
written permission of the publisher, nor be otherwise circulated in any
form of binding or cover other than that in which it is published and
without a similar condition being imposed on the subsequent purchaser.

A CIP catalogue record for this title is available from the British Library.

Printed and bound in the United States.

To Violet Sue, born on New Year's Eve

PROLOGUE

Valeri Fedorov had grown up with his eyes on the stars.

As a boy he had studied the history of space exploration while his friends were playing hockey and soccer. As a young man he had studied engineering and joined the Russian Air Force, distinguishing himself as a pilot and studying at night to prepare himself for applying to become a cosmonaut. His hero was Yuri Gagarin, and when he had felt the crush of liftoff for the first time in 2011, he felt like he was fulfilling Gagarin's dreams, as well as his own.

Now, five years later, he was on Rhea, one of Saturn's moons, and as far from Earth as any human being had ever been… but instead of flying, he was trudging across the moon's hostile surface toward an electrical substation, trying to figure out why the power in the command center kept going out.

As he walked, Valeri surveyed the landscape, looking for any sign of something that might have caused the outage. There were no recent meteor impacts. The base was built along the lip of a giant crater, and the crater walls showed no sign of recent slides or collapses. At first they had suspected damage to some of the equipment from a micrometeorite, but unless it was really very small it would have registered on the base seismometers. Thus he would have to abandon that theory and inspect the equipment to see what it might tell him.

They had emergency power from shielded generators, but that wasn't enough to keep all the lights on, and it sure as hell wasn't enough to keep the Rhea station warm. So Valeri and his crew, another dozen cosmonauts with bruised dreams and bruised knuckles just like him, were out in the near vacuum of Rhea's surface, freezing their asses off and trying to get the lights back on.

There had been several strange power surges of unknown origin over the past few days, perhaps related to Saturn's electromagnetic sheath, or maybe a passing wave of particles from the sun. Valeri didn't know. It wasn't his job to know. He wasn't a scientist. He was a trained pilot and engineer, a cosmonaut, reminded that most of space exploration was far from glorious. It was hard work, turning wrenches and fixing machines constantly under assault from the extremes of vacuum and cold.

Despite all that, Valeri loved it.

He had a girlfriend back on Earth, and someday he would settle down with her, but today he was building humankind's dream of space... and keeping the human race safe from a repeat of what had happened in 1996.

Valeri had been just a boy then, still spending all his time playing hockey and fishing, and then at night looking up at the stars. The aliens had destroyed Moscow, Kiev, and St. Petersburg, but they had not reached Petropavlovsk when their mother ship was destroyed. Because of that, Valeri was alive to go to space and curse the balky machinery here on Rhea.

The power surges were making his life hell and slowing down the construction of the Earth Space Defense base they were supposed to be building.

"You on vacation out there?" one of the techs radioed from inside.

"Shut up," Valeri said. He didn't have much patience for people sitting inside where there were air and survivable temperatures, complaining about the pace of work on the moon's surface. At least Valeri and his team didn't have it as hard as the construction crew working on the base itself. The cranes and arc welders had their own fuel cells, so power interruptions didn't give them any time off. The welders sparked now as a crew member held a ten-meter-long steel beam in place, extending the base's frame toward what would be its final shape.

The armaments were still in transit from Earth. When the base was complete, the Earth Space Defense force would reach to Saturn. Heavy gun turrets engineered from alien technology would ring the base, making Saturn the outermost point in the defense architecture. Other bases were under construction on Mars and on one of Jupiter's moons. Valeri couldn't remember which one. Jupiter had too many damn moons.

Rhea's minimal gravity made it easy to move once you had the hang of how to jump and control your landings without losing your balance. Valeri had figured it out during his first posting off Earth, back on the Moon. Rhea's gravity was so light you could practically throw a rock over its horizon. He'd had to adopt a sort of slow-motion walk, not trying to jump, because each normal step would launch your body into a slow arc that could cover tens of meters.

He reached the substation and opened an electrical panel. He saw a lot of black streaks and knew immediately what the issue was.

"I found the problem," he said. "The power surges blew out most of the fuses." The substations were supposed to be shielded, but apparently their protection wasn't as good as the thirty centimeters of lead that sheathed the emergency generators.

"Get the heat back on before we freeze to death," the tech responded. "This is worse than Siberia."

Siberia was nice in the summer, Valeri thought. He had gone fishing there a few times before joining the cosmonaut corps. Maybe when he rotated back to Earth, he would take a trip there again. The lakes, the endless forests... a marked contrast from what he was looking at out here.

He had to take off the whole panel to replace the fuses. Where was his wrench? He'd had it a minute ago. Ah. There it was, on the ground.

Must have dropped it, he thought. As he picked it up, though, Valeri noticed a strange phenomenon. Tiny particles of ice floated up from the surface, drifting higher. Like a slow motion reverse snowstorm.

It wasn't unusual for small vibrations to kick up little mini-storms like this. A passing vehicle or a launch shook up the surface for a radius of several kilometers—but there was nothing like that going on at the moment. Feeling a strange sensation, Valeri turned in a slow circle to make sure. The only thing he saw was the welding crew, levering another beam into place. That shouldn't have caused this, and it certainly shouldn't have caused what he was feeling—it was as if gravity was starting to disappear around him.

A pang of fear went through Valeri at the thought of floating away from Rhea. He had done space walks before, but he didn't have the gear for one now, and—

Stop it, he told himself. *There's nothing wrong with gravity. What could affect it, after all?*

He looked up then and saw a glowing, pulsating mass in space between Rhea and Saturn. The disturbance was... difficult to describe. It was circular, or perhaps spherical. The boundary between it and normal space was hard to determine because it rippled and pulsed, like a convection current in water, but with color.

What could cause something like that? Valeri was a trained engineer, and had learned quite a bit of physics and astronomy during his years in space. None of his education had prepared him for this sight.

"Command, are you seeing this?" he radioed.

There was no answer. Valeri looked over toward the base and saw that the lights inside were flickering. Another power surge? Was it from the ripple in space? Valeri had never seen anything like it. The energies coming from the ripple had to be intense to affect the power supply even through the heavy shielding.

A thought occurred to him. If the power supply was being affected, what were those mysterious energies doing to his body through the minimal protection of his space suit?

Valeri decided the substation repairs could wait. He looked around and saw the other members of the crew reaching the same conclusion. They dropped their tools and started back for the relative safety of the base. The construction cranes and tractors powered down as their operators broke off work. All around them hung fine particles of ice, drifting slowly and incredibly upward.

Valeri followed, stepping carefully because he was still seeing the ice particles lifting around him, and he was suddenly and irrationally afraid that if he tried to move too fast, he would float away with them.

*   *   *

Commander Piotr Belyaev stomped into the command center as the lights flickered again. The area was still under construction. It was airtight and heated—at least theoretically—but the computer systems weren't fully installed yet, and the furnishings were still minimal. The temperature, he guessed, was somewhere around minus twenty Celsius. He wore a parka and extra socks under his ESD-issue boots.

"What is it now?" he demanded as he entered. The power problems were slowing construction, and that in turn was slowing preparations for the installation of the gun turrets. They were on their way from Earth, and Belyaev was going to catch hell if the gun emplacements weren't finished by the time they arrived.

"Look," the closest technician said. He pointed toward the command center's large bay window. Belyaev walked closer to see what the latest problem might be.

The window was partially iced over, but enough of it remained clear that he could see the disturbance occurring between Rhea and Saturn's rings. The rings themselves looked like a road from this perspective, curving away around the vast arc of the planetary body.

The disturbance partially obscured the rings. At its edges they appeared warped and shimmering, like the distant surface of a road on a hot day back on Earth. It appeared as if space itself was rippling, and colors flared around the phenomenon—which Belyaev guessed was approximately a kilometer across.

It was growing rapidly, and seemed to be taking on a more definite shape, though he couldn't tell for sure. He had never seen anything like it, and his brain seemed reluctant to interpret the images fed into his eyes. One thing was certain, however. There were huge energies there, radiating outward and washing over Rhea and nearby smaller moonlets. The monitors in the command center detected remarkable amounts of radiation across the entire electromagnetic spectrum. Belyaev guessed that if he had neutrino and plasma monitors online, they, too, would be registering substantial energies.

"Call it in," he ordered. Earth Space Defense protocols

dictated that all unusual events had to be reported to the United States Army command and control headquarters. All nations of the world contributed to the ESD, but the United States had taken the lead in the integration of alien technology, and therefore were the de facto leaders of the ESD. In some ways this rankled the other participating nations, but it also made their jobs easier. *When something unusual occurs*, Commander Belyaev thought, *let the Americans handle it*. They wanted the problem, they could have the problem.

"We tried," a nearby technician answered. "Our long-range communications are down."

Impossible, Belyaev thought. They were on the Earth-facing side of Saturn at this point in Rhea's orbit. Only empty space lay between the base and Earth's orbital satellite network, speckled here and there by orbiting rocks. How could communications be down?

Occasionally a solar storm or intense fluctuation in the Van Allen belts disrupted communications, but those disruptions never lasted more than a few hours, and they never occurred across all frequency bands. The ESD had built a great deal of redundancy into its outer-planet communications systems.

"This cannot be," he said. "Try the EHF band."

"There's too much interference," the technician said. He could see that Commander Belyaev didn't believe him. "Listen." The technician flipped a switch, routing the long-range satellite communications through a speaker system in the command console.

All they could hear was white noise. It wasn't the ordinary white noise, however—the kind that came from the background radiation of space. It seemed to have a pattern, to pulse and fluctuate just as the visual disturbance did. Something about the rhythm of this noise gave Belyaev a deep-rooted sense of unease—a feeling in the pit of his stomach like his ancestors must have felt when they saw an eclipse.

He and the entire Rhea Base team were in danger. Of that he was certain. If asked, he wouldn't have been able to explain how he knew it, or what the danger was, but all of his survival instincts were on high alert.

Small objects began shifting and floating away from the table tops where they had been resting. Was the ripple in space interfering with gravity? It would have to be something tearing at the fundamental fabric of space-time. How was that possible?

That was a question for the scientists. Belyaev was a soldier. All he cared about at the moment was that he and his crew were more than a billion kilometers from home, and now they were cut off behind a wall of white noise and the unraveling disturbance over Saturn's rings.

PART ONE
JULY 2

1

Dawn broke over the Rockies. General Joshua Adams sat in the back of a Marine helicopter, irritated at his abrupt summons but reconciled to his duty. He was a career military man, and had done his part to battle the initial invasion that had come to be known as the War of '96. Since then he'd worked for the past twenty years on the integration of alien technology into existing human military hardware. The Earth Space Defense systems were at least partly his baby, and he was a proud father.

Even so, he hadn't been happy when the request had come in from the research site at Area 51. They needed him pronto, they said. No explanation available over unsecured channels. So he had gotten up from the breakfast table, climbed into the chopper, and here they were speeding over the salt flats south of Salt Lake City, on their way to New Mexico.

His wife was still at the bed and breakfast, as far as he knew. He also knew he would hear about this later, when she got things wrapped up and went back to their home just south of Area 51. Janine was an Army wife, and knew what came with the territory, but she also wasn't shy about letting him know when he was putting the work before the family.

"It's one thing to save the world, Josh," she'd told him once when they were arguing. *"It's another to convince yourself that every time you sign a report you're fighting a war. You need to be able to tell them apart."*

She was right, too—he had a tendency to lose himself in his work, and thanks to Janine, he could fight it better. Adams had learned a long time ago that listening and assessing made a good general. Any idiot could point to his stars and bellow orders. A real leader made sure his subordinates understood why the orders were necessary, and made it clear that he trusted the people around him to carry them out—or propose better ideas if they had them.

Janine had a lot of ideas, and they were often good ones. Adams wouldn't have climbed the career ladder so quickly without her, and both of them knew it.

"We're two minutes out, General," the pilot informed him. Adams nodded even though the pilot couldn't see him. It was a distracted reflex. His attention was occupied by the scene below. They crested a pass between two mountains, revealing a sight Adams never got tired of seeing.

Spread out over miles of the salt flats, and still looming large enough to be part of the horizon from Area 51, was the wreckage of one of the alien city destroyers.

In flight, each of the city destroyers had blotted out the sun over a large metropolis—in more than a hundred of those instances, they were the last things citizens ever saw. New York, Washington, D.C.... Four of America's largest cities lay in ruins by the time the sun set on July 2, 1996. Fifteen by the end of July 3.

Fifteen still, on July 4. The same was true on a larger scale worldwide. London, Berlin, Paris, Bombay, Shanghai, Moscow, Lagos... the list went on, and would have been much longer were it not for the heroism of President Thomas Whitmore and the pilots who had flown with him. Because of their courage, the devastated wrecks of three dozen city destroyers lay scattered across the world, monuments to the dangers that came from space and the resilience of humanity in fighting them.

The destroyers' landing arms—petals, the scientists called them, because of the way they had unfolded from the craft before landing—were each larger than three aircraft carriers lined up nose to tail. Or bow to stern, if you were a Navy man... which Adams wasn't. The main body of each destroyer was fifteen miles in diameter, a circle containing huge fighter hangars, labs, facilities for growing the various organisms the aliens had domesticated and engineered for their own use, command and control rooms, and a seemingly infinite number of other inscrutable devices that would keep Area 51's scientists busy for decades.

Scattered across the salt flats, the wreckage still held some of the incredible menace of the ship in flight, when it had seemed impossible that it could be destroyed. Adams had been a staff officer during the invasion. He'd coordinated surveillance and intel for the joint command that oversaw the pilots who flew to their deaths attacking the city destroyer, and nobody had been happier than him to see it go down when that lunatic crop duster had flown his jammed missile right up the barrel of its main weapon.

Russell Casse, that was his name. Adams tried to take a lesson from that moment. He would never have let Casse near one of his jets, if the fate of the planet hadn't been at stake. The truth was, he'd been inclined not to anyway. And then Casse'd come through, sacrificing himself in a manner as heroic as any career serviceman. You never knew about people.

In the aftermath of the War of '96, when the Army had led the war against the surviving aliens, Adams had seen enough combat to put him on the track to the stars he currently wore on his collar. His mission in the Atlantic had been one of the toughest—he hated being undersea even more than he hated outer space. Still, it had been a success, and results were all that mattered.

He'd spent the next twenty years coordinating efforts to reverse-engineer alien technology and put it to use, and that in turn had put him right in the middle of the founding of the Earth Space Defense initiative. He was no-nonsense and demanding, because the work required it, but he was also smart enough not to think he knew everything. That meant he was good at putting the right people in place, and he had taught himself to listen to them even when they spouted crazy theories.

After all, as far back as the 1970s some of the scientists had voiced theories about what would later be the alien invasion.

If more people had listened then...

But that was hindsight. Pointless. What mattered was today, and what ESD could do to keep the people of Earth safe—which was why he was on this chopper, instead of lingering over breakfast with his wife. Not many people on the planet knew as much about the aliens and their technology, and it all began when the city destroyers came crashing down to earth. He had flown over this one a hundred times, and to him the sight of the monumental wreckage would always mean one thing.

Victory.

Thousands of workers were breaking it down, and as the chopper skimmed over the wreck, many looked up. One of them even waved. Adams didn't wave back.

Recovery teams worked around the clock, loosely divided into two different specialties. Inside the vast spaces of the destroyer, dedicated teams of technicians and scientists investigated the ship's systems. The aliens apparently used genetically tailored organisms for a number of tasks, which kept an entire department of biologists and geneticists busy. Extraterrestrial computing systems were built on completely different principles than Earth's, and had spawned a whole new science of mind-based computing.

Even now, after twenty years, scientists were in the depths of the ship, learning more about how those systems worked. Their initial results found their way to the research and development wing of the new Area 51, where applied scientists and computer engineers hybridized the technology and built it into new generations of military hardware.

The structural and materials engineers, on the other hand, had different interests, and for them, teams recovered huge intact pieces of the ship's hull and mechanisms. Military contractors had designed transport platforms specifically to move those pieces from the crash site to Area 51, where a battalion of engineers waited to document them and take them apart, piece by piece, analyzing each component in an ongoing effort to understand and utilize the alien technology.

The invasion had left terrible destruction in its wake, and hundreds of millions dead—but it was also a gift, in a way. Because of it, Earth knew what was out there, and knowing enabled them to prepare for when they encountered it again. Adams had made it his life's work to guide that preparation.

The city destroyer fell away behind them and the chopper followed the main approach road from the crash site to the new Area 51. Not for the first time, Adams reflected on how Area 51—once the focus of so many conspiracy theories—had become exactly what the most wild-eyed kooks of the 1950s had believed it to be. The nerve center of Earth's investigation of alien technology.

In old photographs, the Groom Lake facility was just a few buildings behind a fence. It had grown to include runways, hangars, several small repair and manufacturing facilities, and laboratories. For decades the government had denied its existence. Until the aftermath of 1996, they had continued to deny its true purpose—which had always been to investigate, analyze, and attempt to use bits of extraterrestrial technology. The spy planes and stealth technology were all part of that, the tip of the iceberg that eventually became visible to the public. Yet for every B-2 that thrilled spectators at an air show, there were a dozen other projects that only a few people on Earth knew about.

Then, after 1996, Area 51 had exploded into a small city of its own, built alongside a huge complex of research facilities—the best in the world. Crashed alien fighter craft, pieces of unidentified technology from the alien vessels, even a few surviving invaders themselves, all had been brought here. Now Area 51 was one of the largest military installations on planet Earth. Thousands of military and civilian workers lived and worked there. Manufacturing and testing facilities were getting close to good enough to reproduce alien technologies.

All of it existed for one purpose.

When the aliens came again, Earth would be ready.

And they would come again. Adams knew it. They'd made contact once, and gotten a bloody nose, but any race that would traverse the great spaces between the stars would possess the kind of determination that a single setback couldn't overcome. Adams had studied military history his entire adult life, and there was a truism. The conqueror didn't give up after his first effort failed. The aliens would come back, and when they did, they would be pissed.

The chopper flew toward the helipad next to the fighter hangar. As it swung around to orient itself for landing, Adams could see the destroyer again, a few miles away. He remembered watching it burn after it crashed to the ground.

That crazy drunk crop duster...

His final missile jammed in his jet's own launch bracket, and he'd flown it straight up the aperture of the destroyer's main weapon assembly. Pure guts.

At the time *Major* Adams had been attached to the Area 51 R&D wing, but he hadn't known all of its secrets. What he *had* known was that new technology kept appearing, along with orders to integrate it into existing fighter jets and other military hardware. He'd heard the rumors, of course, knew that Area 51 held secrets to which his security clearance did not entitle him—but when he'd learned the full truth, he'd been astonished.

Area 51 had been doing alien research since 1947.

Incredible.

Once he'd recovered from the surprise, Adams had applied to join the accelerated alien research projects. He'd seen some combat when the survivors from the city destroyer came boiling out in a last murderous attack, but most of his career had been, and was, dedicated to turning the aliens' technology against them. Against whatever else might be out there among the stars.

All enemies, foreign and domestic, the oath said. After 1996, Adams had mentally added *extraterrestrial*.

Now he was one of the officers in charge. Using the alien materials, science, and especially the anti-gravity propulsion systems, humankind had reached out into the solar system. There were bases on the Moon, Mars, Rhea, and others were in the planning stages. Humanity had taken a weapons lesson from the aliens, as well.

Cannons based on the city destroyers' main weapon were the next step in human defense. Dozens of them were lined up at one end of Area 51, in various stages of construction. Dozens of others ringed the Earth in geostationary orbits, linked to the command center here in Nevada. Still more were on the way from Earth to the space-based installations on other planets and moons.

Before Adams retired, he wanted to be able to look at a map of the solar system and not find a hole through which an alien aggressor could get close to Earth—not without humanity knowing about it ahead of time and having the capacity to react.

That would be a legacy worth leaving.

Near the rows of cannons, next to the research complex, a large red cross painted on the roof marked out the hospital named for President Whitmore's first lady, Marilyn, who had died during the War of '96. Adams had met the president only once, and admired him as much as he admired any man on Earth. It was sad to hear about the mental decline Whitmore had experienced in recent years.

The president's daughter, Patricia, would have been a good pilot, following in her father's footsteps, but she'd left flight school to be closer to him, back in D.C. She'd landed on her feet, though, and was an assistant of some kind to the new president, Lanford.

Solid woman, Adams thought. *Better than her predecessor, Bell.*

The hospital in which Marilyn Whitmore had died was now a world-class research and medical facility. Here again, alien research had given humanity new insights. The invaders were so much farther along the biotech learning curve that even after twenty years, Adams knew the human race still had a long way to go to catch up. Even so, new advances were saving lives. Most of that research was centered here, because most of it was based on classified material and couldn't be shared with other medical facilities. Maybe someday, Adams thought, but not quite yet.

The chopper hovered for a moment as the ground crew cleared away from its rotor wash, and General Adams wondered again what had lit a fire under the staff.

He would find out soon.

2

Dr. Milton Isaacs took a break from his rounds in the Marilyn Whitmore Hospital to check in on Brakish. There weren't many patients in the hospital, since it was on the grounds of the alien research facility at Area 51, and outside of the occasional workplace accident or bout of the flu, the local population was quite healthy.

He entered the room carrying a plant he had ordered from an orchid vendor in California.

"Good morning, Brakish," Isaacs said as he took the plant to the windowsill and placed it among the others already there. "I brought you a new one." Most of them were also orchids. Brakish loved orchids. Occasionally Isaacs let himself succumb to magical thinking and imagined that reciting their scientific names would be the incantation that finally brought Brakish out of his coma.

"*Dactylorhiza maculata,*" he said as he approached Brakish's bedside and combed his long gray hair. "The spotted orchid. When it fully blooms the lilac will take your breath away." He paused as if listening, his eyes never leaving Brakish's face. "I made you a gift. I think you're gonna love it.

"No, I'm not going to tell you," he added. "You're just going to have to wait."

He always made a point of pausing in his little monologues, giving Brakish a chance to respond, even though in nearly twenty years Brakish had not once made a sound. Seven thousand three hundred days. Well, with the leap years it was seven thousand, three hundred and five, but to Isaacs the round number was almost more of a milestone.

He had been at Brakish's side, helping to extract the alien from its genetically engineered exoskeletal armor. They hadn't known much about the aliens then, having only been able to study three of them over the years. Brakish had the idea to cut through the suit and attempt direct communication. The presence of President Whitmore, watching from the viewing room next to the surgery, had Brakish worked up into quite a state. He was always proud of his work, and this was his chance to show the president himself what the scientists at Area 51 were doing to justify their enormous black budget.

Then everything had gone wrong.

The alien's telepathic attack came as a complete surprise. Physically, too, it had lashed out and instantly killed or wounded everyone in the room—Isaacs included. He still had the scars from the lash of its tentacles, but for Brakish the experience was far worse. The alien had forced its way into his mind, used him as a puppet to speak to the president and make clear that there would be no peace, no coexistence. Only war, until one side or the other was destroyed.

Isaacs remembered starting to regain consciousness just as the soldiers in the viewing area shot the alien through the surgery's windows, breaking the telepathic hold it had on Brakish. A few days later, when Isaacs was sufficiently recovered to visit Brakish, the man was in a coma.

They'd thought it would only last a few days, until his brain recovered from the trauma, but those days had lengthened into weeks, and then years. Over time Isaacs had been absorbed into the new research avenues. No matter what else occupied his working hours, however, Isaacs always kept his eye out for new orchids, and he made sure to visit Brakish at least once a day. On working days, he stopped in twice, before and after his shift. In that way two full decades had disappeared into the past. Twenty years of Isaacs' life had included tending his comatose lover, and nursing the fragile seed of hope that one day he would awaken.

They hadn't been open then—in 1996 it was a different time, and fraternization among staff was frowned upon no matter what gender the fraternizers might be. To be gay at Area 51 was to be very discreet. Over the twenty years since, the stigma of his sexuality had gradually disappeared, until he could openly mourn and care for Brakish. Isaacs had never been tempted away. Brakish was the love of his life. He didn't want anyone else.

Some day, he believed, Brakish would wake up. He would look around and see the orchids lining his windowsill, and he would know Isaacs had been there for him the entire time.

That was love. Simply that. Being there for someone else no matter how difficult it became.

"Dr. Isaacs report to the ICU," a nurse's voice said over the hospital speaker. Isaacs sighed. It was time to get back to work.

"I'll be back," he said, and he patted Brakish's hand before leaving to answer the call.

Love, he thought. *It drives us to do things we never thought were possible. Like having conversations with a man who has been in a coma for nearly twenty years.* He believed that somewhere deep in his mind, Brakish heard him. That seed of hope lay within both of them, perhaps, ready to germinate and then grow into a new life together.

Twenty years wasn't too long to wait. Someday Brakish would wake up. He would reappear, his eyes still alight with the joy of discovery, his enthusiasm still infectious even when other people didn't know what he was talking about, his good humor still invulnerable to the attacks of pessimists and naysayers. Isaacs had never met anyone like him, and never would again.

Tomorrow, he thought. *Maybe it'll be tomorrow.* He said it to himself every time he was walking out of Brakish's room.

* * *

Isaacs left the room.

He didn't see Brakish Okun's fingers twitch on the crisp white sheets of the hospital bed.

3

A black SUV, standard base transport, was waiting for General Adams when he got out of the helicopter.

He returned the driver's salute and climbed in the back, watching the base go by until the SUV pulled up at the entrance to one of Area 51's central research buildings. Waiting outside the entrance was Lieutenant Jim Ritter, one of Adams's handpicked subordinates in the alien technology research project.

Ritter snapped to attention and saluted.

"Sir," he began.

Adams cut him off. "This better be good. My wife and I were enjoying a very nice morning at a very expensive bed and breakfast."

"I'm sorry," the lieutenant said, "but I thought you should see this."

Despite his irritation, Adams was intrigued. The building housed the prison wing of the research complex—and it wasn't a prison for human beings.

During the course of years fighting against surviving aliens, hundreds had been captured and sent to New Mexico. The most famous capture, of course, was Captain Steven Hiller's. He had dragged a parachute-wrapped prisoner across miles of desert while the initial invasion fleet was still destroying the great cities of the world. That event had passed into legend, as had Captain Hiller himself.

Soldiers and pilots all over the world had also captured aliens during the course of the battles following President Whitmore's heroic last attack. Those aliens had been gathered here at Area 51—most of them, anyway. General Adams suspected that other countries also maintained their own versions of the facility. Information wasn't always shared. Even faced with the threat of collective death from the stars, humans banded together into nations and guarded their secrets jealously.

Many of the captured aliens had died for reasons poorly understood by the scientists assigned to study them. Efforts at interrogation had failed almost completely—the alien consciousness was so different from the human mind that establishing common ground for communication was difficult, even before the interrogators dealt with the visceral hatred the aliens felt for humanity.

In many ways, Adams reflected, they knew as little now about what motivated the aliens as they had in 1996, when Hiller's captured monster had gone berserk in the medical suite, killing or injuring a number of important scientific personnel. It then used one of them as a mouthpiece, communicating from the other side of a viewing window.

What was the man's name? He tried to remember.

President Whitmore had asked the creature what the invaders wanted humanity to do, and the alien had answered simply.

Die.

They had shot it, ending the short conversation.

Since then, not a single one of the aliens had uttered another word. Neither, for that matter, had the scientist— Okun, that was his name. Like him, most of the imprisoned aliens had spent the intervening two decades in what appeared to be a catatonic state. They performed basic biological functions, but so rarely that for long periods of time they appeared dead, although instruments monitoring their vital signs noted continued breathing and circulation.

This entire building had been designed to house the aliens and keep them alive so they could be studied. What little *was* known—or could be inferred—about their preferred habitat had been incorporated into the design. Not to keep them comfortable, but to extend their lives and therefore the opportunity to study them.

They seemed able to adapt to the terrestrial atmosphere and temperatures. As a result, some scientific personnel theorized that Earth-like conditions were necessary for advanced life forms to exist anywhere in the universe. Adams didn't think the sample size was all that convincing.

Right then it didn't matter. What mattered was that one of his junior officers had encountered something of such importance that it warranted dragging Adams out of a very enjoyable weekend retreat. He typically trusted Ritter's judgment, but as he had said when he got out of the car…

This had better be good.

Ritter led Adams inside, through the outer lobby and office areas. Just past those was a central monitoring station. Rows of screens displayed the feeds from various locations within the prison complex itself, including every cell. Several technicians were gathered around one of the monitors as Adams and Ritter approached. One of them saw the general and motioned the others out of the way so he could see what they were looking at.

On the monitor, an alien thrashed back and forth in its cell, hammering itself into the walls, over and over. The walls were slick with its body fluids, but if it was causing itself harm, that didn't appear to be deterring it.

"It started a couple of hours ago," Lieutenant Ritter said.

The techs cycled through other video feeds. Everywhere the same frenzied scene played out. Aliens smashed against the walls, beat at them with their tentacles, pounded against the bulletproof glass and left smears of their secretions.

After a few moments General Adams walked over to a bay window that overlooked the enormous prison block. He was old enough that he preferred seeing things with his own eyes, rather than through the lens of a camera. The cell block was immense, and along its entire length the same chaotic scene prevailed. The aliens had apparently gone insane.

It must have something to do with their telepathy, he thought. They had used it as a weapon in the war, and much of their technology was based on it. They maintained a sort of hive mind, but had fallen into disorganization when the mother ship was destroyed, and they lost their queen. Most of the surviving aliens had fought, but they hadn't fought well—not without the direction from above. Now they were all doing the same thing, as if they were hearing the same voices or directives again.

Adams couldn't think of another reason.

"After twenty years of being catatonic," he muttered to himself, and he didn't like the implications. Then he turned to Lieutenant Ritter. "Get me Director Levinson."

"We tried," Ritter said. "He's unreachable."

Unreachable? That was unacceptable. *If I can be pulled out of a vacation weekend with my wife, Levinson can goddamn well answer the phone when he's called,* Adams thought. *Scientists. You need them, but you can't count on them.*

"Where the hell is he now?"

No one seemed to know.

4

A convoy of jeeps clearly marked with the distinctive logo of Earth Space Defense rumbled northwest along a dirt track—calling it a road would be unwarranted flattery—with the savanna of the northern Congo spreading away into the falling night on either side.

Heavily armed United Nations Humvees escorted the convoy at front and rear. Seated in the lead jeep, Director David Levinson looked at the passing scenery in the convoy's headlights. Flat scrub grasslands as far as the eye could see, which wasn't very far because of the darkness and the clouds of dust kicked up by the vehicles ahead. Even so, it was a landscape he hadn't seen much, and he tried to lose himself in it. Unfortunately, peace was hard to find when you were being grilled by a federal bureaucrat who wanted to pinch pennies while you were trying to save the world.

The bureaucrat in question—who sat in the back seat, leaning up to be heard in the front—repeated a point he had been making continuously since they had left the U.N. base earlier that afternoon. Now it was dark, and he hadn't run out of steam.

"This administration has made it clear that expenditures need to be reined in, and yet you've spent nearly three times your allocated travel budget this year alone…"

"Who are you again?" Levinson asked him. It was hard for him to keep track of all the bean counters who seemed to make it their mission to chip away at his budget. Their navy suits, their earnest faces, their belief that their columns of numbers mattered more than ideas. David found it all confounding and repulsive, but he had learned he shouldn't say that out loud. Instead he just tried to radiate a certain kind of lofty disdain, and hoped they would go away.

The bureaucrat stopped talking.

"Floyd Rosenberg the accountant, sir," Levinson's assistant, Collins, reminded him. Collins was driving. This was one of his primary uses as an assistant, because David didn't like to drive. It took up his concentration when he would rather be thinking about more important things than traffic lights or turn signals.

"Oh," Levinson said, without bothering to hide his scorn. "The accountant."

"We should slow down," one of the U.N. escorts radioed. "We don't want to look like we're posing a threat."

"Collins, tell him to go faster," Levinson said. "We also don't want to show them weakness."

Collins nodded. "Of course, sir." He picked up the radio handset and spoke into it. "That's a negative. The director insists we maintain current speed, and possibly even go a tad faster."

"Must," Levinson corrected him. "We *must*, and not just a tad." He turned slightly, and spoke over his shoulder. "A tad and a scoche. Did I ever tell you that was the name of my first jazz band? I was Tad."

"I have the feeling he's not taking me seriously," Rosenberg the accountant complained.

"He's not," Collins confirmed. "He doesn't take anyone seriously… but himself, of course."

Levinson shot him a look. Collins ignored it, as he always did. It was another of his prized abilities—knowing when to ignore the boss, and when to take him seriously.

"Well, he needs to," Rosenberg said to Collins. Then he turned to Levinson and said, "You should take me seriously. I've been chasing you across the planet for the last three weeks, and now that I have you..." He opened his briefcase, as if they were in a conference room on J Street, instead of bumping across the savanna on the way to meet a volatile warlord.

"Oh God, he's opening his briefcase," Levinson said. "Collins. Do something."

"All vehicles prepare to come to a stop," the lead U.N. escort radioed. "We have visual on the border crossing."

"We're here, sir," Collins said. Levinson didn't bother to point out that he could, in fact, scan their surroundings and see for himself. Collins' skills included repeating of the obvious.

"I know," Rosenberg said, "a lot of people have a negative reaction to being audited, but it can be a very constructive experience."

An audit, Levinson thought. *Out here on the savanna. Someone, somewhere in Washington decided it was a good idea to fly this guy to the Congo, just so he could conduct an audit while I'm trying to do science.*

"Listen, Lloyd..." he began.

"Floyd," Rosenberg corrected him.

"Right," Levinson said. "This is all very interesting."

Rosenberg beamed. "Thank you. We take pride in our work."

"But I have a friend I have to meet," Levinson added. "Great guy. Come say hi." He opened the door and stepped out of the jeep, glad to not be bouncing around anymore. The lead U.N. Humvee swung around to the side, clearing a path toward the border crossing between the Congo and the self-proclaimed Republique Nationale d'Umbutu.

Rosenberg looked up from his papers and his face went pale.

"Where are we? Director Levinson?"

Levinson had seen a lot of border crossings in his life, but for sheer style he had to rank Umbutu's ahead of all the rest. No simple floodlights and customs house here. Huge totems built from the skulls and bones of aliens flanked the road, over which a sign proclaimed the breakaway republic. The U.N. soldiers picked out the totems in the beams of their flashlights, making them seem even spookier than they would have in daylight. The border guards weren't your standard-issue military police, either. They were big and mean-looking, with tattoos and ritual scarring and looking not at all pleased to see a United Nations convoy parked on their doorstep.

Rosenberg got out of the jeep, too. Clutching his briefcase, he came up next to Levinson.

"Who are they?" he asked.

"Umbutu's rebel forces," David answered.

Rosenberg got even paler. "The warlord?"

Levinson shrugged. "Nothing to worry about. The old man died. I hear his son is much more of a moderate." He walked up to the border garrison and said, "Excuse me, I'm looking for Dikembe Umbutu."

Instead of answering, every member of the garrison pointed their guns at Levinson, which provided him with an interesting bit of information. Instead of AK-47s or the other standard armaments a Central African rebel group might be expected to possess, Umbutu's border guards were all armed with alien blasters. The green glow from the energy reservoirs was sharp in the darkness and emphasized the hostile expressions on the guards' faces.

"I see you found their armory," he said. Rosenberg

looked as if he might be about to faint. Collins wasn't happy either, but he stayed close to Levinson, trusting the boss to know what he was doing. That was yet another of the things that made him a useful assistant.

Levinson had been expecting a welcome party, but apparently that wasn't how Umbutu the Younger did things. Maybe it wasn't that much of a surprise, given the facts. He had survived his own father's insanity and attempted murder, his best friend's betrayal, and a series of attempted coups after he took power following his father's death. Now he was firmly in command of his breakaway republic, but the established governments on all sides had no love for Dikembe Umbutu. Under the circumstances, it didn't pay to be too welcoming to anyone, for fear of appearing weak.

A voice came from behind the soldiers.

"The one and only David Levinson."

It was a woman. French accent. Familiar.

Ah. Catherine Marceaux. What's she doing here?

Marceaux approached through the garrison, which parted to let her pass. Even in the unflattering illumination of floodlights and flashlight beams, she was a beauty. David tried to conceal his confusion. He failed. He was congenitally bad at hiding his emotions.

"Catherine? Wow, that's..." He didn't know what he was trying to say. "Uh, what are you doing here?"

"You don't think you're the only expert he called, do you?" She had a little mocking smile on her face. Friendly, but also competitive.

"I'm just a little surprised to see you," David said. Might as well come right out and admit it. She was, after all, a psychiatrist.

"I'm a little surprised you remember my name," she replied, and now she wasn't smiling.

"Come on now," David said. "Let's be professional."

"We both remember what happened last time we tried to be professional." With that, she seemed satisfied that she had made her point, whatever it was. She turned and walked away.

"I'm sensing a palpable tension," Rosenberg commented.

Levinson tried to play it off.

"We've bumped into each other at a few conferences."

"I bet you have."

"Shut up, Floyd." David walked off. He wasn't in the mood for the innuendo of accountants. As he followed after Catherine, however, he heard Floyd call out.

"Wait! Where are you going?" He was cut off as one of the guards stopped him and demanded his papers.

Good, David thought. *That'll keep him off my back for a while. Maybe long enough to get the real scoop out of Catherine.*

Once she was done being angry with him, at least.

They'd met at a conference in French Guiana, too soon after Connie was killed in a car accident. That was the problem, the timing. Catherine was an intoxicating, very intelligent, and quite beautiful woman. David liked to think he had a certain charm himself. They spoke, got interested in each other's research, and later got interested in each other. Intimately.

After that, David had realized that his wife's death was too fresh. He wasn't ready for anyone else in his life. The alien invasion had brought him and Constance back together, and far too quickly she'd been taken away from him again.

David had been angry about it. At the universe, God maybe, everything. Out of the massive tragedy and destruction of the invasion, their marriage had been reborn, and then of all things—a car accident. Completely random. David raged at the randomness of it, the blind stupid chance.

Realizing he had a long way to go before he made any kind of peace with it, he never called Catherine as he had promised to. Looking back on it, he knew he should have handled the situation better, but the past was the past. Now that she had made her point maybe Catherine would be ready to forgive and forget.

David put this theory to the test when he caught up to her. She was climbing a hill just inside the border station, and he fell into step next to her.

"So why does Umbutu Junior need a psychiatrist?" he asked. "Unresolved daddy issues?"

She ignored his little joke—which wasn't all a joke. Anyone with Dikembe Umbutu's history would in fact have enough father issues to keep busy generations of therapists.

"His people fought a ground war with the aliens for an entire year," she responded. "Their connection is the strongest I've ever seen. It's like they're tapped into the alien subconscious."

"Oh, yeah," David said, recalling some of the conversations they'd had at the conference. "Your obsession with the human–alien psychic residue."

"You, calling *me* obsessive?" Catherine shot back. "That's cute."

Maybe, David reflected, he should have said something more professional. *Oh well.* He'd never been particularly good at couching his thoughts in the right phrases. It was part of the reason he'd refused the ESD directorship for so long, allowing himself to be sidelined as the research coordinator so the government could take advantage of his brains, but ignore his policy recommendations.

He had known they were moving too fast with the hybrid fighter program, and endangering the lives of pilots and researchers alike, but they'd been hell-bent to get a working model ready for a July 4 celebration back in 2007.

When it mattered, only one person associated with the hybrid program would listen to David, and that was Steve Hiller. After David had laid out his reservations, Hiller had done the kind of thing you'd expect him to do. Instead of endangering the life of another pilot, he had taken the prototype on its shakedown flight.

It had cost him his life.

While the smoke still hung in the sky from the explosion that killed his friend, David was already acting. Connie was a senator then. Between her influence and David's obvious suitability, he'd been able to force his way into the ESD directorship. Originally he hadn't wanted the job, but after Steve Hiller's death he had bowed to the inevitable. It might be too late to save Steve, but at least he could make sure the hybrid program would proceed at an appropriate pace.

Three years later Connie died, and David was alone with his directorship. Life hadn't gone the way he had wanted it to—not by any stretch of the imagination. Even so, he'd had to make the best of it. There was important work to be done.

"Do you know why he called *you*?" Catherine asked, shaking David out of his reverie. They were both a little out of breath from the climb. They got to the ridge, Catherine a bit ahead of him—most likely because she couldn't stand to be second at anything, David mused. As she spoke she turned to face him. "We found something out here. Something only you might understand."

When he crested the ridge he paused for a long moment. Not because he didn't know the answer to her question, or because he didn't feel like answering, but because he was seeing something that brought back a lot of memories—few of them good.

Apart from his emotional response, David Levinson was detached enough to understand that he was a scientist, right down to the last molecule of his body, and here in Umbutu he might just have found the research project of a lifetime.

"The ship's been dark for twenty years," Catherine said, and he nodded. Straddling the main settlement of Umbutu's fiefdom was a nearly intact alien destroyer ship. Its hull was fifteen miles wide, and its fully extended landing petals were another mile wide and four long, holding it high enough off the ground that birds could wheel and glide underneath it and still be far above the ramshackle tin-roofed buildings that spread between the legs.

Gloom and the hill's steepness had hidden the vessel as they climbed, but now it loomed over them, taller than anything they could see from here to the jagged ridgeline of the Ruwenzori Mountains, the foothills of which were just visible far to the west.

Beyond the ship, the last fading light in the western sky cast shadows over the city that had sprung up around its landing petals. Bright lamps lit the vessel from below, resulting in even more macabre silhouettes that twitched and moved with the activity below.

That alone would have been an amazing sight. Intact destroyers were unheard-of—it was absurd that it had taken him so long to reach this one. He had known, of course, that Umbutu the Elder had fought a brutal war against the surviving aliens after the destruction of their mother ship. He had also known that a destroyer was in this area—that much had been revealed by Lucien Ondekane, a refugee from the National Republic of Umbutu—but to see it now, almost looking flight-ready... it gave him a chill.

He'd been inside one of those ships once, with Steve Hiller back in the War of '96, and they had barely escaped with their lives.

On top of the destroyer's presence and condition, Levinson was also astonished to see that somehow it had been powered up. Lights glowed through ports in the superstructure, and along the landing petals. A broader, brighter illumination fell from the circular weapons port on the bottom of the main hull, bathing the grassland and buildings below in chilly blue light.

"How did they get the lights on?" David asked.

"We didn't," someone said from behind them.

David turned to see Dikembe Umbutu himself. Son of a warlord, perhaps a warlord himself. Educated in England, he had found his way home during the invasion and arrived in the middle of his father's brutal war against the aliens who had landed this city destroyer in what was then the frontier of the northeastern Congo.

Surviving that war, and his father's madness, he had matured into a respected—perhaps even revered—leader of his people, yet he still wore the twin machetes that had been his trademark armament during the conflict. David wondered at that—Dikembe clearly had access to alien armaments, but he chose the primitive route. It was a powerful statement to be sure, but not a statement David could ever imagine making.

He much preferred the lab and the keyboard to the battlefield. On the other hand, that was a choice Dikembe had never been able to make.

According to the reports, the elder Umbutu had been driven insane by telepathic contact with the aliens—lending credence to Catherine's theories—and had turned his revolutionary movement into some sort of death cult, believing that humans and aliens were divided halves of a single whole organism. Unfortunately, that organism could only be reintegrated by killing the human part. Nobody knew how many of his people had died in Umbutu's crusade. Dikembe himself had been marked for death and cast into a pit where he suffered a long series of visions related to the aliens.

However, their telepathic intrusions seemed to have

affected him differently than they did most humans. The people of this breakaway territory believed Dikembe had a powerful connection to the invaders—that much David had been able to learn from afar, but he didn't know how much of the belief was justified.

He hoped to find out on this trip.

Dikembe walked up next to them and stood, contemplating the sight of the gigantic ship. His presence was commanding, and would have been, David thought, even without the machetes. There was a certain magnetism born leaders possessed. Dikembe Umbutu had that quality.

"It happened on its own, two days ago," Dikembe said. David waited for him to reveal more, but the man remained silent.

Two days ago, David thought. That would be twenty years, almost exactly, since he had discovered the signal corruption in Earth's satellite network, and figured out that the aliens were counting down to an attack. *Coincidence?*

He didn't think so, but they had to know more.

It occurred to him to wonder where the accountant—Rosenberg?—had disappeared to. As quickly as the thought flitted across David's mind, it was gone. There was a puzzle in front of him. An unexplored frontier in his expanding effort to learn everything he could about the aliens.

Why hadn't he gotten to Umbutu sooner?

5

To the accompaniment of the classic rock his father had loved, Jake Morrison eased his tug over the blasted surface of the Moon, keeping his speed low in unison with the other five tugs in the group.

They looked like giant metal frogs, with nearly spherical main hulls flanked by long jointed legs. These were actually used as arms while in flight, to catch and hold whatever the tugs were hauling at the moment. They turned back into legs when the tugs landed, sitting on the gripping claws like they were feet with toes splayed wide.

Right now the tug formation was closing in on the Moon. The excess heat from the tug's engines at full load was turning the interior into an oven, even though it tended to lose a lot through the bubble of windows that formed the front of the cockpit. Due to the temperature, Jake had departed from the standard dress code, stripping down to a wife-beater. He'd even considered taking his hat off, but he liked the hat.

He felt exposed without it.

They were carrying a brand-new energy cannon from one of the city destroyers back on Earth, and had been en route for the last four days. Now they were cruising through the final approach to the ESD lunar base, in the

Sea of Tranquility not too far from the original landing site of Apollo 11, back in 1969. As a matter of fact, Jake was low enough that he could just pick out the American flag planted by Armstrong and Aldrin. The much larger and newer Chinese flag flew nearby. The Moon wasn't just an ambition anymore. It was an outpost of human civilization—and human defense.

The tug's radio crackled.

"Morrison, what's your position?" It was one of the Chinese engineers responsible for the cannon's final installation, getting jumpy now that they were so close to completing the project. Jake turned down the music enough to answer.

"Seven miles and closing," he said. He cut the connection and muttered, "Of the slowest trip of my life."

His co-pilot, Charlie Miller, woke up at the sound of the radio. He'd been snoozing on one of the benches at the back of the passenger compartment.

"Three hundred and eighty thousand klicks in four days isn't slow," he said. "It's peaceful." That was just like Charlie. Find the bright side.

Jake wasn't feeling it, though. "Remember when we were kids, and we thought we'd be the best fighter pilots in the world? Now I'm flying a forklift. On autopilot." *Dreams don't always die hard*, Jake thought, *but sometimes, they do die.*

"Hey, cheer up," Charlie said. "Your dreams almost came true—and there's worse things you could be doing than towing a half-trillion dollar weapon."

There were a lot of better things too, Jake thought.

"Yeah, well, I need a little more stimulation."

He left the autopilot to handle the final approach to the cannon emplacement site at the edge of the Moon Base complex. The ship didn't need him at this point, and neither did the engineers. Let them handle it. Jake was a glorified mailman. Moving aft, he sat in the rear-facing turret bubble and tried not to sulk.

Charlie dropped into the seat next to him. "Do you want to play name the constellation again?" he asked, a little too enthusiastically.

"I'd rather open the airlock and watch our heads explode," Jake grumbled.

Charlie gave up. "Yeah," he said. "Me too."

The Moon Base drew nearer as the six tugs maneuvered the immense cannon into position. The base was built around a central tower with spokes radiating out to smaller structures. The command center was in the tower, which enjoyed an uninterrupted view of the lunar plain for miles in every direction. At the end of the main spoke, longer and wider than the rest, sat the turret assembly built to support the cannon.

Because the Moon was tidally locked to Earth, always showing the same face to its parent planet, installing the heavy cannon at the base would ensure that it was always covering any threat that might approach. There were plans to build another base on the dark side of the Moon, facing out into deep space, but for now ESD resources were engaged here. They already had other defense bases under construction on Mars and Rhea. The Chinese were in charge here, the Russians on Rhea, and the French on Mars—but the administration and executive authority of Earth Space Defense rested with the United States. Specifically the Army.

Jake and Charlie knew the crew of Chinese engineers and military officers would be on edge inside the command center, so they had to stay on their toes, even though the tug was on autopilot for the moment. Jake switched the radio to the base command channel, holding the frequency open per regulation.

It wasn't the job Jake had envisioned for himself. He'd

always wanted to be a pilot, and after the War of '96 he'd made it his mission. After his parents died in the war, Jake found himself in an orphanage, trying to stand out in some way that would get him into a better school. That's how he and Charlie had ended up friends. Charlie was kind of a runt, and Jake had stepped in to bail him out when he got in trouble with some bullies at the orphanage.

Turned out Charlie was kind of a genius, too, and after that he helped Jake study, getting him into a pretty selective tech school. That led to a new problem.

He couldn't just leave Charlie in the orphanage—the kid would never stay out of trouble on his own. Jake worked it out so he and Charlie could live together near the school, which was on the outskirts of the Area 51 alien research complex. It was the least he could do. They'd been like brothers, together ever since, their friendship growing closer even when Jake's nascent flight career had gone down the toilet.

That train of thought led to Dylan Hiller, and Jake didn't want to think about Dylan right then. Or Patricia.

"They're in position, sir," he heard a tech say. Commander Lao must have arrived in the command center to oversee the final docking operation.

Jake didn't like Lao, and the feeling was mutual. Lao thought Jake was a failure, a slacker, and Jake thought Lao was a petty tyrant. They had to work together, though, and Jake needed the job. Plus he was flying. He had to keep that in mind. Maybe he wasn't flying the new generation of hybrid fighters, but he was in space. It wasn't all bad.

The tugs got the cannon into position.

"Initiate uncoupling sequence," Lao said.

An engineer got the process started. "Tug One... disengage."

One by one the tugs cut loose and drifted away.

Jake disengaged the autopilot and got ready for his turn to pull away from the turret mount. He put the thrusters into a gentle reverse, holding the tension in the linking arms that extended from the tug's hull to the armature of the cannon. His command console beeped and the engines thrummed, holding the cannon steady while the engineers in the command center figured out whether the cannon was in the right place.

Just like the mail truck it was, the tug beeped when you put it in reverse. Jake itched to fly something else, like he'd been trained to do. But he'd made his bed, and he had to lie in it—at least for now. He hadn't really given up. It just seemed like it most days.

When it was their turn, Jake and Charlie's tug cut loose, nice and smooth, their crane arms opening up just like they were supposed to. Their tug drifted back and then Jake held it steady a short distance from the cannon mount.

"You know, I didn't have to follow you up here," Charlie said, as if he'd been reading Jake's mind, which sometimes Jake thought he could.

"Yes, you did," Jake said. "You get lonely without me."

Charlie watched the cannon as another one of the tugs pulled away.

"I was the youngest valedictorian in the history of the Academy," he responded. "I could've been stationed anywhere. San Diego would've been nice. Beaches, surfing…"

Jake snorted. "You never surfed a day in your life."

"But I'm a fast learner, and I've got great balance. Like a cat." Always looking on the bright side, Jake thought again.

He didn't feel like looking on the bright side.

"Cats hate water, Charlie," Jake said.

Over the tug's radio, they heard Commander Lao say, "Seal the locks."

Jake and Charlie watched as giant clamps started to close in around the base of the cannon. All the tugs but one held their positions a short distance from the turret mount, with Jake still close enough to brace the tug's crane arms against the cannon if that was necessary. Sometimes the clamps shifted things as they tightened, and at least one tug had to stay attached to keep the cannon from moving too far. If they'd set the cannon down a little crooked or off-center, or if it moved too much while the engineers and techs were setting the clamps, they would have to start the whole process over again.

Until then, all they could do was wait. Jake tried not to think of Patricia. Or Dylan. Or all the things he could have done differently.

6

The emergency klaxon blared angrily. Rhea Base personnel filed into a tug, jamming themselves together in its small cargo space after the passenger compartment was full. Commander Belyaev was at the controls.

Outside, the ripple grew into a giant distorted cloud, a hole in space that sucked in everything around it. Base equipment and building material tumbled away from Rhea's surface in a cloud of ice crystals and dust, whirlpooling up into nothingness. Smaller asteroids and other fragments collided on their way in, releasing flashes of heat that disappeared as quickly as Valeri saw them.

None of them knew what was happening. Was it a black hole, suddenly born out of nothing? It didn't look right—or at least it didn't look like what they had theorized a black hole should look like. It was irregular, for one thing, seeming like a tear or a wound in space-time rather than a clean circular singularity.

But what, then? What had caused it?

That was a question for the scientists to wrestle with later, Valeri thought. When he'd seen the drifting ice crystals at first, he'd thought it was strange. When he'd felt the lightness in his step on the way back to the base, he'd thought it was his imagination. Then when he'd seen the ripple in space he hadn't known what to think.

As it grew, he started to understand—deep in his gut, where real intuition lived—that something very bad was about to happen. He just hoped they were going to live. They still hadn't been able to communicate with any of the other human bases in the system. No one knew what was happening to them.

Would they ever know? The tug would get them back to Earth, but it would take a long time, and they didn't have enough room for supplies. So even if they got away from this maelstrom, unless they could reestablish communications, they were going to be in real trouble.

He forced himself into the front part of the passenger area, trying to peer out of the window and get a look at the distortion. All of the seats were filled and people were jammed throughout the tug, holding onto whatever they could grab.

"Hurry!" Belyaev shouted. The ship shook as he fired the engines, trying to hold it steady against the vortex's increasing gravitation pull. "Prepare for immediate takeoff!"

The last cosmonaut was in, and the tug's airlock slammed shut. Belyaev lifted off in a storm of flying construction materials mingled with pieces of ice and stone from Rhea's surface. They banged off the shuttle's hull, none of them hard enough to do much damage, but Valeri jumped every time. It was easy to die in space.

He thought of home. He thought of Kiev, and Natasha. He wanted to have children. Right then, he wanted to go back to Earth, put his feet on the ground, and never get on an airplane or a spaceship again. These last few hours had been enough adventure for a lifetime, and it wasn't over yet.

The ship bucked and shuddered. Belyaev held it steady for the moment. Sparks shot from conduits in the walls behind the pilot's chair. The tug was built to haul heavy loads, and it had enough power to escape the gravity wells of any planet in the solar system—but the engines were straining, and they weren't getting much farther away from the hole.

Below them, the entire base tore apart as it was uprooted from the surface. Modular structures that had held living quarters, machine shops, the greenhouse... all of them tumbled past the ship and broke into pieces as they accelerated into the distortion. Valeri watched a table soccer set spin by, along with a hydroponics bay with fresh tomatoes still sprouting from its mesh. The transformer he had been working on shot past, followed by the crane from the construction site, a seven-meter beam still attached to its hook assembly. Someone's bed, someone else's footlocker. All of it now space debris, and space itself rippled around the vortex.

Incredulous, Valeri saw the nearest of Saturn's rings sprouting a tail of debris, drawn by the gravitational pull of this new wound in space. Whatever the phenomenon was, its power was incredible, far beyond his ability to fully comprehend. His mind returned to the idea of a black hole springing into existence, even though he knew it wasn't possible.

There was nothing else to which he could compare it.

"Give me more thrust!" Commander Belyaev shouted.

The technician in the copilot's chair worked the controls as fast as he could.

"We're at maximum output, sir!"

The tug's frame groaned under the stresses between its engines and the opposing gravity. Smaller cracking sounds made a terrifying counterpoint. If they could get around to the other side of Rhea, Valeri thought, the mass of the moon would protect them for long enough that they could get away. Gravity diminished quickly with distance.

Belyaev seemed to have the same thought. Instead of

steering the tug straight away from the vortex, he kept it at a low angle of ascent. The chunks of the moon flying past them grew to the size of hills. The moon itself was beginning to break apart. Valeri remembered the first time he had seen Rhea, wondering what was inside of it. Was it dead, ice and rock all the way through? Or did the pressures deep inside create heat? Measurements from the surface had been uncertain, and the Russian team had orders to build ESD defense turrets, not indulge their astrogeological curiosity. Valeri had a feeling they might find out shortly, though.

As the tug turned away, it rolled to the right and he saw geysers erupting through the mile-wide cracks in Rhea's surface. There it was. Confirmation of a subsurface ocean. The scientifically curious child in him was glad to see it, glad to be in on one of the solar system's mysteries. The adult in him looked forward to sharing the story over a glass of vodka back home.

The tug slewed to one side, slamming the cosmonauts against each other. As Rhea broke up, its gravitational pull was lessened and became unbalanced. Suddenly Belyaev was fighting different attractions from different directions.

He was a superb pilot. He had survived dogfights in the War of '96, claiming four confirmed alien kills and two other probables. He had flown interplanetary missions, had landed on the Moon, Mars, and Rhea. He had overseen docking operations with an asteroid mining station. Belyaev could fly anything.

Even he couldn't fly a ship straight, though, when the very space around it was being torn apart. The tug started to tumble. The groans in its hull turned into screams. Alarm klaxons went off, warning of leaks. Emergency oxygen pumps kicked in. The cosmonauts sat silent, relying on their commander to get them out of this. They could scream, they could thrash around, they could panic... but what good would it do?

Space flashed by the windows, and then the surface of Rhea as Belyaev shouted orders. The copilot fired impulse thrusters to arrest their tumble, but it was too violent, the forces around them too great. The moon passed through their view again. It was in fragments, torn completely into pieces. Liquid water, freezing rapidly, sped through space toward the distortion. It was one of the most beautiful things Valeri had ever seen, striking in the way the light caught the water in space, and then how that light changed when the water froze...

Then the tug was shaking too violently for Valeri to see. Belyaev was still shouting and the rest of the cosmonauts held their silence. Abruptly a loud metallic scream from the back of the ship got Valeri's attention. He turned, and was looking out into empty space. Instinctively he grabbed a handrail. The ship's atmosphere gusted past him, the cosmonauts screaming now but their voices growing thin as the air fled. Some of them were gone through the hole in the hull, others hanging onto the broken edges.

More of the ship broke away. Through a hole Valeri could see one of its thrusters. The other had been torn off. Valeri held the rail with one hand and the trailing edge of a suit harness with the other. Whoever had been in that seat was gone now.

The violence of the spinning began to disorient him, and he realized he had been holding his breath for a long time. He wanted to breathe again, but there was nothing to breathe.

Belyaev was gone too, the cockpit windows shattered and the two command chairs empty.

The last thing Valeri saw, as the ship disintegrated around him, was the majestic rings of Saturn, tearing themselves apart.

7

Jake held the tug steady. Charlie was still rambling about surfing and parties and women and whatever else. He had an active imagination. One of the things he imagined was that he was a ladies' man.

"You realize there's only thirty-six women on this Moon Base?" he said, and Jake was sure it was true. Charlie would know. The question was, how did he know? Had he counted them? Had he hacked the personnel database to find out? Either was possible.

"I'm sure one of them will eventually come around, pal," he said just to be supportive.

Charlie turned to glare at him. "Hey! It's not like they all rejected me. I happen to have standards."

Standards, Jake reflected. *Good thing to have. If it wasn't for standards, I'd still be in the hybrid fighter program. I screwed up. That was that.*

There was a flare of static over the radio and the voices from the command center cut out for a moment. Jake and Charlie winced at the sharp spike of white noise. The lights on the tug's navigation console flickered, went out... then came back on, still flickering.

The tug dropped and pitched forward as the signals to its engines were interrupted, and with an awful grinding squeal the tug's crane arms plowed into the cannon.

"What did you do?" Jake shouted.

Charlie was working the console. "Nothing!"

"That didn't feel like nothing!"

Jake tried to get the tug back under control. The radio feed from inside the base command center came back on, and a tech was shouting.

"Tug Ten collided with the weapon! It's listing!"

Everyone in the command center was shouting. Jake heard another engineer say, "The clamps have stopped—they're not responding!"

As he got the tug level and stationary again, Jake saw that this was true. The clamps hadn't closed all the way, and the huge turret, the size of a small hill, was starting to tip toward the lunar base. The Moon's gravity was only one-sixth as strong as Earth's, so the cannon wasn't falling fast, but it was still falling, and when it landed…

"Override the system!" Commander Lao bellowed. Then his voice got louder as he spoke directly into the microphone. "All tugs, take evasive action!"

The cannon gathered momentum, its huge mass accelerating it downward. On Earth it already would have landed, crushing much of the base, but the slowness of gravitational acceleration on the Moon meant they still had a chance to act.

"That's a negative, sir!" Jake shouted.

Charlie's eyes popped. "What do you mean *negative*?"

Jake gunned the tug's engines and dropped between the toppling cannon and the command center.

This is all Charlie's fault, he thought furiously. *If I hadn't paid attention when he helped me study, I wouldn't know all the basic physics. I wouldn't know that the cannon would fall slower in this gravity. I wouldn't know all that crap about how every action has an equal and opposite reaction. And I sure as hell never would've had a stupid idea like this.*

As the tug angled around, they came close enough to the command center's bay windows that they could see Lao's astonished face. Charlie caught the commander's eye and shrugged.

Sure, Jake thought. *Throw me under the bus.*

"Morrison!" Lao barked into the microphone. "Get out of there! That's an order!"

Jake toggled the radio off. He had to concentrate.

"Charlie, strap in."

"So we're not even gonna talk about this?" Charlie yelled, but he strapped in, all right, and Jake swung the tug around so it faced the cannon—which was about halfway through its fall that would end in dozens of deaths, and billions of dollars in damage. Plus who knew how long it would take to repair everything and get the cannon defense-ready? Someone had to do something.

That someone was Jake. He flipped the tug's arms around so they faced forward, spread wide like the arms of a wrestler ready to engage an opponent, and then he rammed the thruster control all the way forward. The engines roared and the tug leapt ahead. It wasn't built for speed, so "leapt" was kind of relative, but they sure were moving fast—directly at the cannon.

"This isn't a fighter, Jake!" Charlie screamed.

"Don't remind me!" Actually, Jake thought, it was a good thing it wasn't a fighter. A fighter would go real fast, and then blow itself to tiny little pieces doing what he was about to do with this tug.

The cannon grew in their windows, huge and terrifying and approaching way too fast—and then they collided with it in a shower of sparks and an impact that rocked both of them forward in their harnesses. Jake heard all kinds of popping and snapping noises as little things inside the tug's hull and in the control arms broke under the impact. But the arms held, locked against the turret just above where Jake had gauged its center of gravity to be.

"We're gonna die," Charlie moaned. "This is how I die!"

Jake wasn't sure he was wrong. He held the tug's thrusters at maximum power, listening to the echoing groans of overstressed metal, feeling the heavy vibrations of two huge forces opposing each other—the tug's thrust against the cannon's angular momentum. The tug wasn't built for speed, but it was built to move large masses from place to place. Warning lights flashed in the cockpit as the engines started to overheat.

"Come on! Come on!" Jake said, holding the thrust and hoping the engines could last just a little bit longer.

The cannon started to slow.

The sounds coming from the front of the tug and from the arms weren't good, though. Either this was going to work in the next few seconds, or the cannon's fall would make Jake and Charlie the smeared middle of a sandwich, with the cannon on top and the wreckage of the command center on the bottom.

The cannon slowed a little more, and the engines still held. Hydraulic fluid and sparks shot and spewed from the crane arms, but they held, too. Jake had a feeling they were smashed into place and would never operate again, but replacement crane arms were a hell of a lot easier to come by than replacement moon bases.

Charlie tapped the control to activate the radio again, so they could hear whether it was working. From the inside of the tug, it looked as if it was. They couldn't really see anything beyond the instruments, however, which said they were moving forward at the glacial pace of a few meters per second.

Still, they were moving forward.

The tug pushed the immense cannon slowly back

into place. Over the comm link, they could hear techs shouting about getting the remote turret systems back online. The cannon reached its tipping point and settled back into the mount as slowly and ominously as it had toppled out.

"Commander!" an amazed engineer said. "The locks are reengaging!"

As the cannon settled back into its vertical rest position, Jake slowed the tug and let it go. The bent and overtaxed crane arms still stuck out forward from their mounts. Jake eased his grip on the thruster controls. His hands were cramped.

Charlie sat back in his chair, pale as a ghost but looking relieved. He started to get his composure back. Good old resilient Charlie.

"Was that stimulating enough for you?"

Jake chuckled. "I didn't think that was gonna work."

A huge metallic *thunk* reverberated through the tug as the cannon locked into place. All of the clamps were tight, the cannon was on center. The crisis was over.

Jake eased the tug back around to head for the landing pad and the hangar. It was going to need some serious repairs. Ordinarily denting up a tug like this would be a firing offense, but Jake figured he might catch a break, since he'd just saved the lives of everyone in the command center. Even Commander Lao might stop giving him a hard time.

At least for a couple of days.

8

President Thomas Whitmore woke up screaming. He sat bolt upright in bed, feet tangled in the sheets, sweat dripping into his eyes and soaking his beard. He sat wild-eyed and gasping, looking around, gradually coming back to himself and realizing he was awake in his bedroom in his house in Morristown, Virginia.

It wasn't 1996—it was 2016.

He wasn't in the Oval Office anymore. He was a *former* president, an old man now, haunted by memories and vulnerable to nightmares—and obsessed with a truth that hovered just out of reach on the other side of the visions that plagued his sleep.

He rubbed at his face and wiped away the sweat. Normally when he woke up from these nightmares he just wanted to be by himself, but this one was different. This time he'd awakened with a sense of purpose. He had to tell someone. There was no time to waste.

Whitmore got up and started moving. He looked at his desk as he passed it, momentarily lured by the chaotic piles of sketches and drawings he'd made over the years. The circle, the line cutting through it, in a thousand variations. The symbol he'd seen in a thousand dreams. Were they dreams? Or were they messages of some kind?

Deliberately sent? He believed they were, but from where?

That was the problem. Whitmore knew his psychic link with the aliens had scarred him. It was a wound. Wars caused wounds, but he also believed—and Tom Whitmore had never been a man to fool himself or sugarcoat anything for anyone—that he could see the shape of the wound, and get outside of it. Understand at least *most* of what was going on in his mind.

Even if he couldn't figure out how to say it out loud, to people he was sure wouldn't understand.

Was he getting closer to understanding what it meant? It was in the aliens' mind, that symbol, stronger than almost anything else. Burning like a beacon, like some kind of totem that they called out to. The alien mind was a strange and labyrinthine thing. If they never touched your mind, you never understood that—and if they did touch your mind, you were never the same.

Whitmore wasn't the same.

What was he thinking about? The symbol. Those dreams were back, and more intense than ever. Things like that happened for reasons. Causes had effects, and vice versa. What was the cause here? Whitmore had a bone-deep, gut-deep, feeling that he knew—but he had to be sure.

He formed a plan, but it was really only the beginning of a plan because sometimes it was hard for him to hold long to-do lists in his head. He had to go, and he had to go quickly. If Agent Travis had heard Whitmore's scream, he would be coming to check on him. That was the downside of still having Secret Service protection. They never really left you alone, they never let you do what you wanted to do. But Whitmore didn't have time to deal with Travis.

He'd given a speech, a long time ago. Twenty years ago, was that right? About that. He'd tried to bring people together, focus them on a common menace. He'd given the speech not because he thought it would help the men live, but because he thought it might help them die better.

That had been a time for a speech. He'd been president. Sitting president. Now he was just an ex-president. No speeches. Nobody would care if he gave a speech.

This was a time for action.

* * *

Agent Travis took the stairs two at a time, heading up from the kitchen—where he'd been debating whether to have an afternoon cup of coffee—to the second floor where the president's bedroom was.

Travis had been on Whitmore's detail for almost four years now, and it wasn't unusual for the president to wake up like this. The problem was that sometimes when he had nightmares, he took off into the neighborhood. The old pilot wasn't what he used to be. His mind was going, and he was sinking into all kinds of crazy visions that followed him from sleep into the waking world.

If he wasn't what he used to be, though, he was still crafty, quick, and real, real determined. Physically pretty spry for a guy his age who had been through what he'd been through. It took a lot to keep up with him sometimes, and it took a particular kind of patience because the Whitmore detail wasn't like a lot of the other assignments. The service occasionally took pride—when nobody else was listening—in the fact that they'd only ever lost one president. Compared to some of the others out there now, Whitmore didn't hardly have any enemies at all.

The brass didn't think his safety was a high-level risk anymore, especially since his mental problems had become more or less an open secret. For whatever reason, people got a lot less likely to assassinate public figures who were unwell.

Being on the Whitmore detail was less a security

operation and more a babysitting job, but Travis didn't mind. He was proud to serve the man who had spearheaded the resistance in the War of '96, and destroyed the alien mother ship. Not every agent could say that.

Most other Secret Service agents liked the active presidential detail, because it made you feel like you were defending the free world. Travis thought it was just as important to defend and protect those who had already served. As far as he was concerned, President Whitmore was a living monument to the best of American ideals and values.

But he was also frustrating, and Travis was frustrated again when he banged his way into the president's bedroom and found it empty. Bedding twisted up and flung aside, bathrobe not hanging on its hook. Where was he? Travis noticed a breeze moving the curtains by the bedroom window. A moment later he noticed Whitmore's cane leaning against the sill.

The window was open.

"Not again," he groaned, and he ran out of the room. Why didn't Patty just nail that freaking window shut?

Ten seconds later he was outside, in the front yard of Whitmore's immaculate colonial house. He ran to the street and looked up and down. Quiet houses, someone just turning the corner walking a dog, sounds of a television through someone's open living-room window.

No sign of the ex-president.

"Shit," Travis said. He got out his phone and made a call.

9

The United States Capitol building had been expanded and renovated countless times since George Washington had laid its cornerstone in 1793. Partially destroyed during the War of 1812, it had been completely rebuilt and expanded by 1829. Additional space doubled its size in the years surrounding the Civil War, which was also when the iconic dome was added. A gas explosion in 1898 led to more renovations and structural work. If you knew the inside of the Capitol, you could in a sense trace the growth of the United States as a nation... until the War of '96.

The destruction of the Capitol had been a powerful psychological blow, and one of the first things President Whitmore did after defeating the alien invasion was begin the rebuilding process. Fragments of the original Capitol were saved and made part of a memorial museum. The entire grounds at that end of the National Mall were redesigned and rebuilt around his vision of a new Capitol, bigger and grander than the old, keeping the stately appearance of its predecessor but adding a new and modern strength. This was the building that commemorated the War of '96, those who had died, and the resilience of those who had survived and triumphed.

In two days, it would be twenty years since that triumph, and preparations for the anniversary were in full swing. Workers on anti-gravity platforms were touching up the building, rushing to have it completed and ready for the celebration. All over Washington, D.C., people were gathering for parades and remembrances.

Inside a White House conference room, President Elizabeth Lanford was reading the speech she would deliver on that occasion. She always tried new speeches out on her team before reading them in public. Not every president did this, but she liked hearing how they sounded and seeing how actual human beings reacted to the rhythms and the phrasing.

"On this day, twenty years ago, President Whitmore passionately declared 'We will not go quietly into the night,'" she began. "And we didn't."

She ran quickly through the rest of the introduction, outlining progress made in reconstruction and focusing on the beautiful new Capitol building and other landmark structures rebuilt across the country. Then she touched on the enormous undertaking of the Earth Space Defense initiative, with its outposts on the Moon, Mars, and Rhea, and others being planned. Her administration had faced some public concern about the amount of money it had spent on domestic reconstruction, instead of an accelerated ESD program, and one of Lanford's goals for the speech was to make clear that she thought it was time to move on.

The people of the United States—and all of planet Earth—had poured their energy and resources into defense systems. In Lanford's mind, they had reached the time when it was appropriate to rebalance that effort and divert some of those resources into reconstruction of the cities. It was a fine line to walk, and she needed to make sure the speech would inspire, reassure, and deflect criticism all at the same time.

"Make no mistake, the defense of our planet will remain a priority for this administration," she said, coming to her conclusion, "but your voices have been heard. We've all sacrificed enough. The time has finally come to put the people first again." With that Lanford shuffled her notes back together and looked to her aide and trusted speechwriter, Patricia Whitmore.

"Great speech, Patty." It was true. Whitmore had grown up around politicians, and knew how to strike the right rhetorical tone. Her father had possessed the same gift, in his damn-the-torpedoes way. In Patty it was a bit more nuanced, but she still knew how to connect with people. Lanford was glad to have her on staff.

"Thank you, Madam President," Patty said.

Then Secretary of Defense Reese Tanner, predictably, weighed in with his own concerns. "I have to disagree. It's too premature to announce the defense cuts, and I would strongly advise you remind the people that you lost your entire family in '96—"

No, Lanford thought. She would not do that. This wasn't about her. It was about the world putting itself back together.

"Three billion people died, Tanner. Everyone lost someone." She looked over the rest of the team, not wanting Tanner to feel singled out. He was surprisingly thin-skinned for someone who had spent his life in and around the military. "We've been living in fear for the last twenty years. It's time to change the narrative. The people deserve a little good news. Let's give it to them."

One of her aides popped into the conference room.

"Madam, Captain Hiller has arrived."

Excellent, Lanford thought. A perfect way to end the meeting before there was too much back and forth. She was going to give the speech, one way or another, and if the rest of the team didn't have a chance to air their grievances beforehand, they would have to support it once it was given.

"Thank you," she said, signaling that the meeting was concluded. "Send him in."

The door opened again and Dylan Hiller walked in, looking quite dashing in his Air Force dress uniform. He didn't have the swagger or boisterous humor for which his father had been known, but he did possess a quiet confidence that inspired other people to believe in him. It also didn't hurt that he was quite handsome.

A perfect poster boy for the new ESD flight corps, he was also a genuinely good kid. The world could use a lot more like him. Lanford saw Patricia and Dylan share the kind of smile that only came from years of friendship… and possibly more. She knew they had a bit of a history, dating back to flight school, and she also knew that it was complicated. Stepson of a hero pilot, daughter of a hero president. It seemed like a match made in heaven.

But none of them were in heaven, were they?

Beyond Hiller, out in the hall, Lanford saw the painting President Whitmore had commissioned to commemorate the War of '96. In that painting, fighter planes and alien craft swarmed the skies over a cityscape meant to represent the ideal of an American city. Towering glass and steel skyscrapers reflected the flash and glare of the aliens' energy weapons. Missiles streaked through the sky and the upper parts of the painting were dotted with the fireballs of exploding alien craft.

Seeing that painting must hold particular significance for young Dylan Hiller, Lanford reflected. After all, among the fighter jets represented was surely the one Steve Hiller had flown. It was both an honor and a burden to have a stepfather who had become a legend. Everyone knew about Hiller's heroics during the War of '96, while his untimely death in 2007 told the story of a man who wouldn't let risk pass to another, when he could assume it himself.

Dylan could never equal that, and Lanford hoped he wouldn't try. He had his own path to carve, his own greatness to achieve.

"Captain Hiller. I can't tell you how proud we are to have you flying our flag up there," she said. Some of her staff had already left, but Reese Tanner was talking to one of his undersecretaries—and, Lanford suspected, waiting to greet the young rising-star pilot.

"It's an honor, Madam President," Hiller said.

"Your father was a great man," Lanford said. She decided to throw Tanner his bone. "You know the Secretary of Defense."

Dylan nodded. "Sir."

"And I don't have to introduce the two of you," Lanford said, indicating Patricia.

Another aide appeared. "Ma'am, let's get you touched up for the photo."

While the makeup artist worked, Lanford watched Patricia and Dylan together. They hugged and then held each other at arms' length.

"Moving up in the world," Dylan said.

"Says America's knight in shining armor." Patricia smiled at him.

"You're the one who's back in the White House."

"As an employee, I don't have the same benefits as I did when I lived here," she said, looking around as if she was seeing the rooms the way she had when she was a little girl, her father was still president… and her mother was still alive.

"How did they let us get away with everything we did?" Dylan wondered.

"Because my dad was commander-in-chief," Patricia answered, her tone of voice leaving no doubt that she was adding an unspoken *Duh*.

Dylan grinned. "That probably had something to do with it."

Once Lanford had been made camera-ready, her aide approached Dylan. "We're ready for you, Captain." Dylan nodded to Patricia and started to walk away.

"Dylan," she called after him, "be nice to Jake when you see him."

He didn't answer, but Lanford could see that her words had landed. Lanford didn't know who Jake was, but there was clearly some sort of vexed history there. The dramas of the young. She put it out of her mind as the young man approached her and became Captain Hiller again, standing at her side as flashes popped and their images went out all over the world. If she was going to make her new program work, and begin to emphasize reconstruction and normalization over military spending, she would need all the photo ops she could get. Particularly with young, handsome, and famous military officers. It was a cynical point of view, but that was politics.

While she smiled for the cameras, Lanford still kept an ear out for the conversations around the room. One of the things politics had taught her was that people would speak as if she wasn't there, if they didn't think she were paying attention—and that listening to what was happening with her back turned was a vital skill. So it was that she could appear fully present for the photographers, even joking with some of them about making sure they got her good side, while at the same time hearing another of her aides approaching Patricia.

"Ms. Whitmore, it's Agent Travis—he says it's urgent."

10

Once Jake got the tug into the shuttle bay, he and Charlie looked at each other and took a deep breath. For once in his life, Charlie seemed to be at a loss for words. They'd done something actually heroic, Jake thought. That felt pretty good. Maybe he didn't have to fly a fighter jet to be a hero. He punched in the final system shutdown commands, and they headed for the ramp.

When they got down onto the floor of the bay, they took a walk around the tug to see how she'd fared. Jake had worked some ships hard before, but never anything close to this. The engines were smoking, they could see that right away. The anti-gravity generators in the engine housing tended to give off a lot of waste heat when they were pushed, and in this case they'd given off enough to start little fires in the circuitry and insulation.

Looking at the smoke, Jake realized how close they'd come to engine failure. That would have been lights out, pure and simple. *Do not pass Go. Do not collect two hundred dollars.*

Coming around to the front of the tug, the damage was even more obvious. The hull was dented and gouged from the impact with the cannon. All of the landing lights and other surface electronics were either shorted out or damaged in other ways. One of the crane arms—now legs again, because the tug was resting on the splayed claws—was bent so badly there wouldn't be any way to repair it. The other looked to be in better shape, but would still need some time in the shop before it could lift anything heavier than a sandwich. The tug sat crooked and beat up, kind of forlorn, but Jake was proud of it. He'd asked a lot of it, and it had come through with flying colors, all things considered.

"Shit... don't turn around," Charlie said all of a sudden. "Lao's coming in hot, and he's got that look."

Jake didn't want to turn around. Maybe if he kept looking at the tug, Lao would just be a bad dream that went away. *Ha.* No, it was better to face the music, he thought, and he slowly pivoted as Lao's footsteps got closer.

Charlie was right. He was hot. Hot enough that when he started screaming, it wasn't even English. Jake knew perfectly well that Commander Lao spoke English. Also French, in addition to a couple of different dialects of Chinese, but he was so mad right now that he had reverted to his native language. Probably because he could swear more efficiently, Jake figured.

Nobody ever learns to swear right in a second language.

Trailing Chinese invective, Lao stalked back and forth across the bay as the other tug pilots gathered to watch the show. Lao didn't go off very often, but when he did it tended to be quite a spectacle. Jake glanced over at Charlie.

"He knows we don't understand Chinese, right?"

Lao stopped in front of Jake and Charlie, looking like he was debating whether to have them shot out of an airlock, or kill them himself. Jake thought he might as well start to make his case.

"Sir, there was a malfunction—"

"You almost got us all killed!"

Okay, Jake thought. *But is anyone going to mention*

the power fluctuation and the way the clamps didn't shut right? Anyone? "Yeah," he said, "but then I saved everyone, so I was kinda hoping for a high five—"

Suddenly Lao got in Jake's face, close enough that if he hadn't been the base's commanding officer—and if it wouldn't have caused an international incident—Jake would have decked him.

"You don't get credit for cleaning up your own mess," Lao snapped. "And you destroyed my tug!" he added with a flourish, pointing at the damage.

"That? That's just cosmetic," Jake said, as much for the benefit of the other assembled pilots as anything else. One of the engine mounts chose that moment to fall off and hit the floor with a resounding clang.

Jake looked over at it, then back at Lao.

"He can fix that," he said, nodding over at Charlie.

Charlie must have been feeling guilty, because he tried to cut in.

"Actually, sir, I'm th—"

"I lost my focus," Jake said, putting on his serious in-the-principal's-office face. "It won't happen again."

"No, it won't," Lao said. "You're grounded until further notice." He held Jake's gaze a moment longer, then stalked off in a huff.

"Grounded as in I can't leave my room?" Jake called after him. "Or as in I can't fly?"

"Jesus, Morrison," one of the other tug pilots said. "Screwin' up really seems to be your thing!"

Not for the first time, Jake wondered how stories from flight school had followed him all the way to the Moon. He also wondered if there would be any punishment if he jumped the guy and pounded him with a piece of the broken-off engine housing.

Whatever, he thought, and he just started walking. Charlie went with him.

"You didn't have to take the fall," Charlie said as they left the bay.

"He already hates me," Jake said. "Why break tradition?" He didn't have to add that taking heat for Charlie was also tradition. It dated back to when they'd both been at the orphanage together, and Jake figured that it would continue as long as they knew each other. Friendships were like that. If you couldn't dive under the bus for a friend, then what kind of person were you?

He thought again about the strange burst of interference. It had thrown the tug's navigational controls offline for a critical moment, and clearly it had done a number on the base's electronics, as well. That's why the clamps had jammed. So why wasn't anybody talking about it?

Why the rush to blame him and Charlie?

Jake shrugged. Such was life. Everybody needed someone to blame when things didn't go right, especially when nobody really knew what the hell was going on. In the command center right then, there probably was an engineer diagnosing the problem and tracking the source of whatever electromagnetic burst had caused the shorts. Then he or she would write up a report and file it, and Lao would read it, and at that point everyone would know that the real cause of the accident had nothing to do with Jake or Charlie.

But by then, it would be way too late to say it. The story was already set. And anyway, Lao wasn't really the type to apologize.

Dikembe Umbutu didn't waste any time getting David and Catherine closer to the alien destroyer. In two pickup trucks, the group drove down the back of the ridge and then underneath the giant ship, passing one of the landing petals. By itself that petal was larger than any structure human beings had ever built.

The scale of the whole ship was hard to assimilate. David found that every time he looked at it he had to remind himself that it flew, that it wasn't a fixed monument or a feature of the land. That's how big it was. The human brain had trouble putting it in the same category as the ships human beings had created, defaulting to the idea that it was a thing made by natural processes, rather than by sentient beings.

He had asked Dikembe about Floyd Rosenberg. Dikembe had shrugged, like it was beneath him to consider the whereabouts of whining accountants. Collins, pursuing his own lines of inquiry, found out from their United Nations escorts that Rosenberg was back at the border checkpoint. He was described as irritating and stubborn, which Collins took to mean he was unharmed.

The pickups stopped and they all got out. David looked up at the underbelly of the ship, miles above.

The cavernous space housing the energy-beam generator loomed directly over his head. David remembered seeing what those beams had done to cities all over the world. The largest cities on Earth, collections of millions of human lives, together with their cultural legacies, their art and history... This ship, he knew, was responsible for Dakar, Abidjan, and Kinshasa. Three of Africa's great cities, three centers of the Francophone world.

The destroyer had probably been on its way to Cairo when Tom Whitmore brought down the mother ship. That was an educated guess on David's part, but it made sense. It certainly had been traveling northeast from Kinshasa. Cairo, by far the largest city in the world to survive the War of '96, lay in that direction. Where else would it have been going?

Billions of people dead. Irreparable losses to human culture. Given another week, the aliens would have reduced human civilization to the hunter-gatherer level again. The entire planet dealt with post-traumatic stress.

Astonishing, he thought, taking in the spectacle of the ship from the darkness cast by its shadow. Even twenty years later, digging in the ruins of ships like this one, humankind was just beginning to scratch the surface of the vast technological knowledge that created the destroyers and brought them across the spaces between the stars. What if the aliens had put that to work building something other than engines of war? The universe might have been so different.

He brought himself back to Earth.

"I appreciate you finally granting us access, Mr. Umbutu," he said. "Your father was a tenacious man who really stuck to his guns, no pun intended." David had known for years that there was an alien presence in this part of the Congo—now the Republique d'Umbutu—but it had been impossible to get permission to see it while the elder Umbutu was still in charge.

"My father was a monster," Dikembe answered sharply. "His pride caused the deaths of more than half of my people. Including my brother." He started walking away.

Taken aback, David said, "I'm so sorry." For once he had tried to be diplomatic, and where had it gotten him? He and Catherine followed the warlord. As they walked, they looked around, taking in the scattered alien bones and skulls that littered the site. David wondered if Dikembe had decreed they should be left there as some sort of memorial, or whether the people of Umbutu simply had more pressing problems than disposing of them. He also knew that Dikembe's father had fought a brutal war against alien holdouts. Perhaps the memorial wasn't to the war at all, but to the elder Umbutu, who had left so much damage in his wake.

David wouldn't be able to ask, of course, but the scenario intrigued him. Dikembe was a young and powerful leader with a European education and experience in war. Men like him went a long way if they kept their heads, but the previous generation in this part of Africa had seen so much conflict and human cruelty that only cruel men could lead them. The elder Umbutu was one such man. He died after the aliens died, but because of them in the end.

So his memory *was* scattered here, among the bones.

"He should have asked for help," Dikembe said, his tone softening ever so slightly. "I will not make the same mistakes he did." He stopped and held out his arm to the side. "Be careful."

They had reached the edge of an enormous hole in the ground, hundreds of yards in diameter and plunging into the earth farther than David could see. Even with the lights, blackness took over immediately.

"What happened here?" Catherine asked.

"They were drilling," Dikembe said.

David nodded. "We heard rumors, from refugees who fled the regime."

Catherine asked the logical next question.

"For what?"

"Fossil fuels, minerals, metals…" David speculated. "I don't know."

"That's a first," Catherine said wryly.

David ignored her. "When did the drilling stop?" he asked Dikembe.

"When you blew up the mother ship."

That made sense, David thought. From what they knew of the aliens, there was a collective consciousness, a hive mind driven by a central awareness. Probably analogous to the queen of a beehive or anthill. Individual aliens could act autonomously, but they were subject to commands from whatever that central mind was, and they all shared its knowledge and awareness.

Yet it was important to understand the reasons for the drilling. The captured alien had said all they wanted was the death of humanity, but if that was true, what was the point of this shaft?

"Mind if I send some members of my team down here to run some scans?" he asked.

Dikembe nodded. David looked back up at the underside of the ship. The lights there beckoned him, promising new discoveries and revelations inside. He had never been inside one of these ships—not when it was functional—and had never imagined getting the chance. During his trip to the mother ship, of course, there hadn't really been time. Now, though, David saw a chance to investigate some of the mysteries of the alien civilization. It was a tantalizing puzzle, and the ship also had a kind of irresistible because-it-was-there-ness.

He had to see what they had left behind.

David figured he could order a helicopter from

Brazzaville, but it would take forever to get there, and he wanted to explore as soon as possible. Right then, for that matter. Why wait? They had flashlights. They also had no idea how long the lights would stay on, or what they might miss if they didn't get inside while the ship was still responding to... well, whatever it was responding to.

For a moment he considered contacting Joshua Adams back at Area 51, to see if anything unusual had happened with alien technologies there. Then he discarded the idea. Adams was smart. He could handle things. Collins could talk to him.

Decision made, David turned to Dikembe.

"Is there any way to get up there?"

Some things had changed a lot in twenty years. Some hadn't changed at all. Some things were both different and the same.

President Whitmore knew he had a tendency to lose track of things, but he also knew that there were things he had to tell people. Things that came to him in the dreams, but the aliens were in his dreams, too, and they had forced him to dream in their language, their way of thinking. How could he get that across to people? They acted like he was crazy when he tried.

He was out in the street, knowing he was trying to get somewhere but already confused about what he'd meant to do. The bus stop had distracted him. He stood staring at an advertisement, trying to figure it out. It was a large image of the ruins of Las Vegas, with a crashed alien destroyer covering much of downtown and the destroyed Strip. Whitmore remembered flying over the site after the war. Smoke had hung in the air for months. Now it was a memorial.

In the picture, tourists were lined up to enter a portion of the downed destroyer through a shiny new visitor center. For all Whitmore knew there was a gift shop inside. Probably there was.

Across the top of the ad, in large letters, was a slogan.

VISIT THE RUINS
OF LAS VEGAS

"You weren't there!" Whitmore said. He couldn't help himself. He turned to two teenagers who were waiting for the bus. That was another thing that hadn't changed. Teenagers. They hadn't been there. They weren't even born yet in 1996. To them it was all history, stories their parents and grandparents told them. But they had to understand. Everyone had to understand. They stared at him and he knew he had to convince them of the danger.

"You don't understand what they're capable of! They're coming back, and this time we won't be able to stop them. I have to tell the world!"

The girl shifted away from him. "I don't want to hit you, 'cause you're old and stuff," she said, "but you're big time in our space right now."

"Yeah," the boy agreed, trying to sound tough, but he couldn't keep it up because his curiosity got the better of him. "And what's up with the robe?"

Whitmore looked down. He was wearing his bathrobe. Had he meant to do that? The kids didn't recognize him. That was confusing, too. For years everywhere he'd gone, everyone had known who he was. People had listened to him. He had tried to help them, to lead them, to prepare them. Now he was... he had a moment of clarity. He was an old man in a bathrobe shouting at kids on the street.

As quickly as the clarity had come, it was gone. Whitmore looked around, confused again. Where had he been going? He had to tell someone. What did he have to tell them?

A black car pulled up in front of the bus stop. Two people got out, a man and a woman. On the side of the car was the crest of the Secret Service. The teenagers stared as the man and the woman walked up to Whitmore.

He recognized her. She was his daughter, Patricia. What was she doing here? Whitmore thought he should tell her what he knew, but he had trouble forming words sometimes, trouble making himself understood because his train of thought was always—

The man was talking into a radio. Agent Travis, that was his name. He was supposed to be at Whitmore's house. Who had let him off duty in the afternoon?

"All agents stand down," he said. "Principal is secure."

Principal, Whitmore thought. They were talking about him. They had been looking for him. He looked down at his bathrobe again and remembered leaving the house, avoiding Travis, needing to go somewhere and tell someone. But even though he looked at Patricia, his daughter, and wanted to tell her all of this, he couldn't figure out how to get it into words.

"Come on, Dad," she said, taking his arm. "Let's get you home."

* * *

She was silent for a minute or so in the back of the car and then she said, "You can't keep doing this, Dad. You need to take your pills."

Whitmore looked at her. He had another one of those clear moments, and was amazed at the woman his little Patty had grown up to become. "I know," he said. "I—I know I'm not at my best anymore. I'm sorry. You shouldn't have to bother with all this."

"It's no bother, Dad," she said automatically, but as she turned to look out of the window, Whitmore knew that wasn't entirely the truth.

"I know you gave up flying to take care of me, Patty," he said. "I know how much you loved it."

She looked back to her father. "Yes," she said, "but I love you more. It was my decision, and I don't regret it."

She's a hell of a lot stronger than I am, Whitmore thought. "Patty, my good days are behind me. I did the things I needed to do in my life. You haven't yet. This is your time now—don't waste it on me. Go live your life."

She didn't answer.

13

The aliens were still going crazy down on the prison levels, and the scientists still had no idea why. General Adams had half a mind to have them all shot, just for the sake of peace and quiet. The aliens, not the scientists, although sometimes the lab coats were as much trouble to wrangle.

Even before this, Adams had been debating whether it was worth keeping the aliens. What humankind really needed from them was their technology, and none of them had to be breathing to accomplish that goal. It would be a fine thing to not have ethics, Adams mused. If he was the kind of officer who had no compunction about killing prisoners, Area 51 would run much more smoothly.

Unfortunately he did have ethics, and he believed that doing the right thing was a laudable goal even if you never got credit for it. He didn't need to be in the spotlight. He didn't need anyone congratulating him. He just wanted to serve. That was why he'd joined the Army in the first place, and why he'd stayed here at Area 51 instead of taking a more public career path. He might have been on the Joint Chiefs by now, if he'd made more of an effort to play the political game.

That wasn't him, though, so he had a problem with

the prisoners and he had to solve it. Normally he'd drop an alien issue in David Levinson's lap, since Levinson was the ESD director.

But Levinson was nowhere to be found. According to his office, he was running around the Congo somewhere, though even they weren't sure where. It was just like him to vanish when there was something he needed to address, Adams thought, and with the anniversary celebrations coming up, too.

He'd be expected to take part in the pomp and circumstance, but he wouldn't care about that—might not even show up. He was the classic science type, always focused on the next bit of data that came his way, or the next interesting problem he thought only *he* could solve.

Adams debated involving the president. Maybe she could bring Levinson back from his safari, or whatever he was doing. No, he put that idea on the back burner, deciding to keep the alien situation in-house for now. The president had enough on her plate, not the least of which was the big show Legacy Squadron was due to put on in a couple of hours.

Walking into the command center, Adams spotted Lieutenant Ritter. "Any word from Levinson yet?"

"No, sir," the lieutenant said. Then he added another headache to the day. "Sir, Rhea Base has gone dark again. We haven't had contact in eleven hours."

Eleven hours? "When are they going to learn to follow protocol?" Adams growled. Every ESD base was supposed to check in at specified times, to ensure continual operational readiness. The Russians at Rhea Base were lousy at keeping their schedule—he'd complained about it from the moment construction started out there. Say what you would about the French on Mars, at least they were punctual.

"I spend more time on the phone with the Kremlin

than I do with the Pentagon," he added. "Try bouncing the signal off one of the orbiting satellites."

Communications with the space-based ESD installations bypassed the geostationary satellite network and went via line-of-sight to the Moon, then by a relay out to Mars and Rhea. It was a security precaution put into place because the network was too susceptible to being hacked. Adams preferred to follow protocol, but he had to get updates from the outer bases. What was the use of having them, if you couldn't talk to them?

"Yes, sir," Ritter said. He went to issue Adams's orders to the communications team.

"And let me know when you hear from Levinson," Adams added. He was getting more and more irritated with the man. He couldn't just disappear whenever he felt like it. This was why civilians shouldn't be put in charge. They couldn't keep their priorities straight. He would have kept the operation running tight and smooth.

Maybe one day he would have the chance.

Until then, however, he would have to deal with screaming aliens and incompetent directors and Russians who couldn't follow the rules. This was no way to run planetary defense, and Adams wished—for the hundredth time that day—that he was still enjoying the weekend with his wife. Maybe it was getting close to time for him to retire, and live life a little differently.

14

Jake decided to interpret Lao's command as meaning he had to stay in his quarters unless someone ordered him to be somewhere else, 'cause he needed something to eat. Then he issued himself an exception to permit giving Patty a call. He could only talk to Charlie for so long before that irrepressible optimism drove him nuts.

The base had a room set aside for staff to call home. It was a simple rectangle with rows of video booths that offered a little bit of privacy. Jake found an unoccupied booth and made the call, catching her after she'd gotten home from work, or so he guessed. It was early evening, Washington, D.C. time.

Seeing her face on the video feed made Jake feel better right away. Then it made him feel worse again because it had been so long since he'd seen her in person.

"I'm going crazy up here," he said. "I can't take it. Tell me how much you miss me."

"Actually, the chief of staff just got this new intern," Patty said with a mischievous smile. "He's not quite as tall as you, but he's got cute dimples—and he plays the cello."

"Sounds like a great guy," Jake said, playing along as best he could. "I'm happy for you."

She must have seen something in his expression,

though, so she got more serious.

"You know how much I miss you," she said. "It's been a tough week with my dad."

"You still taking him to the anniversary?" It had seemed like a good idea when the planning began months earlier. The White House seemed to want Whitmore there, but Patty—who knew more than they did about her father's condition—had been torn.

"No," she said, surprising him. He hadn't known she'd reached a decision, and now he wondered if something had happened to make her choose. "I want people to remember him for the man he was, not who he's become."

Whitmore had been a dynamo of a man, a genuinely great and decisive leader, as good in peacetime as he'd been during the War of '96. He'd started to have mental health troubles about five years ago, and they were getting worse. Strange dreams, dissociation from reality, scrawling the same weird drawings over and over without being able to explain why... the doctors didn't seem to know what it was or how to treat it. So mostly they just tried to keep him home and out of trouble, but Jake knew it was hard on Patty.

"I wish I could be there with you," he said.

She sighed. "Me, too."

"That's it," Jake said. "I'm gonna walk out of here, steal a tug, and come and see you right now."

"Last time you did that, they added a month to your tour," she said, but she was smiling again. God, Jake loved her. Nothing in the world was as important to him as making her happy.

"Yeah," he said, "but tell me that wasn't the best three minutes of your life."

She let the innuendo slide. "Yes, but as much as I want to see you, I'd like to have you back permanently."

"Only two more months," Jake reminded her. He

wondered how much of it he would spend grounded. He hadn't told her about the accident. It would only worry her, and he sure as hell didn't want her to call in any favors to try to help him. The other pilots would sniff that out immediately, and he'd never hear the end of it. Better just to handle it, see out his tour, and get home.

"I'm counting the days," she said.

The video feed wobbled and distorted as a strange static flared over the audio channel. It was the same pattern Jake had heard right before the tug went out of control. As quickly as it appeared, it was gone.

"What was that?" Patty must have seen it, too.

"We've been getting these weird power surges lately," Jake said. There were a couple more hiccups in the signal, and then it stabilized. The feed returned to normal. He decided to change the subject because if they started talking about the interference he might accidentally mention the accident. "You take a look at the houses I sent you?"

"I haven't had a chance to, with work and everything going on," she said apologetically. Then she paused and added, in a tone of voice that told him she didn't want to say it but felt like she had to, "I saw Dylan at the White House today."

The last thing in the world Jake wanted to talk about was Dylan Hiller. Patty knew it, but she had this idea that the two of them could patch things up and be friends again.

"I just think tomorrow would be a good chance for you two to talk…"

Sure, talk, Jake thought. *Dylan and I have lots to talk about.* "*Hey, remember when I almost killed you in a training exercise? And then I got scrubbed because you were the golden boy and I was just a nobody? Yeah, my fault, but I was a good pilot. Everybody makes mistakes. Tugs? Sure, who wouldn't love flying tugs? Cool, good talk—let's go have a beer.*"

That was never going to happen. Dylan was a rising star. Jake was a space mailman.

"So he gets to shake hands with the president, and I'm stuck on the Moon," Jake said bitterly. "Must be nice."

"Why do you always have to be so headstrong?" Patty looked like she was sorry she'd brought it up. So was Jake, but there they were.

"Everyone knows he wouldn't be leading that squadron if it wasn't for his father."

Then Patty looked angry, and Jake didn't know why.

"You nearly killed him, remember?" she said. "Give him a little credit, Jake."

Jake didn't feel like giving Dylan Superstar Hiller any credit for anything right then, and he was pretty sure whatever he said now he would regret later. Nevertheless, he started to reply—when suddenly a power surge cut the satellite link. The screen blacked out, then resolved for a moment, then a final burst of white noise faded away into nothing.

"P?" Jake said. Maybe she could hear him, even if the video was out. He didn't want the conversation to end this way, right when it was turning into an argument. "P, you there?"

All over the room, video booths went dark. The power flickered on and off. Jake looked around. This time it was lasting longer than it had before, he thought, and it seemed stronger.

What the hell was going on?

*　*　*

Patricia slammed her laptop shut.

Why was Jake so stubborn about Dylan? He was like a big bundle of resentment when it came to anyone else's successes, like the chip on his shoulder was this secret super power he was afraid to let go of. Sure, Dylan had a leg up because of his dad—but he was also a good pilot. The crash during fighter training had nearly killed them both. Jake ended up scrubbed from the program and relegated to space tugs, while Dylan had caught a break, despite sharing the blame. But Jake had played his part in their childish competition, and he didn't have anyone but himself to blame for the outcome.

On her desk next to the laptop sat a photo of her, Jake, and Dylan back in flight school. They were standing next to a human–alien hybrid jet, smiling and happy, the world full of possibilities. That was before she had dropped out, before Jake and Dylan had become rivals, instead of friends.

Before Steve Hiller had died.

Before Patricia's dad had begun his decline... and before the world had started sending them signals that maybe this adulthood thing wasn't going to be that easy after all.

Patricia wished she'd stayed in flight school. She was good at politics—maybe it was in the blood—but it never gave her the feeling she'd had when the afterburners kicked in during a flight.

She and Jake had almost split up when she'd dropped out to deal with her father's affairs. Jake had assumed everything was over, but the truth was, it was easier when they weren't both officers in the same squadron, competing for the same assignments. She'd needed to send him a signal, back then, so she did, taking him on a road trip to a cabin up in the mountains where they could forget about school, forget about jets, forget about everything but each other for a while.

They'd been together ever since, and she wanted to spend the rest of her life with him... but it sure would be easier if he wasn't so good at holding grudges.

Then another thought occurred to her. *What happened*

to the uplink to the Moon? Frowning, she tried to reopen it, but couldn't get through. After a couple of tries she gave up and decided it was one more worry she didn't need. Maybe someone at work would know what was going on.

She would give Jake some time to cool off, and then talk to him again in the morning.

Julius Levinson had never thought much about being famous until he and his son, David, had helped save the world.

David had gotten all the glory, but Julius knew in his heart of hearts that he was the one who had breathed the last bit of hope into the resistance against the aliens, back in the War of '96. After all, wasn't it his idea to infect the alien computers with a virus? Maybe he'd come upon it accidentally, and maybe he'd just mentioned it in passing, and maybe only David could have made the intuitive leap that brought the invasion to its knees.

Okay. Maybe all that was true.

But it had started with Julius.

That's what he told everyone on his book tour. "In our darkest moment, when all hope was lost," he told his audience on this particular day of July 2, 2016, twenty years after David had cracked the alien code. He paused for effect, standing in front of a blown-up photo of himself—a little photoshopped, okay—and a huge image of his book cover, *How I Saved the World*. "That's when I said, 'Never give up! You have to have faith!'"

Sometimes they cheered then, depending on what

time of day it was and how big the audience was. Julius liked the big energetic crowds.

Today they weren't cheering. He kept going, believing that you gave the same speech to a packed house at Madison Square Garden as you did to a single person sitting at the chess tables over at Washington Square Park.

"And in that moment, *pow*! It came to me like a thunderbolt! That's when I came up with the idea that saved the world—"

Or the common room of an assisted-living facility for the elderly in Galveston, Texas.

That's where he was today. Yesterday he'd been in Corpus Christi, at another old folks' home. He'd seen enough of them over the past few years that when it came time for him to settle down in one, he'd have more than enough information to make a good choice.

Today they weren't cheering. They were snoring gently. A gentleman of especially advanced years was sleeping in the front row, lulled no doubt by the comforting sounds his oxygen tank made.

Frustrated, Julius did what he always did at times like this. He went for the comedic angle. If you couldn't sell books based on the books, maybe you could sell them sometimes just by the force of your personality.

"Are we sure he's not dead?" he asked. "Sir? Excuse me, *sir*?"

The man opened his eyes. "Huh?"

"There he is," Julius said. He wanted to go back to his book spiel, but he couldn't. Not today. Not after all the disappointments had piled up a little too high. Why not just have some fun instead? "You didn't follow the light! Welcome back."

It was time to give up. Once Julius had started up his Catskills shtick, it was hard to get back to the book. He knew when to cut his losses.

"Anyway, my book is a bargain at nine ninety-five. Makes a great gift for the grandchildren. If you're lucky enough to have any."

* * *

Twenty minutes later, after he'd talked to the home's director, Julius carried a box of unsold books across the parking lot to his car. At least he had a decent car, a Cadillac. A car with a little class. He opened the trunk and set the box in with all of the other books he hadn't sold.

Yet. Hadn't sold *yet.*

At least the director had bought two, one for herself and one for the home's library. That brought his total for the day to a magnificent... three.

Standing there in the sun, Julius deflated. Who was he kidding? There were no big energetic crowds. Not for him. He couldn't even get David to come with him. His own son! He'd had to trick him into doing a few appearances when the book was new, and David was still angry about it.

What's he got to be mad about? Julius hadn't included how David was drunk and full of self-pity, back during the War of '96. No, he'd spared his son's reputation, yet still he was angry. He'd always been a temperamental child, and now that he knew how smart he was, it was even worse. You couldn't tell him anything. Julius wondered if he should put the scene back in the book. It would have been a good scene. Powerful, affecting. Full of emotions and then redemption—the downcast genius realizing his full potential, with the help of his father.

Julius had himself convinced. He'd have to do another printing—a revised edition.

Book publishing was a difficult business, but the problem surely wasn't him. He was magnetic. He was funny and captivating. Women loved him. It was a great story.

The problem, Julius decided, was with the rest of the world. They wanted their heroes to have guns and jets, wear uniforms. Be young and handsome. They didn't want to hear about computer viruses, or the geniuses who came up with them—or the fathers of those geniuses who planted the ideas in their stubborn sons' heads.

The more he thought about it, the more Julius seethed. The big publishers hadn't wanted his story. And why not? Oh, they were nice about it, but most of the times he'd approached a publisher he'd gotten a polite email back, crying about how the damage to their corporate and editorial offices made it very difficult to launch new projects. Especially books by unknown writers... blah blah blah *bullshit*.

Julius was a bullshitter from way back, and he knew it when he saw it. Especially he knew it when it was being directed at him.

Sure, most of their offices *were* in ruins, because the aliens had destroyed New York, but wasn't there the Internet? They could have published the story. It was a great story. People needed to know that it wasn't just the pilots and the generals who had fought the aliens. It was regular people like Julius Levinson and his son, David. That was the real story.

The pilots could shoot missiles, but if they didn't have the brains behind them knocking the aliens' shields down, the missiles didn't do anyone any good, did they?

"What's wrong with people?" he asked out loud. "No one reads books anymore. Maybe I should start selling online."

He slammed the trunk and decided that what he really should be doing was fishing. What else was an old man to do? When the readers weren't buying, at least maybe the fish would be biting. And if they weren't, well, Julius wouldn't be offended. At least he'd still be out on the boat.

Also, he reflected, he had to be careful about thinking of himself and David as regular people. They weren't, not really. They had helped to save the world. How many people could say that?

He tapped on the trunk and said, "Ask the fish." Then he went around and started the car and headed for the marina.

Jasmine Hiller was trying to focus on her job, but all the hoopla in advance of the anniversary celebrations made it difficult. She walked down the hallway on her rounds. Pediatric nursing was a long way from exotic dancing, but Jasmine herself had come a long way in the last twenty years.

Wall-mounted televisions were showing the press conference where the president and members of Legacy Squadron were taking questions from the assembled press corps. One of those pilots was her son, Dylan, who had also come a long way. Steve had adopted him after the war, and for the next eleven years they had been a real family—the kind of family Jasmine hadn't stopped hoping for after everything had gone wrong with Dylan's biological father.

About whom, she thought, *the less said the better*. The past was the past.

The room into which she walked was dim and quiet, the only lights coming from a lamp near the bathroom door and the TV on the opposite wall. A small boy, bald from chemotherapy, slept there, clutching a doll tightly in his tiny hands. His name was Lucas, and Jasmine had watched him go through his treatment with courage and good humor that broke her heart every time. This time, though, it looked like there might be a happy ending.

One of the other duty nurses, Emily, was straightening Lucas's covers when she saw Jasmine come in. She nodded toward the object he was holding.

"He can't fall asleep without it."

"How's he doing?"

"He's recovering well. He even watched a little TV."

Jasmine smiled. "Go home," she said. "I'll finish up in here."

Emily left and Jasmine stood at Lucas's bedside, looking down at the small boy and his favorite doll. It was a Steven Hiller action figure. Suddenly her heart was in her throat again, thinking of Steve, and the end of the war, and all the plans they'd made together...

Now Dylan was carrying on his father's legacy.

That was the truth of Legacy Squadron. They were torchbearers, holding up the memories of those who had sacrificed everything. For a while Jasmine had been part of a support group made up of survivors who had lost pilots during the War of '96, but she'd come into the group too late—in 2007, when Steve's loss was so fresh and she hadn't known where else to turn. They had their own losses, and to them Jasmine was one of the lucky ones whose husbands had survived the war. She'd had years with him that they hadn't.

She couldn't make them understand. The fact that Steve died in a test flight hurt just as deeply—maybe it hurt more, in a way, because his death had been so unnecessary. He had died because a bunch of goddamned bureaucrats had refused to put the lives of pilots ahead of their political agenda.

Steve's death was heroic because he'd put himself at risk so no one else would have to fly a plane that wasn't ready. But Jasmine had found that she couldn't explain that to the support group. So she'd left. Since then she'd handled it on her own.

There were plenty of people at the hospital who didn't even know she was Steve Hiller's widow. She didn't broadcast it. On the other hand, when your son was on television getting his picture taken with the president, it was pretty hard to remain incognito.

Jasmine went to turn off the TV so Lucas would sleep longer, but she stopped when she saw that it was a documentary retrospective about the hybrid program… and about Steve. There he was, walking through the shimmering heat on the Area 51 tarmac toward the sleek, lethal shape of a prototype fighter. Jasmine couldn't help herself. She turned up the volume, just a little. She didn't want to wake the boy up, but she wanted to hear what they had to say about her husband.

"The 2007 test flight of the first ever human–alien hybrid fighter was piloted by none other than Colonel Steven Hiller," the announcer said. It was right after he'd gotten his final promotion, Jasmine remembered. He'd been convinced they wanted to move him out of his career as a pilot and into a desk job where he could use his clout to help move the program forward on Capitol Hill.

Steve being Steve, he'd said no way. He wanted to fly. If they wanted a poster boy, he would do that, but only when he wasn't flying. Tensions had heated up when Steve had told the administration that he didn't think the new hybrid prototypes were ready for flight tests. David Levinson had agreed. Nobody had listened to either of them, so when the test was scheduled, Steve pulled rank and demanded that he be allowed to fly it.

He was hoping they would cancel the test, not because he was afraid, but because he knew how valuable he was to the public perception of Earth Space Defense. Even Steve had underestimated the one thing in the world more stubborn than he was—a bureaucrat feeling political pressure. The test had gone ahead.

On the screen, the hybrid fighter streaked through a wide ascending arc, then accelerated upward at a steeper angle.

"His was a decision that would ultimately cost him his life," the voice-over intoned.

Wrong, Jasmine thought fiercely. *It wasn't Steve. It was President Bell and Defense Secretary Tanner who cost him his life. Steve saved someone else.* She was surprised at how quickly the emotions returned.

"These haunting images are forever etched in our hearts and minds—"

Jasmine held her breath.

The fighter exploded, disappearing in a huge fireball that trailed bits of burning wreckage across the sky. Every time it broke her heart. Every time it was like being there and seeing it when it happened. Again. Again. Again.

Over the last nine years Jasmine had watched the footage more times than she could count—and definitely more than she would care to admit. It was a sore spot between her and Dylan. He wouldn't watch it again, didn't want to talk about it. *"Enough is enough,"* he said. *"Past is past."* All they could do was look forward and live. But he'd had a different relationship with Steve. To Dylan, Steve was the dad whose example he was always trying to match.

To Jasmine, Steve Hiller was the one man she had met in the last twenty years who had looked past what she did for a living, and seen the potential for what she might do with the rest of her life. She'd had him for eleven years. A whirlwind, wonderful eleven years that had passed as if it was a single evening, and now was gone.

Steve was gone.

Nothing could diminish the shock of seeing it again,

even though by now she had memorized every detail of the blossoming flames, every individual trajectory of falling debris. Piloting was a dangerous business. She'd known that. Steve had certainly known that—but there was a difference between knowing it and seeing it. That was Steve on the screen, disappearing from this life in a ball of fire.

She turned off the TV and made sure Lucas was still sleeping. She had work to do, and her job was saving lives.

Maybe the past wasn't always just the past, Jasmine reflected as she walked down the hall toward the next stop on her rounds. Not when she had to live with it every day.

Suddenly she wanted very badly to hear Dylan's voice.

Dylan Hiller was itchy to fly. He'd had enough of the parade of photo ops and press conferences and briefings and the rest of the stupidity that came with being the public face of Legacy Squadron.

He wanted to get up in the air, feel the power of the new anti-gravity thrusters carrying him higher than any winged aircraft had ever gone. They'd tested the hybrids in the upper atmosphere, and all the way up to the edge of space. They'd done experimental flights out into hard vacuum and then quickly back down. They'd even flown training missions along the Moon's surface.

Not always with the best results, he mused wryly.

At every step the designs had been assessed and improved. The new generation of fighters was fully able to achieve intra- and extra-orbital flight. The fuselage and wing design could withstand reentry temperatures at terminal speeds. The anti-gravity thrusters were built into gimbals with limited range because too many moving parts meant they didn't hold together very well at high speed in thicker atmospheric conditions. That had been a problem in the first vacuum tests, so the new generation had impulse jets at various points along the hull that improved maneuverability in space, where wings didn't do any good.

Weapons systems also featured the best of alien and human design. Dylan and the rest of the squad had practiced for hundreds of hours targeting air-to-air missiles and alien-derived energy cannons. He didn't know if he'd ever have to fire either of them, but if the occasion ever arose, Dylan was confident that he had the training and skills to handle it.

After the press conference he'd flown from Washington, D.C. to Area 51, where he and the rest of the squadron were facing their last few hurdles before they could climb into their jets and be gone from the bounds of Earth. By tonight, Dylan Hiller would be on the Moon. That was something his father had never done.

His father's "legacy"—the word was starting to get on his nerves, but there it was. It weighed on Dylan. He wasn't even Steve Hiller's biological son, but everyone assessed what he did by comparing it to what Steve might have done.

Dylan was grateful that Steve had come into his life, and his mother's. He'd been good for them, and they'd been good for Steve. Family obligations had settled down the wilder cowboy aspects of his personality and centered him around what was really important in life.

That was one reason he'd demanded to take the prototype up in 2007—paradoxically, having people who cared about him made him more likely to risk his life on behalf of other people. Selfishly, Dylan wished he hadn't done it, but at the same time he was proud of his dad, and he knew that if Steve hadn't gone up in the prototype, somebody else's spouse and children would be mourning.

Family life had taught Steve Hiller to be selfless, and Steve had taught that lesson to Dylan.

Leaving the briefing room where a senior ESD official had outlined the parameters of their flight—all for the sake of the assembled reporters—they took a long and photogenic stroll down the wide hallway. Then the photographers scampered ahead of them to catch them coming out of the hall into the main hangar... where nobody in Legacy Squadron had to fake their enthusiasm.

The hangar was filled with hundreds of hybrid fighters, lined up in rows that extended practically as far as the eye could see. Dylan sometimes thought the place was so big it must have its own weather.

The pilots gathered together for another photo op, with the rows of fighters forming their backdrop. Ranks of hybrid craft stretched off into the distance. As impressive as it was, though, Dylan could not wait until the public relations part was done so he could get back to what he did best.

Flying. That was all he wanted to do. Maybe Steve Hiller hadn't been his biological dad, but he had passed on to Dylan a love for the air and the machines that speared through it.

One of the reporters got tired of following the herd and singled out Rain Lao, who Dylan thought had as interesting a history as he did.

"Captain Lao," the man said, "China has been integral to the Earth Space Defense program. Anything you want to say to the folks back home?"

Dylan watched, wondering how Rain would handle the spotlight. He was used to the attention, but it gave some people problems. Rain was the young, beautiful daughter of a pilot who'd been killed in '96 over Wuhan... making her the perfect media fodder. He didn't know whether she'd had any preparation for this kind of questioning, other than the media relations meetings every member of Legacy Squadron had to attend.

Hearing the question, more reporters gathered around her, waiting for her response. Rain replied in what Dylan recognized as Chinese, and they all waited for their translators to speak.

"It's a privilege to be a part of a squadron that symbolizes the unification of our world," one of them said in English.

Another of the pack stayed focused on Dylan.

"Captain Hiller, how do you feel taking off out of a hangar named after your father?"

How do you think I feel? Dylan wanted to say, but he'd been better prepared than that. ESD had put him through drills about dealing with questions that struck an emotional nerve, and by this point it was pretty much routine. "I'm proud," he said simply, "but it's also bittersweet." He might have said more, but his phone rang.

Not many people had his number, and they all knew he was in the middle of flight prep. That meant it was either a crisis, or his mother. Dylan glanced at his phone and winked at the assembled reporters.

"Saved by my mother."

"He's our mama's boy," Rain said, this time in English. The press gaggle laughed.

"Yeah, that's right," Dylan said, going along with the joke. He walked over to his fighter so he could get a little privacy, and answered the call. "You caught me just in time."

"Hey," his mother said. "I just wanted to hear your voice." Right away he could tell there was more to it than that. His mother was good at a lot of things, but hiding her feelings wasn't one of them.

"What's wrong?" he asked.

"Nothing."

Which meant something. A particular something.

"You watched it again, didn't you?" She didn't answer. "Why would you put yourself through that?"

Because she couldn't help herself, was the answer. Dylan knew it and he knew his mother knew it. Neither of them was going to say it out loud, though, so instead Jasmine changed the subject.

"They put your picture with the president on the front page," she said, her tone brightening. "My boy, making a name for himself."

Dylan wasn't quite ready to let it go. "You gonna be okay?" She got depressed sometimes and didn't like to talk about it, but it was real, and he worried.

"I'll be fine," she said, like he'd known she would. They'd had this whole non-conversation before. "Just tell me you'll be careful up there."

"I will," Dylan promised. Then he had to hang up because it was time to fly.

Around him, the other members of Legacy Squadron were climbing into their cockpits and running their preflight checks. Dylan did the same.

The new generation of fighters had optimized the interface between the human operator and the alien technology. Much of the aliens' command and control software was designed along lines suitable for a collective consciousness. Studying and understanding that part of their tech had created an entire new department within the Area 51 complex, and they were just getting to the point of being able to use it efficiently.

An individual operator interacted with the flight systems differently than an element of a hive mind, and those differences weren't always apparent until a human pilot tried to fly one of the hybrid planes. Twenty years of trial and error had gotten them finally to fully operational status… at the cost of more than a few lives.

Dylan deliberately changed his train of thought. Knowing his mother was still watching the footage of his dad's last flight bothered him, but he couldn't help her right then. He had a mission to execute.

He powered up the engines, feeling the thrum of the anti-gravity generators as they came online. The cockpit heads-up display lit up and everything looked exactly like it was supposed to. Dylan called it in, and got permission to take off. He eased the fighter out of the hangar, lifting it just a few feet off the ground as camera flashes popped all around. This was one huge advantage the new hybrids had over traditional thrust-and-lift designs. You could fly them slow if you had to. No need for long runways and the dangerous moments of takeoff and landing.

Some of the reporters followed the planes right out through the hangar doors to the landing pad before ground crews chased them back to their designated viewing areas.

Once he was outside, Dylan amped the thrusters to about half-power and the fighter accelerated, smooth and strong, nose angled up at thirty degrees. When he hit a thousand feet, Dylan really unwound. Four gees pushed him back in his seat—"eyeballs in," as the old test pilots had said. He broke the sound barrier a few seconds later, and a few minutes after that he was on the edge of space.

The fighter bumped just a little through jet stream-level turbulence, but there was another advantage of the anti-gravity propulsion system. When you weren't relying on a controlled explosion and linear discharge of thrust, your plane was a lot more responsive to small adjustments in angular momentum. That translated into a much smoother ride in turbulent atmosphere.

Even the limited turbulence didn't last long, because Dylan and the rest of Legacy Squadron were through the highest levels of the atmosphere less than ten minutes after taking off from Area 51. They flew in formation through near-Earth space, arcing away from their home planet toward the Moon.

This is it, Dylan thought. *This is what I was born to do.*

It was long after nightfall when David, Catherine, and Dikembe reached the upper portion of the city destroyer. They had been climbing for hours, and were miles above ground.

If they'd had to climb all the way from the ground, they never could have made it. Not a human being alive, David thought, could climb fifteen thousand vertical feet in a day, or even ten. Maybe ten, but if that person existed, his name wasn't David Levinson. Thus it was a good thing that Dikembe had led them back up to the ridgeline between the destroyer and the road. There he'd loaded them into an ancient Sikorsky single-rotor helicopter that must have been left over from a colonial engagement in the 1960s.

Despite its dilapidated condition, it stayed in the air long enough to get the three of them across to the joint where the nearest landing petal bent to become nearly horizontal. Even with that head start, they'd had a long way to go before getting anywhere near the main hull of the ship. That was where Dikembe said the entry point was.

They could look out over miles of the surrounding savanna, with the lights of human settlements revealed as tiny pinpricks against the vast landscape. It was an amazing experience, David had to admit. Like climbing a mountain, only the mountain was made of an extraterrestrial alloy, and instead of a summit they were looking for a way into an alien ship. What would they find?

He privately worried that some of the aliens might still be alive inside, although he knew that was practically impossible. After President Whitmore had destroyed the mother ship twenty years ago, most of the aliens had died in the crashes of the other ships, and the rest were killed in the long series of ground battles that followed. Dikembe and his father had fought one of the most prolonged and bitter of those wars. If anyone had left aliens alive, it wasn't going to be them.

Still, David was nervous. Ahead of him, Dikembe and Catherine nimbly jumped over a crevasse at the juncture of one of the enormous landing petals and the main body of the ship. David trailed behind. He was starting to feel some serious vertigo. He didn't think he could just jump across that gap. He knew he would fall. In fact, he wasn't even sure he could take another step.

"Come on, David," Catherine called to him. "We don't have all night."

"This is not safe," David said. "We should definitely be, um, tied to something." *Or back on the ground*, he thought. What had he gotten himself into?

Dikembe waited as Catherine tried to help David work through his sudden paralyzing fear.

"You're not going to fall," she said. "Look, I'm right here. Dikembe's right here. Get across this last little gap and we're home free. See?" She pointed across the expanse of the city destroyer's upper hull. There was an opening there, a broad doorway. Inside they would be safe, David thought.

Unless there were still aliens.

He closed his eyes for a moment and took a deep breath. There was no climbing back down, not at this point. He had to go forward so they could get inside. And to go forward, he had to—

With one lunging step, he cleared the gap and got his balance on the far side. Catherine caught his arm.

"Okay," she said. "See, I knew you could do it."

If only she'd been that encouraging when they were lovers, David thought. But that was unfair. Just his nervousness talking.

"Yeah," he said. "Okay."

*   *   *

It was another hour or so, once they'd made their way into the ship's interior, before they reached the cavernous command center of the vessel. David had been inside several of the crashed destroyers, and he still had vivid memories of the trip he'd taken with Steve Hiller up to the mother ship in 1996. So he knew the way.

When they got to the command center, however, seeing it alive, powered up and waiting for orders, he had chills. And not the good kind. This was a great opportunity for scientific discovery, but he also had a bad feeling that when he learned the reason for the ship being powered up, he wasn't going to like it very much.

All around them, lights oscillated in complex patterns. A background hum of released energy filled the air. David walked up to a console and examined the displays. What he saw there both exhilarated and frightened him. Exhilarated because it confirmed something he had been wondering about for twenty years. Frightened because that confirmation meant that maybe the War of '96 hadn't been the final word in human–alien interactions.

"My God," he said. "It's the same pattern. The distress call came from *this* ship."

Dikembe and Catherine peered at him as if he was

speaking another language, and he was familiar with that look. He got it a lot, particularly when he let his mind run, and the free associations came out of his mouth like a conversation he was having with himself. He stopped long enough to explain.

"When we destroyed the mother ship twenty years ago," he said, "we detected a burst in the X-band frequency, directed toward deep space."

"A distress call," Dikembe suggested.

Right, David thought. *Coming from this ship.* One of the few that had not been damaged in its fall from flight, or destroyed by Earth's forces after David's virus had crippled the alien fleet's defensive shielding. A distress call, yes.

But what had it said? What was it saying, even now?

Relying on his knowledge of the aliens' information structures, David tapped in a command, getting access to the communications log. A holographic image was spawned above the display, a huge sweeping image of the solar system, with the planets animated and rendered in precise detail. He, Catherine, and Dikembe watched as Earth spun past them, complete with continents and oceans and the swirling white of cloud patterns. David wondered whether he was seeing the Earth's weather as it had been twenty years ago, or whether he could match these cloud patterns to weather service data from today.

It was entirely possible that the destroyer's systems, upon awakening, had once again made contact with Earth's satellite network, just as the invaders had twenty years before. Another detail of the animated image also gave him pause. Earth was rendered not as a solid globe, but as a translucent sphere. Below the surface of blues and greens, the Earth's core appeared a brilliant, pulsating red.

There's a reason for that, he thought. *Nothing the aliens do is accidental.* He thought of the hole in the ground, miles below their feet, and wondered again what the aliens had really been after when they started drilling the shaft.

"And it looks like someone picked up the phone and answered," Catherine said.

David nodded. It did indeed look like that. This ship had sent its distress call and then shut down. Only an answering signal would have powered it back up, which meant that the aliens were still out there. They were still communicating with their ships across whatever immensity of space separated Earth from their home system.

Which meant in turn that David had some phone calls to make. And the people on the other end of those calls probably weren't going to like what they heard.

PART TWO
JULY 3

19

It was bright and early on the morning of July 3 when Dylan Hiller and the rest of Legacy Squadron made their approach to the Moon. The flight from Earth had gone flawlessly—not a single hitch. The new fighters were beautiful machines, handling equally well in atmosphere or vacuum.

Along the way they'd done a quick series of flight tests to get final data on performance and maneuverability. Everything checked out as close to perfect as human engineering could make it. The Moon loomed in front of Dylan as he led the squadron into their orbital insertion and landing protocol. He radioed ahead to the Moon Base, knowing Commander Lao would be on edge awaiting the fighters' arrival.

Lao had his entire career wrapped up in the lunar outpost and its role in ESD's planetary relay system. If Dylan knew the man, the hangars and facilities would be spotless and ready for whatever the squadron needed. Not only was he an excellent leader—if a bit stiff—he had a keen sense of the fact that he represented China and its people to the world.

"This is Legacy Squadron," Dylan announced. "We're on final approach. Requesting permission to land."

"Permission granted," Lao answered immediately—
just as Dylan had expected. He'd probably been standing
next to his communications console for the last hour,
awaiting the call. "Welcome," Lao added almost as an
afterthought. He struggled with the niceties of diplomacy.

Dylan led the squadron into a loop around the base,
just so the photographers and the base crew could get
a good look at the fighters. He was proud of how they
looked, and he wanted his people to know their work was
appreciated. Taking the long way around was his way of
saying hello.

He also wanted to get a look at the big cannon, which
was the base's primary reason for existing. It loomed over
the stark landscape near the central command tower,
its barrel angled up and away from the horizon. At the
moment it was pointed more or less at North Africa,
but from what Dylan understood it had full 360-degree
coverage of the space between Earth and the Moon, with
an effective range of hundreds of kilometers.

Part of him wanted to see it in action, but he also
knew that if they ever had to use it, that would mean
another war. Earth didn't need that. They'd barely made
it through the last one.

He steadied the fighter into its final approach, feeling
the anti-grav engines readjust to the counter-force of
a planetary body. They continuously readjusted their
thrust and lift to account for the fundamental behaviors
of gravity. Since the pull decreased with the square
of distance, it had picked up quite a bit in the last few
thousand kilometers as the Moon's influence took over
from the zero-g interval after Legacy Squadron had left
Earth's gravitational field.

The hangar had designated spots for each of the
fighters, and as Dylan had expected, it was in perfect
condition. Not a mote of dust anywhere to be seen, except

what the fighters kicked up and brought in with them on their landing approach.

Each of the ships set down as gently as could be. He ran a system shutdown and waited just long enough to make sure it checked out. Then he pulled off his helmet and popped the cockpit open. The air was dry and smelled faintly of machine oil and cleaning products.

He swung himself out of the fighter, noticing that the base had Earthlike gravity. That was a useful bit of tech they'd taken from the aliens. A long-term presence on the Moon was made a lot easier by normal gravity. If they'd had to put a base there in one-sixth gravity, there could be serious consequences for the health of the crew and officers.

As his boots hit the floor, Dylan looked around and saw the other pilots disembarking, as well. Several of them had never been up here before, and even those who had were taking in the progress Lao and the crew had made in recent months. The base was just about fully online.

At the moment, however, most of the ground crew had abandoned their posts to swarm around the pilots. Dylan signed an autograph here and there, and posed for some pictures, but he noticed one difference right away between the Moon and Earth. Down at Area 51, he was one of the main attractions. Not here. This was a Chinese base, run by a Chinese crew and Chinese officers, and as far as they were concerned Rain Lao walked on water.

Dylan didn't understand a word of Chinese, but he could tell adoration when he heard it. Rain looked a little embarrassed by the attention, but he could see she enjoyed it, too. And why shouldn't she? All of them had worked hard their whole lives to get where they were. They'd earned everything they'd gotten. Legacy Squadron didn't have any pilots who weren't the best of the best, no matter what their last names happened to be.

He passed her on his way into the base proper.

"When you're done being a superstar, meet us for the debrief."

She shot him a look, but was overwhelmed again by the attention and couldn't find a quick response. That wasn't like her. Usually she was among the sharpest at coming up with stinging replies.

Cutting through the chatter, Dylan heard Commander Lao's voice. In English, no less.

"Do I get an autograph too?"

"Uncle Jiang!" Rain ran over and embraced him. The ground crew's response was quite a bit different, though. All of a sudden they all remembered they had somewhere else to be.

Dylan moved on, too. Let Rain have her moment. He would have to meet with Commander Lao soon, but it had been a long flight. He wanted to stretch his legs a little first, and let the initial excitement die down.

*   *   *

Commander Lao looked his niece up and down, amazed at how far she'd come. Her youth had been troubled, and he had feared for a while that she would fail to live up to her potential. His fears, it seemed, had been groundless, but in this rare instance Lao was perfectly happy to be proved wrong.

"You look more and more like your mother," Lao said, as the crew started working on the fighters.

Rain rolled her eyes. "There's nothing a girl wants to hear more than that."

He nodded at the other pilots. "You holding your own with these cowboys?"

"Please," she scoffed. "They're the ones who need to hold their own with me."

"Where's Captain Hiller?" he asked.

Rain glanced around. "Maybe the mess hall," she suggested. "That's where most of the pilots are heading." After the flight, they were hungry and in need of some time sitting around doing nothing.

He nodded, and gestured for her to lead the way.

*   *   *

Jake knew Legacy Squadron had landed, but he hadn't felt like watching the fighters come in. It was too hard to see them, and know that he should have been up there with them.

He was good enough. Everyone knew that—but you couldn't cross Dylan Hiller and make it through the program. That was just a fact of life. Another fact of life was that the last thing in the world Jake felt like doing right then was watching everyone celebrate the son of a hero.

So he took a carton of Moon Milk from a vending machine and sat down to look at his lunch. Maybe he would even eat it. He was still deliberating when Charlie rushed up to him.

"I've been looking all over for you," he said.

Jake gave him a look, like, *Where else would I be?*

"I've got good news," Charlie went on, ignoring the look.

"What is it?"

"The pilot China sent is my future wife."

Jake gave him another look.

"Seriously," Charlie said. "I think my heart exploded." He put a hand on his chest as if to make sure. "She's perfect. Her eyes, her hair, it's like our spirits were communing..." He stopped talking, and Jake saw him tracking something over near the mess hall entrance. *Great*, he thought. *Just great.*

"He just walked in, didn't he?"

"Yes, he did," Charlie replied in a wary tone.

Wonderful, Jake thought. *All I want to do is get on with my life, and I can't even do that because Captain Perfect has to drag his ass all the way to the Moon and show up in my mess hall.* He'd known it was coming, but it didn't make it any easier.

He didn't want to make a scene, though, and he didn't want to be a drag on the squadron's big moment. The best thing to do was leave.

"You're not gonna finish this?" Charlie asked as Jake got up. He didn't wait for an answer, grabbing Jake's carton of milk. "This is the only thing I'm gonna miss from this cold rock," he said, and he downed it.

Jake had to pass near Dylan to get out of the mess hall, but he kept his eyes straight ahead and pretended he wasn't seeing anything. *Don't mind me*, he thought. *Just the loser making way for his famous one-time friend.* It didn't work out that way.

Dylan stepped right in front of him. He didn't say anything, just stood there.

Jake stopped. The mess hall chatter stopped as everyone present saw the two of them, face to face. They all knew the story. It was legendary among ESD spacers, and had percolated out from there. Jake felt like it followed him around, and would his whole life.

He'd had it. He'd tried to do the right thing and leave, and here was Dylan, deliberately not letting it go. Hadn't he already won? He was flying point on Legacy Squadron, and Jake was a mailman. Did he have to show Jake up now, in front of the people he had to work with?

This wasn't Dylan's world. He was a famous tourist here, but when he was gone, Jake would still have to deal with everyone watching on a daily basis. He'd have to hear their snide comments and feel their scorn.

All right, he thought, when Dylan kept staring at him

and standing in his way. *If this is the way you want it, this is the way we'll do it.*

"Mind moving?" he asked quietly. "We both know what happens when you get in my way."

Dylan kept his eyes locked on Jake's for a long moment. He bit his lip. Jake could have turned around, gone the long way, past the other tables—but he wasn't going to do that. He'd committed. He'd called out the star of Legacy Squadron, and he wasn't backing down. Not now.

Jake never saw the punch coming, but he felt it. A light flared in his head and he felt himself hit the floor hard. It was a good shot, a straight right to the face. Jake tasted blood. Then he sat up, and saw Dylan staring down at him.

"Been waiting a long time to do that," Dylan said.

Charlie had seen the whole thing and now he ran over and helped Jake get to his feet. Jake shrugged him off, not wanting Dylan to see how badly the punch had shaken him. He could barely keep his legs under him, but that wouldn't last.

"Morrison!" Commander Lao stood in the doorway. Jake didn't know how much he'd seen. "What's going on here?"

He walked up to Jake, standing next to Dylan. Both of them stared hard.

It felt just like it had when everyone had blamed him for the tug crash. Nobody cared about the burst of white noise that crippled the tug, and nobody was going to care that Dylan had started this just to show him up. It didn't matter. When you were Dylan Hiller, you got your way.

"I asked you a question!" Lao snapped.

"These floors are really unpredictable," Jake said evenly. "Be careful, sir." He turned slightly. "Dylan, great seeing you."

He could feel his lip swelling. It was split pretty good. Jake wiped the blood away and started for the door, brushing past Dylan on the way. He could have sworn he saw regret on Dylan's face, but it didn't matter. *Whatever.* Jake was going to take his fat lip back to his room, crank up some tunes, and contemplate life.

Blamed for the cannon accident even though he'd saved everyone's lives, girlfriend mad at him, then his one-time pal busted his lip in front of all his coworkers… it had been a hell of a twenty-four hours.

"Captain Hiller," he heard Lao say behind him. "I'm so pleased to have you here. I once had the honor to meet your father…"

Blah blah blah, Jake thought. Lao would love this scenario. Captain Perfect shows up the chump who once imagined he might be a space pilot too, but couldn't even fly a tug. But everyone was wrong about Jake.

One of these days, maybe he'd show them.

20

Charlie gave Jake a little while to cool off—by which he meant sulk—and then he headed back to their quarters to do what he privately called a "Jakervention."

Jake was a good guy. Charlie liked him, and admired him, and certainly owed him for the way he'd helped him out back when they were kids. Jake had been a big brother to Charlie when the kid had badly needed one. But Jake also needed to get out of his own head once in a while. He got all wrapped up in self-pity sometimes, and it was up to Charlie to get him out.

So he kicked around the base, checking out the knockout Chinese pilot. Rain Lao. What a name. What a woman. The fact that she was Commander Lao's niece deterred Charlie not one bit. Maybe she was out of his league, but how would he know until he gave it a try? It was the truest thing anyone had ever said to him.

"You gotta shoot to score."

That was one of the volunteers back at the orphanage, on one of the occasions when they'd dragged all the kids out to get some exercise. Charlie liked playing soccer, but he wasn't very good at it, and after he'd had a couple of chances to score and muffed them badly, he'd stopped trying. He passed every time. Finally the volunteer, an older guy named Leonardo, came over to him.

"Oye, Charlie," he said, "you gotta shoot to score, man. Don't you ever want to score?"

Charlie did. After that, he'd still been lousy at soccer, but he'd decided it was better to try and fail than not try at all. That was one of the few life lessons he'd taken away from the orphanage.

Most of the others had to do with Jake—and later, Dylan and Patricia. So here he was trying to help. He opened the door and saw Jake staring at the wall. Music was playing in the background, some classic rock tune from thirty years before Charlie was born, and on the screen was the helmet-cam footage from the accident. Jake always watched it when he was depressed. Charlie knew it by heart at this point—Jake cutting too close on Dylan's left, the sharp metallic bang of their wingtips touching, then Dylan shouting that he was ejecting…

Charlie waited until it was over. Then before Jake could start the video over again, he spoke up.

"You okay?"

Jake didn't say anything. This was bad. He'd had a rough couple of days, what with the tug incident and now the Dylan thing.

"I was so close to punching him back," Charlie said, making a fist.

"I think you made the right choice," Jake said, with a ghost of a smile.

Aha, Charlie thought. *Progress.* He plopped next to Jake on the couch. "When is he gonna let it go? It was a training accident. I mean, yes, you did almost kill him, but that's why they have ejection seats."

"I went too far," Jake said softly. "I just wanted it so bad."

"It was never gonna be you. The world doesn't work like that. He's—" Charlie couldn't find the word right away. What did you call a guy like Dylan Hiller? "He's royalty. We're just orphans, Jake."

Charlie knew Dylan had lost his father, too, and then his stepfather. His life hadn't exactly been a bowl of cherries—but there was a long, long distance between having a heroic pilot adopt you and see you through to adulthood, and the kind of childhood Jake and Charlie had experienced.

"When they dropped me off at camp," Jake said slowly, "the last thing I said to my parents was that I hated them. Two days later, L.A. was incinerated. They saved my life."

There were a lot of ways to go with that, Charlie thought. Jake's parents hadn't meant to save his life, after all. They'd just wanted him to go to camp. Charlie hadn't even been at camp. He'd been a toddler at day care when the aliens killed his parents at their jobs. He and Jake had met at an orphanage school, Jake with his big dreams and Charlie just trying to survive. He was small, and smart, and maybe had a bit of a big mouth, and life at the orphanage was hell.

Then one day Jake was there, chasing away the worst of the bullies. He was that rare thing in Charlie's life, a big strapping kid who also had a big heart. Once Jake got involved, the worst of the bullying stopped. Charlie could go through his days without fear of being beaten, or worse. In return, he'd figured out something he could do to help Jake.

Study. Jake had dreams of being a pilot but the top-flight—so to speak—tech schools weren't exactly trolling the orphanages for their next generation of the best and brightest. Still the dream kept Jake going, so Charlie jumped in. And it worked! Jake got into the Area 51 flight-prep academy.

The problem was, Charlie hadn't finished school yet. If Jake left him at the orphanage, Charlie was going to be in for a serious shit storm. Five years' worth of stored-up frustration his tormentors were just waiting to take out on him. So Jake came through again.

He found a place where they both could live, and Charlie found his way into the Academy's engineering track. After that, they'd been inseparable. Jake had saved Charlie, Charlie had saved Jake.

Then the Dylan Hiller thing had happened.

It was stupid, but they'd both been stupid. A simple exercise, scored by the observing officers deciding which cadets would move on to the next round of Legacy Squadron training. Jake tried to cut in on Dylan as they flew through a canyon, and in the ensuing collision Dylan nearly died. Because Jake was Jake and Dylan was Dylan, guess which one of them got scrubbed out of the higher program, and reassigned to space tugs?

The orphan without the famous last name.

To be fair, it *was* Jake's fault. He should have yielded and taken his chance the next time they ran the drill. Problem was, Jake wanted the win as badly as Dylan, and he had a chip on his shoulder as big as his whole life. He was *never* going to back down.

Things had ended with a hundred-million-dollar burning wreck, and everyone had pointed fingers at Jake. Competitive fire was part of the pilot personality, but Jake had gotten carried away, and he knew it.

The worst thing about it was that it had ended their friendship. They'd all been friends. Jake, Charlie, Dylan, and Patricia Whitmore—who also wanted to be a pilot. She was already gone before the Dylan incident, dropping out to take care of her father, but her relationship with Jake had survived. So had her friendship with Dylan.

For a while, they'd been a fine little surrogate family, Charlie thought. But then…

That got him thinking about parents again. About how

neither he nor Jake had any, and what Jake had just said about how his parents had saved his life.

"I'm glad they did," Charlie said. "'Cause you're the only family I got."

Jake nodded. He was too far down to perk all the way back up, but Charlie could tell he was helping. So, true to form, he started joking around before everything got too serious.

"And don't beat yourself up, man," he added. "Enough people are doing that already."

Then Jake *did* smile. *There we go*, Charlie thought. *Another successful Jakervention.*

21

After they'd spent all night trying to figure out what was going on in the newly reawakened alien destroyer, Dikembe brought them back to his house. All of them were still riding the wave of energy from their discoveries. David knew he should be tired—he hadn't slept in twenty-four hours—but sleep could wait. His brain needed to solve problems, not dream.

Catherine, of course, related everything they'd seen to her scholarly work on the alien consciousness and its relationship with the human mind. As they walked from the two trucks toward Dikembe's compound, the monumental shape of the alien destroyer casting a long shadow over the savanna, she brandished her tablet at him, pointing at a series of drawings.

"This symbol comes up more than any other I've encountered," she said. "Look at the similarities. How can you not see the relevance?"

The symbol in question was a circle with a sharp line cutting through it. She was right, they had seen it up in the ship, but David wasn't a psychologist. He was more interested in hard data, and in actual machines.

"It's not that I don't see it," he said as they kept walking. "I just feel like there are more pressing matters than analyzing, uh, doodles. You know, like a giant spaceship turning back on."

He could tell that she was irritated by the word "doodles," but as far as David was concerned, that's what they were. Sure, people were affected by the alien presence in their minds. And sure, they tended to draw the same things, over and over. But that was standard obsessive behavior—a response to frightening or incomprehensible stimuli. It might not be related to the aliens at all. It might be an artifact of how the human brain processed the alien telepathy.

That's what he'd said to her back at the xenology conference in Lisbon, and again in French Guiana. She'd been irritated then, too. Something had interrupted them. David couldn't remember what, until the expression on Catherine's face triggered the memory.

It was a pilot, the famous Chinese one. Rain Lao, that was her name. She and another pilot were flying around the Earth in a publicity stunt to raise support for Earth Space Defense's research activities. The other pilot's propulsion system failed as they were approaching reentry. Rather than leave him to die, Lao had pulled off something David wouldn't have thought possible. She'd matched the falling fighter's speed, nudged herself underneath it, and then decelerated slowly and smoothly enough that both aircraft survived reentry.

They had both crashed, somewhere in Montana, but since they both survived that had only added spice to the story. Legacy Squadron heroics, before Legacy Squadron was even put together.

Anyway, Catherine had been frowning at him in the same irritated—*and, let's face it, beguiling*—way when the video feeds in the conference bar area had cut away to Lao's daring rescue.

Shaking his head, David got himself refocused on the

present as Collins came out to meet them from the front of Dikembe's palace. The word was a little too grand, but "house" didn't seem to quite do it justice.

It was a big, colonial-style structure, and more impressive now that Dikembe had personalized it with his own stylistic touches. Mostly those had to do with adding alien bones here and there for accents. David thought it was quite an intriguing look. The combination of the colonists' architecture, the alien trophies, and the valiant son of a post-colonial warlord presiding over it all…

That made for quite a spectacle.

"Sir," Collins said, his tone setting off alarms in David's head. Normally the man was all but unflappable. If something was worrying him, it likely deserved David's concern, as well. Before they'd made it all the way across the compound's huge driveway, Collins let David know just how concerned he should be.

"We've lost contact with Rhea."

"When? Why didn't you call me?"

"You left your sat-phone in the jeep."

Fair enough, David thought.

There could be a number of reasons for communications failure with Saturn's moon. From Rhea Base, signals went to local satellites, which relayed signals via Mars to Earth. There was a lot of redundancy built into the system, because a lot could go wrong with signals traveling two billion kilometers in an environment filled with different kinds of electromagnetic radiation. Everything from cosmic rays to background dark-matter emanations to X-rays… David figured the best approach was to assume it was a local failure, and see if there was a workaround using the Saturn-based resources ESD had in place.

"Get me images from the satellites orbiting Saturn," he said.

Collins looked even more worried. "They're also offline."

This got David's full attention. Two points of failure in the system were much less likely than one. For both the base comm system and the satellite network to fail simultaneously, something massive must have gone wrong. Either that, or there was a problem with one of the other links in the communication chain—but Collins would have run that possibility down.

If he wasn't saying it, it hadn't happened.

"We have to notify the president," David said. She wouldn't want the distraction as she was gearing up for the twentieth anniversary celebration, but there was no other choice he could see.

"Already tried," Collins said. "Tanner said they'll get back to us after the press tour."

"A press tour?" That pissed him off. Satellites were failing for unknown causes, at the most distant settlement human civilization had ever known. What could be more important than that? David had never thought Tanner was suited to his job, and now he was more certain than ever.

"It's frustrating when someone doesn't take your call, isn't it?" Catherine remarked.

David shot her a look—*this is not the time*—and turned to Collins. "Bypass Tanner however you can, and get General Adams to reconfigure Hubble. We need eyes on Rhea." He knew he could count on Adams, who was remarkably open-minded for a general. David's experience with other high-ranking military officers was that they had shed their originality and creativity while learning the games of promotion and politics on their way up the ranks. Adams was different. He was a fine leader and willing to listen, even if he didn't always understand the finer scientific points.

They entered Dikembe's house and walked through the hall into a spacious foyer, where David's team had set up workstations. They had everything they needed for field research—monitors, satellite transponders, portable laboratory equipment for basic analysis of any unfamiliar materials they might encounter, databases of previously known alien technology, and so forth.

The house made for a strange working environment. It was a museum of stuffed animals, preserved because Umbutu the Elder had been a devoted hunter. David found the activity incomprehensible and repellent, but he understood that it was popular. A sort of throne stood against one wall, under the watchful eyes of a giant portrait showing Dikembe's father with his sons.

"At least your father spared the elephants," David said, taking in the collection. It occurred to him then that Umbutu might well have hunted elephants. The compound was large enough that it could have a separate building just for stuffed elephants and other large animals.

He put it out of his mind.

They had to understand what was going on with the powered-up destroyer, and also with Rhea Base. Were they related? Correlation didn't necessarily imply causation, of course. To assume so was to commit an elementary fallacy. To reject the possibility out of hand, however, was to be blind to the fact that coincidence existed. They didn't know enough to say either way, and wouldn't until they had a solid idea of what had happened on Rhea.

Catherine approached David and held up her tablet again. This time it displayed another variation of the circle image, painted on a barn.

"The Roswell crash in '47," she said. "The farmer who made contact drew the same circle. And every time I interview one of my patients who had physical or mental contact with the aliens and show them this, they express one feeling, one emotion."

"Fear," Dikembe said.

They all turned to him as he went on.

"And I don't think it's a circle. The night the ship turned on, I experienced the strongest vision I've ever had."

David knew some of Dikembe's story. He'd returned from England during the War of '96, arriving in time to take part in his father's ground battle against the aliens who had emerged from the destroyer that now loomed a few miles distant. Then his father's madness had taken over and Dikembe had nearly died in a prison cell of some kind. The son had experienced prolonged and overwhelming visions during his imprisonment, and one of the reasons David was here instead of back in Washington—or at Area 51—was that he wanted to know what Dikembe might have learned.

He didn't believe Catherine's thesis that all humans kept open a psychic link to the aliens after contact, but it was obvious to anyone with eyes that the aliens' telepathic intrusion left some kind of lingering effect. Dikembe might be able to shed some light on it.

Quite a bit of light, as it turned out.

Dikembe led them through a set of massive oak doors into his study. It was more opulent than David would have expected from a man of Dikembe's demeanor. Perhaps he hadn't redecorated after his father's death. The furniture was leather and expensive, the rugs hand-woven, the other furnishings of the highest quality. The room made David want to sit down and study something. He wondered if they could move his workstation in here.

Scattered on every surface, and pinned to the walls between pricey oil paintings, were sketches of the circle.

"And I drew this," Dikembe said, guiding them to the middle of the room. As if set up for display, a more intricate and detailed version of the circle symbol was there on a table.

Catherine started taking pictures of it.

"I've never seen it drawn like this," she said, in a

tone David knew well. This was what scientists sounded like when they first saw something that blew up one hypothesis, and gave a tantalizing glimpse of a much more interesting one.

On the bookshelves, David noticed three of Catherine's books. So Dikembe was a kindred spirit. Also a well-read man, at least in this area. Or maybe not just this area—next to that shelf was a framed diploma from Oxford University.

"An Oxford man," David said. On the wall near the diploma hung numerous images of alien symbols with translations underneath. French, Swahili, Lingala, Kikongo, all the common languages of the region. "Incredible," he said. "You've deciphered more of their language than we have."

"The residual connection," Dikembe said. Catherine glanced up. David refused to look at her. Just because Dikembe believed her… "They were hunting us," he went on. "We had to learn how to hunt them."

And so you did, David thought.

22

General Adams got the armor-piercing message from Levinson's assistant, asking for the Hubble reorientation, and almost fired back an angry reply.

He wanted to point out that if Levinson was here, instead of in the Congo of all places—or the Republic of Umbutu, if the U.N. had recognized it as such—he could do it himself.

Then he decided that wouldn't do any good. The priority had to be finding out what had happened to Rhea Base, and reestablishing contact with the Russian commander there. Despite his initial grumbling about the Russians' punctuality, Adams knew Commander Belyaev and believed him to be a fine officer and a reliable partner in Earth Space Defense.

He felt the same way about the French and Chinese garrisons on Mars and the Moon. One thing their cooperative work had taught him was that international partnerships could succeed if the right people were involved. That was part of ESD's mission from the very beginning. President Whitmore had laid it out in his famous speech during the War of '96, and it was still true today.

What it meant was that if Belyaev wasn't communicating, something had gone wrong. It was one thing to be late for a scheduled report. Being incommunicado for a full twenty-four hours—more at this point—was something completely different. And much more worrisome.

Adams returned to the command center and found Ritter, who was consulting with staff officers.

"Anything from Hubble?"

Ritter walked over to a dedicated monitor.

"We're uploading the image now."

On the monitor, an image slowly resolved itself as the computer compiled the data feed from the Hubble telescope. When it was finished rendering, Adams stared at it for a long moment, unable to believe what he was seeing.

"When did this happen?" he asked.

"We don't know," Ritter replied. "Should I up the alert level?"

Damn right, Adams thought. "Let's go to Orange until we know more."

"General," a staff officer called from the other side of the command center. "Air Force One has landed."

Perfect timing, Adams thought. Aliens going crazy in their cells, this—event—on Saturn, and now the president had arrived. He didn't have enough attention to devote to all these problems at once. "Send that image to Levinson," he ordered Ritter. "Make sure he sees it, and make sure he contacts me immediately."

Then he went to meet the commander-in-chief.

*   *   *

Jake was still grounded, but as it turned out he wasn't excused from repair duty. That was fine. It gave him something to do other than mull over everything that had gone wrong in the last day. He was working on the tug, pulling off damaged plating to get a better look at the burned-out circuitry inside, while Charlie avoided doing any actual work by telling Jake what to do.

"You have to remove the subsonic inlets if you want to reconfigure the thermalized plasma cartridges," he was saying. Jake couldn't follow the torrent of jargon, and Charlie knew this, but that never stopped him from talking. In fact, nothing ever stopped Charlie from talking.

"Oh my God," he said abruptly, interrupting his lecture. "There she is. It's happening. The chemical reaction, the pheromones... all the blood in my body is rushing to my head."

Ah, the Rain Lao infatuation, Jake thought. The only thing Charlie was better at than aerospace engineering was falling in love with unattainable women. "You sure it's rushing to your head?"

"I'm gonna introduce myself," Charlie said, taking off without another look at the tug.

"Sure," Jake said. "I got this. Even though I didn't understand anything you just said." As if to underscore this, a shower of sparks flared in the damaged engine housing. "Son of a bitch!" he shouted. He turned to complain, but broke it off because Charlie was making his move.

He sidled up to Rain Lao while she supervised a crew of technicians. They were rolling out a large Chinese flag next to her fighter.

"You must be the pilot China sent," Charlie said.

She tossed him a classic side-eyed glance.

"Did the giant flag give it away?"

"There's that," Charlie said, taking it in stride, "and the fact that I heard you speak Chinese to some of the crew. Anyway, I was wondering if you wanted to get a drink, and maybe fall in love?"

Now she gave him a more appraising look. Jake admired Charlie's gumption. He never got anywhere with his peculiar approach, but that never stopped him from trying.

"Aren't you a little young for that?" Rain asked.

Before Charlie could answer, the lights in the hangar dimmed, flickered, and then went out, leaving only emergency lighting. Pilots and ground crew alike looked up at the ceiling, then around the space, waiting for them to come back on.

Jake looked from Charlie and Rain back to the tug's battered and disassembled engine housing. This was the last straw.

"Can someone please pay the electric bill already?" he griped.

23

Like the rest of the new generation of military aircraft, Air Force One had been heavily modified with alien technology. Now it was powered by massive anti-gravity thrusters, taking the place of the traditional turbine engines.

It sat cooling down on the tarmac of Area 51 as President Lanford and Secretary Tanner led a group of journalists toward the command center.

"Now that our Orbital Defense System is fully operational, we can initiate Phase Two of the Space Defense Program," she said, following the schedule she'd rehearsed with her team over the past few days. She had to strike a balance between giving the public useful information and steering clear of classified data. Tanner hadn't wanted her to say anything, but Lanford believed in erring on the side of transparency. "On the left are the destroyer cannons that will be ready for deployment across the solar system over the next ten years."

Sensing an opening, a reporter jumped in without even looking at the rows of weapons.

"So you're not exactly delivering on your promise to scale back on this program."

"The money's already been spent by my predecessors," Lanford said smoothly, "but now that the bulk of the infrastructure is in place, we can finally start spending elsewhere." Camera crews angled around to get pictures and video of the president against the backdrop of the cannons. While she continued her conversation with the press, General Adams approached Tanner and drew him aside.

"We need to cut the tour short," he said.

"I'm sure it can wait," Tanner said, annoyed that Adams had maneuvered him out of the pictures. Adams didn't have time to deal with his love for the spotlight, though. The news from Saturn was much more important, and if he couldn't get to the president directly, he was for damn certain going to make sure he got the information to her cabinet.

"I'm telling you, it can't," he said, and started toward the command center with a reluctant Tanner in tow.

*   *   *

David Levinson was hard at work trying to figure out exactly what Dikembe had learned from his study of the alien language. According to the warlord, the circle represented "fear." As he considered the ramifications of that, Collins rushed into the room waving a tablet.

"Sir, this just came in."

David glanced up, then took the tablet from Collins and looked closely at the image it displayed. It was Saturn. He could tell that much. The color, the striations on the surface—or what passed for a surface on a gas giant—those matched, but where he'd expected to see Saturn's majestic ring system, and the dozens of moons and moonlets that orbited with it in a complicated gravitational dance…

All he saw was debris. The rings were torn into wisps of their former selves, scattered in long strands over thousands of miles of space—maybe millions of miles in some cases. David immediately tried to reverse-engineer what he saw, understand the process that had caused it, and he quickly understood that not only were the rings deformed, but some of the moons were gone. Or if not gone, definitely not where they were supposed to be.

What the hell could move a moon?

Catherine leaned in next to him.

"Is that Saturn?" she asked, her voice incredulous. "What happened to the rings?"

"A meteor, an asteroid maybe…" David trailed off. He knew that wasn't the case. Passing asteroids cut through Saturn's rings all the time. Most of them didn't even leave a trace visible from Earth. The only thing that could have disrupted the rings like this, torn them apart across tens of thousands of miles…

Well, he didn't know *what* could do something like that. A huge gravitational disturbance of some kind? But what would cause it? Maybe a collision between two of Saturn's larger moons would have an effect like this, but none of Saturn's moons had been on collision courses. On the other hand, if there was a passing body large enough to cause that kind of havoc, it would have been visible from Earth. Certainly it would have been visible from Rhea, well before the base there went silent.

A planetary-scale event like this should have been visible from Earth, and should have been predictable. Satellites and telescopes were constantly scanning the solar system for large rogue bodies. David checked quickly and confirmed what he already knew. There was nothing large and unaccounted-for near Saturn.

They were dealing with an unknown phenomenon, and one that had unleashed an incredible amount of power. All the energies of human civilization put together couldn't have shredded Saturn's rings this way.

So what had?

* * *

By the infernal glow of the emergency lights, Jake made his way from the hangar toward the command center. Was this the same thing that had happened yesterday, and shorted out his tug's guidance system?

Maybe it was some kind of electromagnetic storm? They had monitors on the sun for solar storms and flares, but who knew what else was out there. The universe was big enough that there were probably a million different things capable of knocking out power—things that humankind hadn't even thought of.

He got to the command center and saw half the tech crew pounding away at keyboards and touch screens, trying to get the power back on—and the other half staring out of the huge bay window. Jake looked that way, and couldn't believe what he saw.

Just above the Moon's surface, only a few miles from the base, the fabric of space itself looked like it was twisting. Something was happening to gravity, as well. The dust and heavier bits of regolith directly under the... whatever that thing was... spiraled up and were sucked into it. How was that possible in a vacuum? The disturbance had to have its own gravitation.

It might be a black hole. If a black hole was coming into existence, it would do exactly what they were witnessing. At least he thought it would, because black holes had basically infinite gravity, so as one grew from a tiny little pinpoint singularity, it would start eating up all the matter around it. Including ex-fighter cadets who crashed their tugs. Jake remembered Charlie shouting yesterday, *This is how I die!*

Well, maybe it was. Charlie would know if this was a black hole. When it came to astronomical phenomena, Charlie had it all figured out.

The disturbance grew and took a shape like... what, a mouth? A hole of some kind. A few moments ago it had looked like a tear, but now whatever had caused the tear was ripping it wider open. But if space was ripping open, what the hell was going to be on the other side? Jake didn't have the kind of mind that could easily come to grips with ideas like that. Charlie, he would already be spouting complicated formulas about string theory and wormholes or something. That was what he did.

Well, that and put the moves on unattainable women, Jake thought as he saw Rain Lao come into the command center. Dylan came in with her, a whole group of Legacy Squadron pilots entering together. For once Dylan didn't look cocky. In fact he looked just like everyone else—nervous, confused, wondering what to do next. Jake could practically read his thoughts.

He would have bet everything he owned—not that he owned much—that Dylan was having to hold himself back from making a dash for the hangar to get his fighter off the ground. That's what a pilot always wanted to do when things got uncertain. If you were flying, at least you could take action if action was needed. Then you could always land if it wasn't.

But if you never took off, things had a way of running away without you and making you a spectator.

It occurred to Jake that there was some kind of life lesson in that, but then he saw Charlie and nodded toward the window. Charlie, taking in the sight, cut among the feverishly working technicians to stand next to Jake. Neither one of them said anything. They didn't need to.

The storm intensified as the giant hole reshaped space around it. Larger rocks began floating up away from the Moon's surface. It was definitely more whirlpool-like than it had been before. Was it going to suck all of them in? Or would it just spin in space, without influencing the gravity any more?

How did anybody here know what to do?

Jake watched the techs, wishing there was some useful action he could take. Scientists would be going crazy at this, like they always did when they saw something that disproved a bunch of stuff they'd always taken for granted. That was the scientist's state of mind, always looking for the new thing that would make something else wrong. Jake wasn't like that. Once he knew something, he liked it to stay true.

What he was seeing—that he didn't like.

From the look of the command center crew, many of them felt the same way. Some were still working to get the main power back online, but more and more of them were joining the pilots and other outside crew, gazing at the strange phenomenon and wondering what it could be.

Lao had been commanding the tech crews, until he seemed to realize that whatever they were doing wasn't working. He looked back out of the window and said something in Chinese. Jake had picked up a few words of the language during his time on the Moon, but he didn't know exactly what Lao had said. The general tone of his voice was easy to interpret in any language, though.

What the hell is that?

Something began to take shape inside the anomaly. Jake watched and waited, a cold knot in the pit of his stomach. The twentieth anniversary of the start of the war was yesterday. This couldn't be a coincidence. There was just no way.

And if it wasn't a coincidence, then it was a damn good thing he'd wrecked his tug getting that cannon into place, Jake thought. Even if nobody was ever going to give him credit for it.

Then there was motion inside the anomaly. That was when things really started to get out of hand.

24

David was still trying to make sense of what he was seeing on the monitor when Collins called over to him.

"We have a priority feed from the Moon Base."

"Put it on screen," David said. A few keystrokes from Collins' workstation transferred the feed to another monitor. David, Catherine, and Dikembe gathered to watch.

On the monitor, they saw a swirling vortex in space, seen from the Moon Base. Radiant colors crackled around the vortex's core, and a long tendril of dust was visible trailing upward from the surface toward it. David instantly made the connection to Saturn's rings. He looked back at that image, which still showed on another monitor.

Yes, he thought. The rings had all been pulled out of alignment by a point-source attraction with a huge gravitational pull. Was the cause another spatial disturbance, like the one now active near the Moon?

If they were the same phenomenon, the lunar base could be in critical danger. Anything that could destroy Saturn's rings could probably also reduce the Moon to a debris field. And what might it do to the Earth…?

He looked back to the feed as a motion caught his attention. From the vortex, a spherical shape emerged. The immense energies of the vortex flickered around it and then snapped away, like arcs of electricity, as it separated itself from the phenomenon and hung in space.

Several things occurred to David at once.

The first was that he had just seen empirical proof of the existence of wormholes. What else could it be? A hole opened up in space-time and a massive physical object passed through it. The sphere had to have come from somewhere. Either another point in the universe, or—the string-theory explanation—another universe. It didn't matter really. The relevant fact was that the disturbance was a wormhole, and what had come through it was a spaceship.

The aliens were back.

Or were they? As David got a closer look at the ship, he saw that it didn't resemble the aliens' design in any way. They built in giant disk shapes, and this ship was spherical. The markings on the sphere's hull were patterned differently, as well. The ship had a long, unbroken line of bright blue light along what would have been its equator if it were a world, extending halfway around its circumference. As it cleared the wormhole and began to turn, orienting itself toward the Moon, David caught a brief view of its other side, where a trio of circular thrusters glowed the same blue. From that angle it also appeared as if part of the ship's hull was transparent, revealing complex machinery within.

Its orienting maneuver revealed something else to David—and more immediately to Dikembe.

"It was a spaceship," the warlord said slowly, referring to the circle-and-line sketch he had drawn so many times over the years.

Colors began to cycle in a clear pattern on its surface. Some sort of communication? The aliens had never attempted that either. Or if it wasn't a communication, what reason could there be for the change in hue?

David had too many questions, and no way to get the

relevant answers. What he *could* do was loop in everyone else who needed to be part of the conversation, and fast, so they could at least be acting in concert. If this was the aliens returning, humanity needed to present a decisive and united front. If it was not—if this was another extraterrestrial race—the way forward was different, and much less certain.

Perhaps much more positive. Not all alien civilizations would be predatory. In any event, David had to speak to Adams, and if possible President Lanford.

"Patch me through to Area 51," he said, not taking his eyes off the monitor, where the ship was now moving toward the Moon Base.

"You're already on," Collins said.

General Adams, Secretary Tanner, and the president appeared on another monitor. David could see from the background that they were all gathered in the command center at Area 51.

The president didn't waste any time with small talk. "David, are you seeing this?"

"Yes, Madam President. I'm looking at it right now." Next to him, Catherine was scrutinizing the ship's light sequence on the monitor.

"It's a pattern," she said. "It's repeating itself."

David nodded. That's what he'd thought too. "Yes, it is." He looked into the camera feeding his image to Area 51 and said, "It looks like they're trying to communicate."

"They could be initiating an attack," Tanner shouted. "We need to strike first!"

"Hold on a second," David said, studying the ship. It was huge, fifty kilometers in diameter, according to the chatter from the Moon Base, and circular, which fit the aliens' design, but there was something... He looked at it more closely, testing his initial impressions, realizing that whatever he decided in the next few moments might well have an impact on millions—or billions—of lives. No, he was sure. "The design, the tech, it looks completely different than the ones who attacked us."

Tanner wasn't buying it. "So they've upgraded!"

David leaned over to center himself in the viewing window. He'd anticipated that Tanner would want to shoot first and ask questions later, and the bellicose secretary was acting true to form. David needed to stake out his position, and insist on the credibility of the work he'd been doing since 1996.

"I know more about their technology than anyone else," he said firmly. "To my eyes, I don't think this is them."

Tanner's incredulous reply was again along the lines David had expected.

"We've spent the last twenty years building these weapons," he said, looking furious, "and now you don't want us to use them?"

That was the problem with men like Tanner, thought David. Because they had guns, they wanted to use them. It was the old saying come to life. *If all you have is a hammer, everything starts to look like a nail.*

Adams cut into the conversation.

"At this point, we have to assume Rhea Base has been destroyed," he said. "Madam President, this could be a coordinated attack."

David agreed that Rhea Base was probably gone. He didn't agree, however, with Adams's second assumption. The general was falling into the old fallacy that correlation implied causation. Nobody knew what had happened to Rhea Base. Superficial resemblances were just that, and in the absence of hard data, David didn't intend to support a knee-jerk impulse to start shooting.

"They wouldn't be trying to communicate if they wanted to attack us," he insisted, raising his voice a little. President Lanford peered at him through their connection.

"What if you're wrong?" she asked.

"And what if *you're* wrong?" David shot back. That was the whole point—they didn't know. How could they initiate a combat response without knowing? "We could be starting a war with a whole new species. Imagine that!"

Abruptly a different screen spawned a view of the U.N. Security Council. President Lanford must have pressed some kind of panic button to convene them so quickly. David was glad to see this. At least she wasn't just going to listen to Tanner and Adams, who because they were military would be inclined toward a military response.

"We should be cautious and listen to Director Levinson," the Chinese president said.

"How does the rest of the council feel?" Lanford asked.

The British prime minister was the first to respond. "Let's hold off until we know more."

"We need to be decisive," the Russian president countered. "I vote to attack!"

"I also vote to strike," the French representative added. That was unexpected. The French weren't ordinarily given to hasty responses.

Two for attacking, two for learning more.

Lanford was the swing vote.

David saw her considering, the weight of the decision plain on her face. On the other monitor he watched the spherical ship, colors still coruscating across its surface in the pattern Catherine had identified. It was nearing the Moon. Dikembe stood back, watching the proceedings but also lost in his own thoughts, seeing his vision come to life. What did he think? He'd been in closer touch with the aliens than any of them, and he had seen this sphere a thousand times in his dreams.

If only the Republic of Umbutu had a voice on the Security Council, David thought. But he had to deal with what was. President Lanford would make the decision. All David could do was hope he had made his case compelling.

25

Packed into the command center with the rest of the Moon Base's crew, Jake and Charlie shot each other a look as they waited for President Lanford to make her decision. It occurred to Jake that usually this kind of stuff took place in situation rooms, hidden away from the view of plebs like him.

On the other hand, watching politicians and diplomats argue kind of paled next to seeing a giant alien spaceship come out of a freaking wormhole from another part of the universe. He was equal parts exhilarated and terrified. If this was another alien invasion, the human race was in for a rough ride, and just thinking about it dragged Jake all the way back to when he was six years old, at summer camp, watching the fighter jets and the pillar of smoke rising from the conflagration in Los Angeles.

Maybe he was a grown man now, but that scared little boy would always be there inside of him, about to find out that his parents were dead and he would have to make his own way in the world.

Maybe this was different, though. Maybe it was different aliens, bringing not war but some kind of science-fiction paradise. If that was it, Jake was all in. He wanted jet packs. He wanted to see other planets. He wanted to

teleport and do all the other stuff he'd imagined when…
well, when he was that little boy who didn't yet know that
his parents were about to die.

There went his little flash of optimism.

Commander Lao was tracking the ship's trajectory.
It was definitely approaching the Moon. Not fast, but
it was getting closer. Jake watched it nervously for signs
of a weapon powering up. Even twenty years later, he
would never forget the green of the city destroyer's energy
cannon energizing over Los Angeles.

"Madam President, I need an answer," Lao said.

Lanford looked at the ship for a long moment before
turning back to the video feed that showed David
Levinson, who looked like he was in a study that could
have belonged to Sherlock Holmes.

"David," she said. "I need you to tell me with absolute
certainty that this isn't them."

Jake knew enough about scientists to know that they
could almost never answer a question that positively.
There was a long pause as Levinson glanced off to the
side, where Jake could see a woman and man at the edge
of the frame. Both of them looked like they had a lot to
say, and were trying very hard not to say it.

"I can't do that, Madam President," David said.

President Lanford swallowed hard. After another
pause, she reached her decision.

"Take them out, Commander," she said, her tone quiet
and decisive. Maybe even a little sad.

Commander Lao turned to the cannon's lead
technician.

"Get the cannon into firing position!"

Outside, the enormous weapon swung up and over,
lining up on the alien ship, which was still on a steady
path approaching the Moon. The rest of the crew initiated
targeting calculations. Monitor feeds from Area 51 and

the Republic of Umbutu held steady, as for the first time since its inception, the armaments of the Earth Space Defense initiative were prepared for action.

"We're locked on," General Adams said from Area 51.

The president nodded. "Engage."

From the Umbutu feed, Jake heard the woman pleading.

"This is a mistake! Please! They're trying to communicate with us!"

She had a French accent, and that struck Jake as strange for some reason, though he didn't know why. It was a weird thing to notice under the circumstances, but little details like that always stood out to him.

"This is a mistake," Levinson said. "Let's take a minute here to think this through—"

"Shut him off," Secretary Tanner ordered from Area 51. Man, was that guy an asshole, Jake thought.

A second later, Levinson's feed went black.

Outside, the Moon Base's cannon spun up, and the familiar green light started to coalesce at the end of its barrel. Jake got a chill seeing it. Even though he knew human beings were in control, he could never see that shade of green, that particular way the energy built and intensified, without remembering the alien invasion.

That was why they had the cannon, though, and all the other ones like it that would soon be strung all the way out to Saturn, and maybe even farther than that. Humanity had taken charge of its own defense, turning the enemy's weapons to human uses—and this was going to be the first proof that nothing like the War of '96 would ever happen again.

"Fire!" Lao commanded.

A burst of green energy flared out and crackled across the miles between the cannon and the ship, faster than Jake's eye could follow. It hit its target almost dead center, just above the luminescent blue line that ran around its midsection. The impact was silent in the vacuum of space, but Jake filled in the sound on his own, remembering what it had sounded like on old videos of the destroyers unleashing their weapons on Washington, D.C., New York... and Los Angeles.

The spherical ship spun out of control, tumbling and trailing bits of wreckage as it veered away over the bleak landscape of the Moon. Some of them spun down slowly to raise plumes of regolith as they hit the surface near the cannon and around the base. Others scattered behind the falling ship, which was still glowing in different-colored patterns. It disappeared over the Moon's horizon, and a long silence held in the command center...

Then everyone burst into cheers.

It had worked! Earth Space Defense was live, and viable. The aliens couldn't just waltz through a wormhole and flatten cities anymore. Planet Earth wasn't to be messed with. Jake felt the pride of the occasion, and the huge relief of knowing that the next alien invasion would end in the shattered wreckage of the invading ships, instead of the burning ruins of the world's great cities.

Cheers came over the feed from Area 51, too. General Adams leaned into the frame, raising his voice over the celebration.

"Commander Lao. Status report."

Lao studied the initial readings coming in from the sensor arrays on the far side of the Moon.

"It crashed into the Van de Graaff Crater," he reported. "We're not picking up any signs of life."

Amid the cheers, President Lanford looked somber. "Let's hope to God we did the right thing," she said.

Her jubilant Secretary of Defense leaned over to her

with a grin Jake thought was a little… unseemly. Yeah, that was the word.

"You just guaranteed reelection," he said jubilantly. "Let's make a statement to the press."

President Lanford sighed. There was an insight Jake hadn't expected to have. The ship had barely hit the ground on the Moon, and Tanner was already doing political calculations. Lanford wasn't like that, was she? Jake didn't think so. She still looked worried— preoccupied with the gravity of the situation and the action she had just taken.

Then she got down to business.

"How should we handle Rhea?" she asked.

"Let's keep it classified until the Russians notify next of kin," Adams suggested.

There were still backslaps and handshakes and hugs all around, both on the Moon and in Area 51. Charlie had an arm around Jake's shoulders, and even though he wished he hadn't seen the political stuff, Jake really felt the spirit.

Yeah! They'd shot down an alien spaceship!

And it hadn't been the fancy cowboys and cowgirls of Legacy Squadron, either, Jake thought, tossing a look over toward Dylan and Rain and the rest of them. They were sitting on the ground with him, and their fighters had never gotten out of the hangar, and the best part of it was that Jake Morrison knew that he had made this happen. If he hadn't taken the chance to get his tug under the falling cannon and drive it back into place, the command center would be in pieces, and the cannon would still be lying in the wreckage. How would it have fired then?

He glanced over at Charlie, and saw Charlie thinking the same thing. *That's right, partner*, Jake thought. *We did this. Without us, this doesn't happen. And even though we'll never get the credit, we know that it was us humble tug pilots, washouts from the big-shot pilot school, who saved the world this time.*

Hell, yeah.

One of General Adams's officers interrupted the celebration, inserting himself into the group between Adams and Tanner.

"Director Levinson is asking to be patched through."

President Lanford nodded. They still had all the feeds live in the Moon Base command center, and a moment later Levinson reappeared. Jake thought he looked pissed, but—he wouldn't have noticed this if he wasn't so close to Charlie—also hungry for the new revelations the alien ship might hold. *Scientists, man.*

"Madam President," he said. "We need to send a team up to investigate the wreckage. We need to know who we just shot down."

Tanner shook his head. "There are no signs of life. The threat has been neutralized. We can send a team up, but David needs to be in D.C."

"Can we not make this political?" Levinson snapped. "I need to go up there and get answers! Elizabeth… please."

"You're talking to the president," Tanner said in a huff at Levinson's use of her first name. Jake wondered how long they'd known each other.

President Lanford held up a hand.

"Tanner, it's fine. We'll declare it a no-fly zone for the time being. David, you can lead a team up there after the celebration."

Her decision made, President Lanford walked away out of the frame. Jake watched as Tanner, visibly gloating, leaned into the camera.

"You heard her. I want to see you next to us tomorrow, wearing your best smile. Understood?"

"You want to see my best smile?" Levinson echoed. Then his feed went black.

"Levinson?" Tanner said. He looked over at General Adams. "Did he just hang up on me?"

"That's affirmative, sir," Adams said. He kept his voice steady, but Jake thought he detected a little bit of satisfaction. General Adams had a reputation for being a straight shooter, a fair and careful leader who had no patience for bullies because bullies didn't consider what was best for the unit, or the team. They cared about themselves.

Defense Secretary Tanner was exactly that kind of bully, and David Levinson had called him out on it.

Suddenly inspired, Jake realized that if Levinson really wanted to get over to Van de Graaff Crater, there was a way to make it happen. He turned and started working his way through the crowded command center toward the door. Looking puzzled, Charlie followed him.

26

Patricia and Agent Travis watched the coverage of the president's announcement from Whitmore's bedroom. Every network on Earth, it seemed, carried the announcement live.

"Today, at 11:19 central time," she said from a hastily constructed podium outside the Area 51 command center, with the rows of cannons forming a powerful backdrop, "Earth's Space Defense program repelled an alien attack on our planet." She didn't get much farther after that, as the room exploded with reporters' questions, and the networks all cut that initial sound bite out to use it as a lead-in to their own coverage.

Patricia flipped through all the channels and landed on Fox, where the anchor recapped the president's speech over footage of cheering crowds all over the world.

"…The president confirmed the successful use of the Moon's defense cannon," the anchor read, continuing to narrate over clips of what looked like a worldwide party. Times Square looked as if it was New Year's Eve, a rippling sea of humanity celebrating human strength and the joy of knowing that they were safe from a repetition of the War of '96. The same scene repeated itself all over the world. Red Square, Tiananmen Square, the Champ de Mars… Patricia got a little chill, remembering her father's speech twenty years before in which he had called for human unity in the face of the alien threat.

Now they were seeing it.

Cutting back to the studio, the Fox broadcast settled on the anchor, who couldn't resist a little quip.

"It seems that Independence Day has come one day early—"

Whitmore shut the TV off.

"It wasn't them," he said in the silence that followed.

Patricia was wary about this topic, knowing how apt her father was to fall into one of his fugues. "You can't know that for sure," she said gently. It would be better for all of them if he could feel secure. When he got worried, that made his episodes worse.

Also, she was sure *it had been* them. How likely was it that another alien race had chosen the twentieth anniversary of the War of '96 to show up? The coincidence was too hard to believe.

"Sir," Travis said, glancing at his watch. "It's time for your meds."

"I don't need any goddamn meds!" Whitmore snapped. Then he lapsed into silence, sitting on his bed and staring off into space. It struck Patricia how old he looked, how far removed from the powerful figure who had led, not just the United States, but the entire human race through the War and its aftermath.

"Can you give us a minute?" she asked Travis.

He left, shutting the door quietly behind him.

"You shouldn't be wasting your time with a crazy old man," Whitmore said when they were alone. "You should be with Jake."

"He's on the Moon, remember?" Patricia reminded him. She did want to talk to Jake. She felt bad about the way their last conversation had ended, and on top of that she wanted to know everything about what the cannon shot had looked like from the Moon Base. Jake had been in a front-row seat, and Patricia was a little bit jealous of that.

"Then you should be with the president," her father said.

She sat by his side on the bed and smiled. "I am with the president—and you're not crazy."

He was visibly struggling not to fall into his visions again. She knew the expression on his face—that haunted anticipation that made him look even more haggard than worry and long-term lack of sleep. It got worse late at night, like now, when he was tired from the day. She hoped he would sleep tonight.

"I've seen it in my dreams," he said softly.

"That's all they are," Patricia said. "Just dreams."

"No, Patty, they're coming back," he said, and he was fully present again. He looked her in the eye and added, "And we won't be able to beat them this time."

She thought of all the drawings he'd made over the years, the circle with a line through it. He had seen the ship in those dreams, and he had been correct. The ship shot down over the Moon had looked just like that. Realizing this, Patricia grew uncertain. If her father's vision of that ship had been true, was he also right that the ship was different—and that the real menace was still out there?

Could that be?

Watching her father lost in his thoughts, Patricia felt the celebratory mood ebb away, replaced by a foreboding she didn't want to feel but suddenly could not shake.

Tomorrow was Independence Day.

PART THREE
JULY 4

PART THREE

27

Albert Lemieux paused in his work to take in the peak of Olympus Mons, the highest mountain in the solar system, looming over the horizon to the east of the Earth Space Defense base he had been building for the last three years.

It was a sight he never tired of seeing, because the mountains reminded him of home. He had grown up in Grenoble, hiking and skiing the Alps, taking the cable car up to the old Bastille fort and the caves that riddled the mountainsides there, imagining he was a bandit hiding out from the King's soldiers. That sense of adventure had never left him.

He had taken to the skies as a pilot, then to space as an astronaut, and after surviving the destruction of Paris during the War, Albert had joined the newly formed Earth Space Defense the moment it had been internationalized. Through the years he had worked on successive generations of spacecraft designed at first for near-Earth operations... then Moon landings and return... and then, at last, voyages to Mars.

When Albert saw Olympus Mons, he imagined future generations of children growing up on its slopes the way he had grown up on the slopes of the Chartreuse Mountains. The aliens had tried to destroy Earth, but instead in their defeat they had given humanity a great gift. They had left behind the technology that unlocked space, and now Albert was living the life of his dreams. Mars!

Even though he wasn't flying now, he still felt the sense of adventure. Three years on Mars hadn't dulled Albert's sense of the marvelous. He was millions of kilometers from home, building a defense outpost that would oversee this part of the solar system the way Grenoble's Bastille had once overseen the Isère River. He was part of the grand enterprise of space exploration, and if that meant he spent some of his days leveraging pieces of steel and polymer into place, Albert had no problem with that whatsoever. He loved what he did.

Today he was part of a crew tasked with finishing the clamp assemblies on a turret mount that one day would hold a cannon identical to the one that yesterday had shot down the alien vessel approaching the Moon. Like every other human being in possession of a computer, Albert had seen the video, over and over, hardly able to believe his eyes. The reappearance of the aliens gave urgency to his work, but the success of the defensive action gave him confidence that the human race would repel any new full-scale invasion. The aliens would find that the human race of 2016 was much better prepared than the human race of 1996—and after all, hadn't they won in 1996 even without the benefit of the aliens' own technology?

Humanity stood on the edge of a new golden age. Albert felt privileged to be part of it.

He thought again of the brilliant green flare and the explosion when the cannon blast hit the alien ship, and he got goose bumps inside his space suit. He wanted to watch the video again and feel the fierce joy that he had felt when he saw it the first time. Instead, he climbed back up into the open driver's platform on the crane he operated every day, and swung its arm around so the rest of the crew could attach a huge hydraulic joint for the last of the clamps. In another week or so, the turret mount would be ready.

The delivery of the cannon was scheduled for August 1.

Then any new aliens would have not just the Moon, and the orbital satellite cannons, but Mars to contend with. By New Year's Day of 2017, Rhea Base would be online, giving humankind a defense presence beyond the Asteroid Belt.

Albert wondered if the aliens on board the ship shot down last night had been able to send a signal home. The scientists at Area 51 were still trying to understand how it had appeared out of space. The working hypothesis was via a wormhole, but as far as Albert knew, no scientific team had salvaged wormhole creation technology from any of the alien ships. That wasn't entirely surprising, since ESD guarded the details of its research quite jealously until they were ready to release them to the public.

But people were people. They tended to talk, and although Albert had conversed with the Russians who stopped on their way to Rhea, and the Chinese on the Moon while Albert was there on his way to Mars—and the American staff coordinating the base construction from Area 51—he had never heard a whisper concerning wormholes.

Maybe that technology would turn up when ESD investigators got a look at the crashed ship on the far side of Earth's Moon. Albert hoped so. That would mean he could live to see humankind, not just spreading into the solar system, but beyond. Into the stars! Was he too old to sign up for that? Not a chance.

In any case, if the aliens had sent a message back, Albert hoped it had been simple.

Steer clear. They were ready for us.

Because we were, Albert thought proudly, *and we get more and more ready every day.*

A shadow passed over him. That was odd. There were no transports scheduled to arrive near this time, and in any case their landing paths never took them over the construction site. Albert couldn't look up at it. He had the hydraulic joint on the end of his crane arm, and it was a delicate operation to get it into place.

The shadow did not disappear.

Uneasy, Albert realized that only something massive could be causing it. Either of Mars's moons—Deimos or Phobos—would have passed by now. So what was it? The crew on the turret mount looked up. So did Albert.

When he saw what was casting the shadow, his unease turned to terror. Reflected in the visor of his helmet, a green glow began to build.

28

On the morning of July 4, Independence Day, Milton Isaacs showed up early for his rotation because he had a gift for Brakish. He'd been working on it for some time, and had finished in time to bring it in on the big day—the celebration of twenty years since the decisive battle in the War of '96.

The occasion was a somber one for Milton, because every anniversary of the war also marked another year that Brakish had remained in a coma, all but lost to him.

He produced the gift with a flourish, even though he knew Brakish wasn't looking. It was a scarf. A silly thing, maybe, but he had brought Brakish so many plants that the hospital room was starting to look like a greenhouse. Also, Isaacs recently had taken up a variety of different arts and crafts activities to pass the time he spent alone. He was now a competent potter, an enthusiastic woodworker, and when he looked at the scarf he thought maybe he had a little talent for knitting, too.

Of course, he would never say that out loud. Not unless someone else said it first.

Isaacs lifted Brakish's head just enough to get the scarf under his neck. He swept aside the long hair, now completely gray, moving it out of the way, and then set his head back on the pillow. He tucked the scarf around Brakish's neck just right, and knotted it in the European style.

"I took a knitting class," he said. He'd selected the yarn carefully to go with Brakish's complexion, and he thought it looked very distinguished—not that things like that had ever concerned Brakish. The only thing he was vain about was his hair. Clothes, shoes, everything else a human being might put on his body, all of them were afterthoughts. Indeed, what mattered to Brakish was his work.

Suddenly Isaacs was worried that the scarf would irritate Brakish's neck.

"Is it itchy?" he asked. "You'd tell me if it was itchy, right? I won't be offended."

Brakish sat bolt upright in bed, screaming.

Isaacs screamed, too.

First in fear, and then out of the raw emotion of seeing consciousness return to the man he still loved after twenty years. A thousand things went through his mind all at once, but first among them was the simple astonished thought that he had never really believed this day would come. He'd told himself it would, told other people it would, but when he was alone at night and there was no one who needed him to put on a brave face, Milton Isaacs had privately admitted to himself that Brakish was probably gone forever.

Only he wasn't.

Isaacs' eyes filled with tears.

"You're awake?" he said, even though it was so obvious as to be stupid.

Still coming to his senses, Brakish looked at him and asked a question that in three words encapsulated all of the time they had missed.

"Did we win?"

Oh my God, Isaacs thought. *He's really back*. He shouted out of the door to a passing nurse. "Eric, get a medical team! He's awake!" Then he turned back to Brakish, who was staring around the room wide-eyed and with a dazed grin, as if he was remembering a crazy dream—which maybe he was. Isaacs couldn't wait to hear about it.

"That was a trip," Brakish said. "Where are my glasses? I can't see anything."

His glasses were right on the side table next to his bed, where they had been for twenty years. Isaacs polished their lenses once a week because when they got dusty it made him miserable to think of them not being used. He had just polished them the day before, in fact. Now he handed them to Brakish, so filled with gratitude that he could do this simple little thing that his hands shook and he started to cry again.

"Here."

Brakish put them on and looked around the room before settling his gaze on Isaacs.

"How long have I been out?" he asked, his tone full of wonder as he looked Isaacs up and down.

"A long time."

It was all Isaacs could say. He was too overwhelmed to get into the details, and he was trying to keep the doctor part of him from being affected. If he told Brakish that the coma had lasted twenty years—*to the day*—the psychological impact could be unpredictable at best.

Better to ease into it.

Which Brakish did, and quickly. "Yeah, I can tell, baby," he said. "You got bald. And really fat."

Well, Isaacs thought, but he couldn't find a reply. That cheerful candor was something he certainly hadn't missed. Except he had.

Abruptly Brakish looked concerned, and he reached up to his own head. When he felt his hair, and ran his fingers down its length to his shoulders, a look of pure relief washed over his face.

Same old Brakish, Isaacs thought. *Calls me bald, and then worries about his own hair.*

He was the happiest man on Earth.

*   *   *

Tugs like Jake's took a long time to drag a cannon up and out of Earth's gravity well, then to the Moon. Unencumbered, however—and piloted with a certain, um, zeal—one could get from the Moon back to Earth in a matter of hours.

With Charlie sitting nervously at his side, Jake brought the tug through a long approach, hitting Earth's atmosphere somewhere over Baja California.

"Lao's never gonna let you make this run again, you know that, right?" Charlie said it out loud, over and over again before they left, until Jake had to snap at him that he didn't have to come.

"Of course I'm coming," Charlie replied. "I just need to know you'll take the blame if we get caught."

"No problem," Jake said. So far everything he'd tried to do right had gotten him in trouble anyway. He figured he might as well try to do something wrong, and see if people would like it.

They hit the west coast of Africa before dawn, or at least before dawn on the ground. From their altitude they could see the sun, far away, rising over the Great Rift Valley.

I take it all back, Jake thought, as he soaked up the magnificent sight. If he'd made it into Legacy Squadron, he never would have had a chance to do this.

*   *   *

Dikembe Umbutu had a lot on his mind. Mostly what he was thinking about was the alien vessel, and how he had seen it so clearly in his visions.

During the course of his adult life, Dikembe had fought both humans and aliens—though mostly aliens, since at the time the invasion began he was in Oxford. He'd had to come home by boat, and arrived just in time for his father to begin going mad and the aliens to pour out of their starship.

The next year and more was in his memory as a swirl of blood and betrayal. Then it was over... except inside Dikembe's head, where the visions never went away. Perhaps he was learning to control them. Not control what they showed, but at least prevent them from driving him insane the way his father had gone mad.

He watched the pale Moon against the indigo sky that the sunrise had not yet reached. He looked down when a cab pulled through the gates of his compound, bouncing on bad springs and squealing to a halt on bad brakes. The accountant—or auditor or whatever he was, who had tagged along with Levinson—got out looking at his change.

"Sir, I did the conversion, and I think you may have overcharged me," he began. As he spoke the cabbie slewed around into a U-turn and left a rooster tail of dust on his way out of the compound. "Hey, hey, hey! I need a receipt!" the accountant shouted. *Rosenberg*. That was his name.

Dikembe thought about sending him away again. He needed Levinson's full attention. Then he was distracted by a loud group of children coming around the corner of the main house with a storm of shouts and fingers pointed at the sky. He followed the direction where they pointed and saw one of the space tugs that were common around the Moon Base. As he watched, it decelerated to begin a landing just inside his front gate.

Dikembe had received a great many unexpected visitors in the last few years, but this was surely one of the most unusual. The tug hovered for a moment as its gripping arms reoriented toward the ground, becoming legs that rocked under its weight as the ship came to rest. A ship shaped like a frog, that could fly to the Moon and back, Dikembe thought. Human ingenuity was something to behold.

*   *   *

David walked out of Dikembe's house when he heard the whine of the servos preparing the tug's legs for landing. Collins and Catherine came with him.

"I'll send you the data we get back from the hole once it's processed," Collins was saying.

"Good," David said. The tug's engines powered down but didn't turn all the way off. "And if you speak to Tanner, just make something up. Be creative."

They still didn't know what was at the bottom of the shaft under the destroyer here in Umbutu. Collins would lead that investigation, though, because David didn't have time to stick around. In general, he had to be anywhere in the solar system other than with the president and Secretary Tanner, for whatever star-spangled mutual admiration fest they had planned.

Specifically, he had to be on the Moon.

Jake Morrison, who David knew through their mutual connection with Patricia Whitmore, had made an offer that he was only too happy to accept. He could focus on the science, and if they were lucky, both he and Jake could piss off their bosses.

The tug's ramp opened out and Morrison popped his head out.

"Someone call a cab?"

"Thanks for doing this, Jake," David said as he got to the bottom of the ramp.

The young man shrugged. "No sweat, but let's get moving, 'cause I kinda stole this thing."

David gave him a grin and turned. "Well, Catherine, as always, it was a pleasure." He stuck out his hand. She just looked at him. "Good luck with everything, and let's try to keep in touch this time."

Out of the blue, Dikembe, who had been watching nearby, spoke up. He moved to the bottom of the ramp.

"I'm coming with you."

They all turned in his direction.

"Oh no, no, no," David said. "This is an ESD operation. Strictly off-limits to all civilians and..." He hesitated, not knowing how to sugarcoat what he had to say next, then decided not to bother. "...and warlords." There was no way he was taking a head of state on a tug to the Moon. Especially not a head of state from a country whose recognition was still a matter of some dispute within the United Nations. David was far from the sharpest political operator, but even he could see that would end badly.

Dikembe didn't step away. "You need my help," he said. "I let you in. It would be wise of you to return the favor."

A group of Dikembe's soldiers moved closer, sensing possible tension in the air. *Ah*, David thought. *So this wasn't a request, per se.*

How many people do the tugs hold, anyway?

Dikembe turned to his men and said something in Swahili. They roared out a cheer, and a few of them fired their weapons into the air as Dikembe brushed past David and went up the ramp into the tug.

"It's time for our nation to join the world and end this war before it begins again."

Already things weren't going according to plan, David thought. Maybe that was inevitable when the first part of your plan was hanging up on the Secretary of Defense, and blowing off a mandatory appearance with the president… and then the second part of your plan involved a not-quite-legal tug ride up to the surface of the Moon.

"I'm coming, too."

Now this was too much.

"Catherine—" David began, but she wasn't having it.

"Something is drawing him out there, and I'm going to find out what. I think you owe me that much." She, too, walked past him and up into the vessel.

What next? David wondered, and that was when Floyd Rosenberg walked up.

"Do you know where I've been for the last fourteen hours?" he asked, all petulance and nerd menace. David tried hard, but he couldn't think of anything he cared about less than Floyd's recent whereabouts. Floyd told him anyway. "In a holding cell, waiting to get my visa so I could talk to you. There's no way you're getting on that thing—wait. You're not sanctioned to use that space tug, are you?"

Off the rails, David thought. *It's all going off the rails. So why not step on the gas.* He stood aside and gestured, as if he was a doorman. "Why don't you join us, Floyd? Everyone else is. Might do you some good." He started walking up the ramp.

"No," said Floyd. "I am not boarding that ship! And neither are you."

David kept walking. Floyd looked from Dikembe's elite soldiers back to the ramp… which was starting to close.

"I'm coming with you," he said, and he ran aboard, his feet clattering all the way.

The ramp shut behind him.

29

"Everyone buckle up," Jake said as his passengers—there were more of them than he'd expected—found their seats. Charlie helped them get the harnesses straightened out and fastened. "Take a seat, David," Jake added when he saw the scientist still standing, his head nearly banging against the ceiling. The tug wasn't built for guys as tall as Levinson. Jake pointed to an open seat next to his.

"Really?" David didn't look thrilled. "Front row? Okay…"

"What's the matter, you nervous?" Jake woke up the pre-flight systems, which he'd put on standby instead of shutting them down.

"No," David said, in exactly the tone of voice a guy used when what he really meant was *Yeah, but can we pretend I'm not?* "It's just… not my favorite thing," he added.

"Nothing to worry about," Jake said expansively. "I haven't crashed in…" He realized too late that maybe he should have tried another way to settle David's nerves. "Well, a couple of days, but that was intentional."

"What?" Levinson stopped trying to hide his fear, but Jake didn't have time to deal with it. He had flying to do.

The engines fired up, blowing a rolling wall of dust around the courtyard of the big-ass house that apparently

belonged to the guy in the back—the one with the machetes.
Jake didn't know who he was, or what connection he had
to the aliens, but both he and Charlie had seen the alien city
destroyer sitting just beyond the next ridge, all powered up
like it was ready to get back to leveling cities. Something
weird was going on here, having to do with the invaders.
Levinson had found out about it, and Machete Guy was
part of it.

Jake glanced over at Charlie, who gave him a thumbs-
up. *Passengers locked in. All systems go.* Jake eased back
the control stick. The tug lifted a few yards off the ground,
hovered as it swung around, and then he hit the gas. The
tug blazed off across the morning sky, pinning all of them
into their seats.

He loved this part. It was like the world's greatest
roller coaster, combined with the thrill of driving way too
fast, and knowing the cops wouldn't bust you.

David offered another angle. "I forgot how much I hate
this!" he shouted over the thunder of the engines and the
sound of rushing air. They cracked the sound barrier, then
hit Mach 2... 4... and kept accelerating, angling up into
the sky. Escape velocity from Earth was around 25,000
miles an hour, and Jake wanted to get there fast, because
he already had visions of Lao, standing in the tug's empty
parking spot and swearing revenge.

"That wasn't so bad," David said as they reached the
edge of space. They had plenty of speed for a stable
low-Earth orbit, and as gravity started to lessen the ride
smoothed out quite a bit.

But the show wasn't quite over yet. Jake shot David
a grin.

"I haven't kicked on the fusion drive yet."

The look on Levinson's face was priceless. Jake hit
another button next to the control stick and the tug
rocketed away. David screamed loudly enough that for

a minute, Jake was sure someone must be able to hear it back on Earth.

They only needed about fifteen seconds of the fusion burn to achieve escape velocity, and after they did Jake throttled back the drive. Even so, they were moving mighty fast—he was going to get them to the Moon quicker than a 747 could travel from L.A. to New York. A lot faster.

"Gravity field engaged," the tug's onboard navigation system announced. Jake didn't always engage the system's verbal functions—not when it was just him and Charlie—but it seemed like the right thing to do with three new people on board.

Four, with the nerdy guy.

They all had a few minutes to enjoy the ride. The view was like nothing else. It even beat watching the sun rise over the Great Rift Valley. Stars as far as the eye could see in any direction. Until he'd been there, he never really knew what it looked like. As great as the telescope and satellite pictures were, they couldn't do justice to the feeling of seeing it out of the window—and the tugs had great windows.

Something clanged hard against the tug's hull, reverberating through the craft's interior, and just like that David was all jumpy again.

"What was that?"

"We're flying through the old mother ship's debris field," Jake said, as if he did it every day. "It'll give us cover from the Moon Base's radar." He didn't want Lao to know where he was going, and David didn't want Tanner to know where he was going. So they'd play it cool among the wreckage until they could perform an orbital injection burn unseen by the base's prying radar eyes.

Another loud clang. "These are basically space tanks," Jake said, referring to the tug. It was true, but he still sounded more confident than he felt. After all, this wasn't his ship. He hoped whoever usually piloted the tug had kept up on the maintenance.

* * *

Whitmore hadn't meant to get up and leave his house again without telling anyone. But he'd done it, and now he was getting off a bus at the stop across from the Smithsonian Air and Space Museum on the National Mall.

It was a steamy morning in Washington, D.C. The Fourth of July always was. He remembered sweating in his suits when he delivered holiday speeches, and he was glad he wasn't president anymore. Immediately upon disembarking, he could hear President Lanford's voice, echoing out from banks of speakers over the throngs assembled on the Mall.

"Twenty years ago, the world escaped the clutches of extinction," she was saying.

Goddamn right, Whitmore thought.

"And yesterday, we did it again—but our victory came at a heavy price. Our hearts go out to the families of those brave cosmonauts we lost on Rhea."

It was a shame about Rhea Base, Whitmore thought. He hoped Lanford had called the Russian president. She was good at protocol, though, and didn't need him to tell her how to do the job. Whitmore walked up the Mall toward the Capitol building, where a huge video screen gave a view of the president at her podium.

"We must never forget their sacrifice," she continued, "along with the brave men and women who defied the odds and led us to victory two decades ago." The screen cut to shots of officers who had served with distinction in the War. Whitmore recognized General Grey and his wife. Solid people.

"Our survival is only possible when we stand together. We found strength in unity as a planet, and this strength has brought us hope for a better future." The broadcast cycled through a series of feeds from the world's great cities. All were rebuilding, and today they were full of people celebrating, partying, rejoicing in the fact that they were all still alive.

The president's tone changed, and Whitmore realized he'd missed some of her speech. Now he caught up again.

"Let's get a bird's-eye view of our Moon Base defense system," she said, "courtesy of Captain Dylan Hiller and his squadron of the world's finest!" Images appeared of the lunar landscape, with the cannon turret artfully framed and lit by massive floodlights. The whole celebration was choreographed, down to the second. The cameramen shooting the landscape would soon time a pan upward and—*presto*! There was Legacy Squadron racing overhead, corkscrewing toward the turret in a complicated and dazzling formation they'd been rehearsing for weeks.

The crowd went nuts. "How's it looking up there, Captain Hiller?" President Lanford said, her voice booming over the speakers.

As soon as she finished the question, the huge screen switched feeds again. Now everyone on the National Mall witnessed a live feed from the cockpit of Dylan's fighter.

"It's truly humbling to see how beautiful Earth is from here, Madam President," Dylan replied.

Good kid, Whitmore thought. *He says the right things, and he means them.* His dad had been a real pilot. That was the highest compliment Whitmore could give. He'd reached the front of the crowd now, at the Capitol steps, tired and a little overwhelmed by the noise and the spectacle, but he had to talk to President Lanford.

He had to.

He picked out a Secret Service agent near the cordon

holding the audience back from the president's podium. The agent recognized him, waved him over, and called in support. A moment later, Whitmore was surrounded by Secret Service, keeping his immediate vicinity clear as he got the rest of the way through the throng of the crowd.

Some people noticed him, recognized him despite the beard, the bedraggled clothes, and the wild look in his eyes. One man said his name. It spread. Soon enough hundreds or thousands of people shouted "Whitmore!"

Whitmore!

Whitmore!

Lanford noticed. She nodded and signaled the Secret Service agents to get him up on the steps so he could stand with her on the speaker's dais. As he stepped onto the dais, Lanford abandoned her prepared remarks. She leaned into the microphone and said, "Ladies and gentlemen, another great war hero. The one and only President Thomas Whitmore!"

The people went wild. Whitmore stepped forward, feeling the heat of their admiration and knowing that everyone was going to think he was crazy. But he was old enough now. He could take it.

He had to tell them. The information he possessed could mean the difference between life and death.

30

"We're coming up on the Van de Graaff Crater," Jake said as the tug skimmed low over the far side of the Moon. They'd successfully used the old mother ship debris field to sneak past Lao's surveillance. Now they just had to… well, find whatever David thought he was looking for, and then figure out what to do next.

Although it was called the "dark side of the Moon," it wasn't always dark out here. People called it that because it could never be seen from Earth, but sometimes the sun shone out here. Morrison guided the tug over the rim of the crater, which was more than two hundred kilometers long and four deep. Actually it was two craters overlapping to form kind of a figure-eight shape, and—

"There it is," David said eagerly, as the wreckage of the downed alien ship appeared scattered across the crater's rocky floor. The ship had broken apart upon crashing, and David realized how huge the task was they had set for themselves. The debris covered dozens of square kilometers, and without any idea what they were looking for, it might be impossible to prove that the ship came from a different culture than the aliens who had tried to exterminate humanity.

That was science, though—looking for subtle clues

hidden in oceans of noise. Jake landed the tug he and David suited up, and out they went onto the surface.

"First walk?" Jake asked him.

David shook his head, then realized Jake couldn't see the gesture because of their helmets.

"No," David said. "Just never been to the dark side."

They reached the debris field, and continued on together.

"What are we looking for?" Jake asked.

"I'm hoping we'll know when we see it," David said, which was just like him, and he knew it. Why couldn't he just give a straight answer? Or maybe that was as straight an answer as he could give. After all, it was honest to admit when you didn't know what the hell you were talking about.

*   *   *

Inside the tug, Dikembe was watching David and Jake work their way through the wreckage. Some of the pieces were the size of small buildings.

The accountant came up to him and glanced at the tattoo on his arm. It was an alien's head, with notches below it in a series that went all the way down to his wrist.

"Nice ink," Rosenberg said. "So all those notches represent alien kills, huh?"

Dikembe ignored him. He was more interested in what was happening outside, and in learning whether it would solve the mysteries locked away in his own mind.

"That's impressive," Rosenberg persisted. Then, when Dikembe kept watching David and Jake, he added, "Not much of a talker, are you?"

It was all Dikembe could do not to unsheathe one of his machetes.

*   *   *

David had answered Jake's question truthfully, because he didn't know what they were looking for. If this ship had been made by the aliens they already knew, he would recognize certain technological components he'd seen before. If not, there was no way to anticipate what pieces of wreckage might be useful or informative.

He poked around, seeing nothing resembling what he knew of the aliens' tech, and growing more and more certain that President Lanford had made a mistake. Then something caught his eye.

"Catherine, I think I just found another one of your doodles," David said as he made a complete circle around a large piece of wreckage. It was a framework of some kind, a cage, built into the external hull of the spherical ship. Inside it was a smaller sphere, partially exposed but to David's hurried and untutored eye looking quite a bit like the large ship itself. It even had a line across it, blazing with the same blue energy as the larger ship.

Also like the larger ship, lights flickered across its surface. Whatever had befallen the rest of the vessel, this—device?—had survived. What was it? To find it intact was a great prize, assuming they could learn anything from it.

"David, we need to take it back with us," Catherine said from the tug. He sized up the piece of wreckage and tried to match it against what he knew of the tugs' thrust and carrying capabilities... Then he realized he was standing next to an expert. He turned to Jake.

"You think the tug could handle the weight of this whole section?"

"There's only one way to find out," Jake said.

That was what David wanted to hear. "Charlie, tell Area 51 to prep the lab. We're bringing this thing back to Earth."

* * *

President Lanford stood respectfully aside as her distinguished predecessor climbed the Capitol steps and reached the podium.

"Why don't you say a few words?" she prompted. Whitmore looked awful, like a homeless version of himself, but the decorum of the occasion demanded that she give him a voice if he wanted one. He was the hero here. She had pulled the trigger on the most recent alien ship, but if he hadn't fought off the initial invasion, humanity wouldn't have had the weapons to answer the aliens' next incursion.

Whitmore stepped up to the microphone and the crowd went quiet, save for a low, expectant murmur.

"I—I just wanted to…" Whitmore began, then he trailed off. Beyond him, Lanford saw Patricia Whitmore and Agent Travis working their way through the crowd.

Good, she thought. *With any luck he'll say something inspiring and then they'll get him out of here before people start asking too many questions.*

From the crowd, someone screamed out, "We love you, Whitmore!" Whistles and clapping followed. Whitmore looked disoriented, uncertain…

Come on, President Lanford thought. *Come on, Tom. Give them what they want.*

Then out of the blue he grimaced and fell to his knees, grabbing at his head. Audible gasps came from the dumbstruck crowd. Lanford looked around for a doctor—there was always one on call when she made a public appearance. Patricia rushed out of the throng and up the steps, crying out for her father.

* * *

Dikembe dropped to his knees, hands pressed to the sides of his head, screaming in agony. Floyd stood frozen, not knowing what to do. Outside, Director Levinson and the pilot, Jake, were still hooking up the piece of wreckage. They didn't appear to know anything was wrong.

"Um, Mr. Umbutu?" Floyd said.

Dikembe kept screaming.

* * *

In his hospital room within the Area 51 complex, Brakish Okun frantically scrawled symbols on the walls. He had to get them out of his head, out into the world where he could look at them and start to understand where they had come from.

He paused and stared at one of them—a circle with a line through it, the line slightly curved—when a white light flashed behind his eyes and crippling pain seized his brain.

Okun screamed and clutched at his head, the symbols forgotten and new visions stabbing into his mind.

* * *

A few hundred yards away from Okun's room, in Area 51's command center, Lieutenant Ritter approached General Adams with some bad news.

"Mars has gone silent like Rhea, sir," he said quietly, and he touched the screen of a nearby terminal. "This was just uploaded from the Moon Base."

On the screen, an image appeared like something out of humanity's worst collective nightmare. It was an alien ship, and this time there could be no doubt. It was miles in diameter, a flattened disk like the city destroyers and the mother ship of the War of '96—only bigger than any of them.

Much bigger.

Only a few hundred kilometers from the Moon.

"How the hell did we miss this?" General Adams said, as much to himself as to anyone else. Then he grabbed his phone and gave the order for Legacy Squadron to scramble. Earth's orbital defenses had to be brought to bear.

War had come.

31

David and Jake felt rather than heard a low rumble building around them. The scattered debris of the alien ship started to shake and the dusty top layer of the regolith shook itself smooth, obscuring the footprints they had just made.

Then a shadow passed over them, plunging the wreckage site into darkness.

"Holy shit!" they heard Charlie say over the comm from the tug's cockpit. Jake looked up and saw the alien ship, bigger than any city, bigger than any man-made object that had ever existed.

"Charlie, I think you better come and get us," he said, trying to keep his cool. "Sooner the better, as in *right now*!" He and David started shoving at the piece of wreckage, seeing if they could get it loose enough to make sure the tug's arms could grip it.

"Already on it," Charlie called.

Jake and David watched the gigantic ship approach. It was… the brain couldn't even handle how big it was. Watching it was like watching a moon loom over you, threatening to crush you, just getting bigger and bigger until it blotted out the entire sky and everything vanished behind it.

"This is definitely bigger than the last one," David said.

The alien leviathan pushed into and through the old mother ship's orbiting debris field, sending thousands of pieces of wreckage hurtling toward the lunar surface. Charlie had just lifted off as the first wave of debris began kicking up plumes of dust and stone around them. Some of the pieces were bigger than the tug.

"Everyone strap in, it's gonna get rough!" Charlie called out.

From where Jake stood, the falling debris pushed ahead of the titanic ship looked almost like a solid wall approaching them. The tug was coming, but it wasn't going to get there in time.

"Um, should we maybe start running?" David said.

"That's probably a good idea!" Jake agreed, and he took off toward the tug with David right next to him, crossing the distance in huge Moon-gravity leaps with pieces of debris pounding down around them. "Charlie, where the hell are you?" he shouted.

"Just flying through my worst nightmare!"

A chunk of debris hit David in mid-leap, sending him careening out of control. Something was weird with the gravity and Jake realized that if he didn't do something, the scientist might well fly away into space. He jumped from the top of a boulder and barely managed to get a grip on one of David's feet. The two of them tumbled in slow motion back to the ground with more debris punching into the regolith around them.

"You okay?" Jake asked.

"Yes," David said. "No. There's, um… more!"

A huge piece of the mother ship hurtled toward them. Jake pulled David to his feet just as the space junk crashed down. The impact propelled both Jake and David up and away from the surface, spinning out of control—

This is how I die, Jake thought, remembering again what Charlie had said. Only this time it was for real. They were going to float away into space like Major Tom, and that would be that.

Charlie had other ideas. He dipped and swerved through the nearest falling wreckage and swung the tug around so its ramp stuck out in front of Jake and David. "I got you!" he cried out.

They hit the ramp hard. Scrabbling madly, Jake managed to grab hold, but David was sliding off. Reaching out, Jake caught his hand and dragged him the rest of the way up into the cargo area.

"We're in!" he shouted. "Close the ramp!"

The door closed, and the two of them took a moment to catch their breath. When he had composed himself, David looked over at his companion.

"But we're going to get that one piece, right?"

Scientists, Jake thought darkly.

* * *

Legacy Squadron was in the middle of a choreographed maneuver, preparing to fly their flags up and over the massive cannon turret, when Dylan saw the alien ship.

He knew right away what it was—the shape and the color of the lights were unmistakable. If there had been any doubt about the ship from last night, there was absolute certainty now. The immense object, hundreds of miles in size, loomed over the horizon, approaching from the far side of the Moon.

"All fighters take evasive action!" he ordered. As one the squadron jettisoned the flags and went into combat mode. Over the comm channel, tuned to a frequency shared by the president's staff, he heard Secret Service agents shouting to get the president somewhere safe. In the background there was mass panic.

Humankind was beginning to realize what was coming.

*   *   *

Inside Jake's tug, he piled into the pilot's chair as Charlie got out of the way.

"We gotta move!"

"Not without that piece!" David said from behind him. Through the tug's cockpit windows, Jake saw the alien ship coming even closer. It was on a collision course with the Moon, and it was big enough that Jake wasn't sure which of them would survive the impact.

But they might just have enough time to swoop under it and nab the piece of wreckage. The derring-do of that idea appealed to Jake. Also, if David Levinson thought it was that important, it probably was.

"I was afraid you'd say that," Jake said. "Charlie, get on the arms."

Shooting him a glance that said *Are you fucking crazy?* Charlie strapped himself into the rear turret that controlled the tug's gripping arms, while Jake gunned the tug into a sharp turn back toward the spherical ship's wreckage. Huge chunks of falling debris from the old mother ship exploded around them as each hit the surface.

None of the falling pieces had hit the precious thing, whatever it was. Jake pulled the tug into place over the top of it and hovered there. Charlie extended the arms and drew them in around the wreckage. *Almost there*, Jake thought. He'd never wanted anything as badly as he wanted Charlie to get that thing on board, so he could fire the fusion engine and get them the hell out of there.

The tug lurched as falling debris hammered into it. Jake swung it back around and steadied it. The alien ship was closer, way too close. Jake felt like it was going to squash them any second. Charlie got the arms out and Jake held the tug perfectly still...

Kachunk! The arms closed around the piece of wreckage.

"Got it!" Charlie called.

Jake slammed the thrusters to full speed and the tug leaped up and away just as a huge piece of the alien vessel plowed into the surface right where they'd just been. He hauled ass away from that spot, pieces of debris bouncing off the tug as he took a direct approach to Somewhere Else.

"Please stop hitting things!" Floyd Rosenberg shouted.

Sure, Jake thought. *You bet. No problem.*

The alien ship was so big that it seemed to have its own gravity. Huge chunks of the Moon, torn loose by its proximity, tumbled toward the tug. As the gargantuan vessel scraped along the surface, even more of the landscape was torn loose and sent hurtling in every direction.

"There's a flying mountain coming right at us!" Charlie screamed.

"I am aware!" Jake dove out of its way, pushing the tug to the absolute limits of its maneuverability.

"This is gonna be tight!" he said. The tug eased under what was, indeed, a flying mountain, barely skimming over the Moon's surface and emerging just as the mountain ground itself to pieces upon impact. The alien ship continued its inexorable progress toward them.

"Now would be a good time to kick in that fusion drive!" David suggested.

"There's too much debris!" If he fired it now, Jake knew they'd be moving too fast to avoid all the pieces of the Moon and the mother ship pelting the lunar surface. They had to get underneath it and away.

The alien ship ground along the Moon's surface, tearing up new mountain-sized pieces of rock and flinging

them out in front of it. Then Jake saw daylight—or more
accurately, starlight. Open space between the bottom of
the ship and the surface of the Moon.

He went for it, and they made it, just barely, the tug
roaring only a few meters from the hull of the alien ship
with the precious piece of wreckage still gripped firmly in
its cargo arms. Then they slowed down.

Jake gunned the engines.

Still they slowed down.

What the hell…?

Finally he understood. The alien ship was dragging
them back, holding them in its own gravity as if the tug
was just another piece of debris. He struggled with the
controls, trying to ease them free of the ship's pull, but it
wasn't working.

"Shit! I can't get free!"

"Jesus, it has its own gravity!" David marveled. "It's
pulling us in."

"What does that mean?" Catherine asked. Jake
wasn't sure what she meant. The answer seemed pretty
clear to him.

"It means we're going for a ride, lady," he said. *But
maybe not for long*, he added mentally, as he saw the
Moon Base cannon powering up and pointing right at
them. They were about to take their shot at the alien ship,
and everyone aboard the tug had the misfortune to be
right in the crosshairs. "They're gonna shoot at us," he
added, in case everyone hadn't already figured that out.

"That's good, they should shoot at us!" Levinson
said. He leaned into the radio and shouted, "Shoot at
us! Stop us!"

"So this is how I die!" Charlie shouted.

Jake thought maybe this time he was right.

The cannon's blast was a green flash that blinded
them to everything else for a moment. Then it vanished.

Everything vanished. For a split second Jake thought this was what it was like to be dead... then the world reappeared, and he figured out what had happened.

Just like last time, in the War of '96, the alien ship had shields that could handle human weaponry—even if that weaponry had been "borrowed" from the aliens themselves.

Then why did it work on the spherical ship, he wondered. *If it was made by the same aliens, why didn't it have the same shields?*

Jake hoped they would live long enough for him to ask David about that. Right then, he wouldn't have bet on it.

* * *

"Arm the primary and fire again!" Commander Lao ordered in the Moon Base command center.

Dylan had cut the feed from Washington, D.C., figuring it was more important for Legacy Squadron to coordinate with the Moon Base and possibly Area 51. He was filled with a fury so deep it was as if he had always been carrying it, and was only now letting it out.

On the twentieth anniversary, they came *back*?

The alien ship, still moving on its inexorable track around the Moon, opened a portal in part of its hull. Thousands of moving parts rearranged themselves, revealing a monstrous cannon, larger than the Moon Base's turret weapon by a factor of... fifty? A hundred?

The scale of it beggared the imagination.

Come on, Lao, he thought. *Fire that cannon. Maybe they have to let their shields down to use their weapon.* He and the rest of Legacy could only watch uselessly as the alien ship shifted its aim, pointing directly at the Moon Base. Rain Lao shouted something in Chinese. Dylan recognized the name Jiang—her uncle Lao's name...

Then the alien ship discharged its cannon, and the

Moon Base disappeared in an explosion that tore away a kilometers-long swath of the Moon's surface.

Through his initial shock, Dylan realized they had to act. They couldn't hit the ship, not if its shields could handle the turret cannon. More importantly, they now had the expanding field of debris to contend with. Away to his left, one of the squadron's fighters veered to avoid a spinning chunk of rock the size of Long Island—and didn't quite make it. The flash of its explosion was tiny next to the massive new asteroid.

Rain's fighter was going in a straight line, like she didn't even notice the debris. Another nearby fighter got caught by two pieces and couldn't make it between them.

"Rain! Watch out!" he shouted. She was about to collide with another piece.

Nothing.

Dylan dodged through the debris field toward her and fired, blasting the enormous rock into a thousand smaller pieces that fanned out around her. Her fighter angled to one side as she snapped out of it. On the comm he could hear her crying.

"There's nothing you could have done," he said, knowing it was useless. Yet it was true. Against that ship, there was nothing any of them could have done. "Rendezvous at Area 51," he ordered, and Legacy Squadron shot away from the alien ship, away from the gaping wound in the surface of the Moon, toward Earth.

All of it, gone so fast. They had all been so proud of what they'd done, and the alien ship had erased it in a single shot. Dylan hoped the brain trust back at Area 51 had some ideas, because if they didn't, the second alien war wasn't going to end as well as the first. The aliens had upped their game.

Could the human race do the same?

32

The crowd on the National Mall dissolved into a screaming mob. Agent Travis helped Whitmore get into a limo. Patricia hung back, staring at the huge screen. It had gone blank. The feed from the Moon was gone. That could only mean the Moon Base was gone.

And Jake was gone, too.

"Patricia!" Travis shouted. "We have to leave!"

She climbed into the limo and Travis squealed away toward the White House. They arrived as President Lanford and Secretary Tanner were being rushed toward the hybrid choppers Marine One and Two, their engines whining and rotors cutting the air. A military aide was briefing them as they ran across the South Lawn.

"You mean it's gonna ram us?" Tanner said incredulously.

"It's projected to enter Earth's atmosphere in twenty-two minutes," the aide answered. "If it doesn't alter its current velocity, it could crack our planet in half."

"Initiate the Orbital Defense System. Throw everything we've got at them." Lanford didn't have much faith it would work—not after what had just happened on the Moon, and Mars, and Rhea—but they had to try.

The aide ran to execute her order as she and her entourage boarded Marine One. As she got on board,

Lanford saw Tom Whitmore, with Patty and Agent Travis, climbing into Marine Two. Then they were in the air, and she had a moment to plan for what she would have to do next.

* * *

Jake and Charlie and the rest of the group on the tug—including Dikembe, who had recovered from his episode and was staring stone-faced out of the cockpit windows—had a great view of the approaching line of orbital defense stations as the alien ship approached them. They were Earth's near-space line of defense, a geostationary ring of cannon turrets just like the one that had been installed on the Moon.

The tug was still stuck to the bottom of the alien ship, but their comms were working, and they had an open feed from Area 51. An officer was in the middle of issuing firing orders.

"All orbital defense cannons, power up your primary weapon and prepare to engage."

David got Adams's attention. "General, you have to make sure the cannons fire simultaneously." They wouldn't be powerful enough to do sufficient damage otherwise.

"Will you be able to get clear in time?"

"Don't worry about us," David said. "Just stop them."

"Copy that," Adams answered after a brief pause. "All orbital defense cannons initiate simultaneous countdowns."

Each orbital station boasted a small crew to maintain and aim the cannons. Within seconds, the lead officers on each station reported back.

"Ready to fire." A tech down at Area 51 started the countdown.

David nodded at what they were hearing.

"Good," he said. "We're coordinating our attack."

"What's good about that?" Charlie yelled. "They're gonna shoot at us again!" But they never had the chance, because just as Charlie spoke, a barrage of energy beams lanced out from the alien ship and annihilated the entire picket of orbital turrets.

*   *   *

Shortly after lifting off from the South Lawn, Marine Two landed between Air Force One and a looming hybridized C-130 Hercules transport aircraft. Travis had his Secret Service earpiece pressed tightly into his ear as he listened to a report from somewhere. He turned to Patricia, who was staring out of the window, feeling empty from the loss of Jake.

Why had they fought the last time they'd talked? Now she would never—

"Jake's alive!" Travis said. "He's with Director Levinson. They're on their way to Area 51."

Tears of joy filled Patricia's eyes. She couldn't believe it. All that destruction, the entire base gone, and Jake had survived? Maybe that was a good omen. They got out of the car and headed toward the Hercules, which was going to Area 51. Air Force One, with the president, would be on its way to the nuke-proof command center at Cheyenne Mountain.

Lanford and her staff were passing the limousine as Patricia got out.

"Madam President," she said, "can you take my father to Cheyenne Mountain?"

"Yes, of course," Lanford answered.

Whitmore shook his head. "I'm coming with you, Patty."

"Please, Dad, you'll be safer there," she protested, but he was already walking toward the C-130. She gave up and turned back to the president. "Good luck."

President Lanford nodded somberly. "Good luck to us all."

They separated then, and Patricia wondered how many of these people she would see again.

*   *   *

Jake had perhaps overstated things to the lieutenant at Area 51 when he said they were on their way. That depended on their being able to get free of the alien ship, which wasn't yet a done deal. He'd just wanted to make sure Patty knew he was okay, and what did it hurt to spread a little optimism around?

God knew they all needed it.

The front of the alien ship had started to breach Earth's atmosphere, glowing red from the resistance. Violent cloud fronts began to roil along the ship's leading edge. The tug shook so violently that Jake started to wonder if it would survive. Reentry was a lot easier when they weren't attached to an object five hundred miles wide.

"Director Levinson," Floyd Rosenberg said. "For the record, I will definitely recommend to my superior that you have all the money you need to make them go away."

David didn't even look at him. Right then, with giant pieces of lunar debris disintegrating into fireballs around them and an alien ship on a collision course with Earth, money was the least of their problems.

*   *   *

"Sir, the alien ship has entered the Earth's atmosphere over Asia!" an aide reported as Lanford and her staff climbed the stairs to Air Force One.

Another aide chimed in. "We're getting reports it's slowed considerably."

"Finally, some good news," Tanner said.

"Not exactly. The slower it gets, the more gravity it seems to gain. The ship's gravitational pull is fighting with Earth's, creating some… side effects." The aide showed them a tablet with video feeds from ESD fighter jets scrambled out of European and Asian bases, and Lanford realized just how euphemistic the phrase *side effects* had been.

*   *   *

The evacuation order issued by Earth Space Defense got to the salvage ship *Alison* at absolutely the worst time.

They had just received a visual showing a World War II-era freighter that had been torpedoed off the Maldives, years earlier, with what Captain McQuaide suspected was a hold full of gold. McQuaide and Boudreaux—his tech specialist who was operating the remote submersible—took pictures of the shipwreck. His radio operator Ana-Lisa stuck her head into the room.

"They're ordering all ships out of the area, Captain!" she said.

"*Putain*," Boudreaux swore.

McQuaide tapped the monitor. "There's a hundred million dollars' worth of gold on that ship. If they think I'm going to leave it, they're out of their minds."

His first mate, Jacques, called from the deck. "Captain, you better come see this!"

McQuaide left Boudreaux to his work and went out onto the deck.

The sky had disappeared. From horizon to horizon, the vast hull of an alien spaceship loomed behind a roiling layer of fiery clouds.

Suddenly McQuaide understood the evacuation order.

He crossed himself reflexively... but he wasn't pulling *Alison* out. Not just yet.

* * *

Jasmine moved through the chaos in the hospital hallways, trying to coordinate evacuations, and find out where Dylan was. He'd been on the Moon, she knew that much, and she knew the Moon Base was gone. One of the nurses had told her that she saw Legacy Squadron flying before the base was destroyed, which gave Jasmine hope. If Dylan had made it into the air—well, vacuum—anything was possible.

She turned to a nearby TV, where a newscaster was talking over a graphic plotting the trajectory of the invader.

"It seems the alien ship is making its way over the Middle East. These are the latest images sent by Al-Jazeera..."

The graphic disappeared, replaced by shaky footage of the Burj Khalifa, the tallest building on Earth, being torn free of its foundations and coming apart as it was sucked up into the burning clouds above. Next the same scene was repeated from Singapore, Dubai... All over Asia and the Middle East, the alien ship was uprooting and destroying cities just by passing over.

God, she thought. *What will happen if it actually decides to attack?*

* * *

Jake was concocting a plan to break free of the alien ship. He didn't know what that plan was, exactly, but he was busy concocting anyway. Sooner or later the gravitational grip would have to lessen, or else it would end up covered with bits and pieces of the Earth. Surely the aliens didn't want that. If they'd wanted a collision, they wouldn't have slowed the ship down. So, Jake reasoned, there would come a chance to escape. He wanted to be ready.

He also wanted it to be worthwhile. It had occurred to him that the piece of wreckage from the spherical ship might not have survived reentry, so he'd sent Charlie back to look at it.

"Give me some good news, Charlie," he called out.

"It's still there!" Charlie answered.

Excellent, Jake thought. So he hadn't commandeered the tug and risked death for nothing. Now he could concentrate on figuring out how to get the hell out of there. Behind him, he heard Floyd Rosenberg ask Charlie a question that had in fact been on Jake's mind, as well.

"Don't you think it's strange that they're back on the same day, twenty years later?"

"It's quite simple, actually," Charlie said, as if he'd spent a lot of time thinking about it—which maybe he had. Jake wouldn't be surprised. "Orbital mechanics. If they're using wormholes, our relative position in the rotation of the galaxy could be a factor. June 30th, 1908, the Tunguska Blast, July 3rd, 1947, the Roswell crash, July 2nd, 1996, the Invasion." He paused, thinking it over. "Or it could just be a coincidence."

Got it, Jake thought. *Orbital mechanics. Coincidence. Same diff.*

"Uh-oh," David said. "That's not good."

Out of the window they saw that the ship wasn't just dragging along pieces of the Moon and the mother ship anymore. Dozens of passenger jets appeared below them, spinning up from the ground and breaking apart as they got closer to the vessel or collided with each other. A massive hangar emblazoned DUBAI INTERNATIONAL AIRPORT in English and Arabic rose with them.

One of the planes was close enough that Jake could see the panicked faces of the passengers inside. It was a sight he would never forget.

*   *   *

The new hybridized Air Force One got from D.C. to Cheyenne Mountain in the time it used to take to go from the capital to Baltimore. President Lanford and her entourage fought through fierce mountain winds toward the massive steel doors embedded in the rock face. Inside was the most secure facility in the world.

"It's touching down over the Atlantic," Tanner said after a brief consultation with one of the aides.

Lanford needed more detail. "Which part?"

Tanner paused. "All of it, ma'am."

My God, she thought. "We have to expect major seismic activity. Issue an evacuation order for every coastline."

"There's no time," Tanner protested as the door finished swinging open.

"Just do it! If we save one life, it'll be worth it." Enough people were going to die, Lanford thought, anger welling up inside of her. Too many already had. Every single life had to be treated as the most precious resource they had.

The presidential entourage walked into Cheyenne Mountain and the steel doors swung shut, sealing them inside.

*   *   *

"We've just been given a full evac order!" Jasmine called out as she raced down a hallway. She had already been moving out every patient who didn't need to be there, but now she had to empty the entire building, and fast. "We have less than twenty minutes to get every patient out of here!"

"We still have two in surgery," one of the charge nurses said, consulting the operating-room schedule.

"Get them into post-op as fast as you can!" Jasmine answered as she turned into a nearby delivery room where a young woman was in the middle of having a baby. She was alone. Jasmine swore that when she found out who had abandoned her, there were going to be some job openings, if not criminal proceedings.

"They just left me here!" the woman shrieked. "Please don't let my baby die!"

"I got you, honey," Jasmine said, examining her. The baby had already crowned. "Your baby's going to be just fine, but I'm going to need you to push, with everything you got!"

The woman screamed as the next contraction hit and she pushed with everything she had. Jasmine looked over her shoulder. She had scissors, blankets, the whole delivery setup in place. She could do this herself, as long as the mother-to-be didn't have any complications. If she did...

Jasmine refused to think about that. As the young woman's scream trailed away, she worked the baby's head free.

They might just make it, she thought.

33

God, Jake thought. *How much bigger can you build something?* It didn't seem impossible to him that when this ship landed, it would tip the Earth off its axis. It was that big.

Some of the debris sucked up by the ship's passage over Asia started to fall away, and the tug also started to move.

"What goes up must come down..." David muttered.

Sourpuss, Jake thought. "We're free!" he shouted.

"We're upside down!" Catherine said.

"Don't worry," Jake said. "We're in a controlled dive."

David gripped the armrests of his chair, his flight panic back in full force.

"We're falling!" he cried. "It's called *falling*!"

Jake eased the tug away from the alien ship and maneuvered through what seemed like a never-ending barrage of obstacles appearing from the clouds. After the shock of seeing the fleet of passenger jets destroyed, it was almost an anticlimax when Kuala Lumpur's famous Petronas Towers appeared out of nowhere—except they were aimed right at the tug. Everything seemed to be flying in every direction, as if the vessel had scrambled gravity, instead of just letting them all go.

He gunned the tug's engine and did a barrel roll

between the two towers just as the sky bridge between them collapsed and they crashed into each other. Pieces of the Moon and human cities pounded against the tug's exterior. Nevertheless, Jake could tell they were moving. They were free!

A moment later they came out of the debris field, and Jake was shocked to discover that they were above London. A giant statue of Buddha had decapitated Big Ben, and the London Eye toppled toward him as he kept the throttle maxed out, hauling the tug out of the ship's gravity.

"Hold on!" he bellowed, and everyone else screamed, too, like they were on some crazy roller coaster as they shot under the falling wheel and breasted a huge wave of spray from the Thames. Jake turned away from the river, heading southwest over the city, at last free of the alien ship.

Hey, he thought. *Turns out I was right. We actually are headed for Area 51.*

Pushing maximum speed for the thick atmosphere at sea level, Jake rocketed across the Atlantic Ocean toward the east coast of the United States. Above them, the alien ship stopped its descent. Huge landing petals, each one a hundred miles long, began unfolding from its underbelly and descending toward the surface. It was awe-inspiring, and also freaking terrifying, and Jake couldn't wait to get out from under the ship and see the sun again.

Behind him he heard Catherine crying.

"Are you okay?" David asked.

"My mother lives in London," she said quietly through her tears.

David was silent for a moment. "Maybe she made it out," he said, even though none of them believed it.

His phone rang. Frowning, David answered it.

"Dad! Where are you?"

* * *

As soon as David answered, Julius started right in.

"David! This is definitely bigger than the last one!"

"You can see it?" David's voice crackled through a bad connection. "Where are you?"

"On my boat, where else?" What was he going to be doing? Selling books? Going to fancy anniversary celebrations? No. And not catching fish, either.

He'd gone out on the boat to avoid people and catch fish, but he had only managed one of those things. At least he'd been by himself, but even the pleasure of solitude was ruined when he turned on the radio. Every station he could get was broadcasting the big shindig in Washington.

"The world has turned today's twentieth anniversary memorial into a victory celebration," a radio announcer had said, going on and on as Julius Levinson floated in the Gulf of Mexico off the Texas coast. He was irritated, and not just at the guy on the radio.

At his son who never called.

At the people who never bought his books.

At the fish who never bit.

"And what a day for it," the announcer added. "All weekend we're looking at blue skies for most of the Gulf." Julius cast again, and retrieved. Behind him in the cabin sat boxes of his book. He carried them everywhere he went.

"That *verkackte* celebration!" he shouted at the fish who weren't biting. "You know that they didn't invite me? Me! My son just saved the world. Twice! And that's the thanks I get." He quieted down before he went on, feeling a little self-conscious about yelling, even though there was no one to hear him. "Instead I'm here talking to fish. They never bite. If I want fish, I have to go to the fish store."

*   *   *

An hour or so later he'd changed the station, not wanting to hear anything more about the celebration. He'd also given up on fishing and was in his cabin frying a steak on the small stove. Maybe it jinxed him, bringing so much extra food on a fishing trip, but it was sure as hell better than being hungry.

The radio crackled in the middle of a song that had been popular when Julius was younger than David. *Must be a storm somewhere*, Julius thought, remembering the weather report from a while ago. "Schmucks can't even get the weather right!" he groused as he saw dark clouds through the cabin window, distant in the east.

Stepping out of the cabin to get a better view, Julius understood right away that there had been nothing wrong with the weather forecast. The clouds were full of fire, roiling as something immense, spanning much of the horizon, moved within.

"That's not bad weather," Julius said out loud. He'd seen it before. "I have to call my David."

But first he got the boat moving.

*   *   *

"Listen to me," David said when Julius caught him up. His voice was deformed and wobbly, almost robotic from the interference. "You have to get to shore as fast as you can—Dad?"

"I'm here!" But the cell connection failed. Julius shouted into the phone for another minute, then gave up.

Looking back over his shoulder toward the alien ship, he watched the landing foot extend, unfolding out and down, wider than... he didn't know. Bigger than anything he'd ever seen. Miles wide. When it hit the water, the wave it created looked like it could crest over the Eiffel Tower. Julius kept the throttle rammed all the way open. He didn't know how fast the wave was moving, but it was faster than he was. He had to try to ride it out somehow and hope he could drift down the back, instead of getting caught inside of it when it finally broke over land.

He buckled himself into his fishing chair as a nearby oil rig bent and tore apart. Farther away a tanker disappeared into the wall of water.

Julius somehow made it to the top of the wave, riding incredibly high. There were buildings approaching. How long had he been doing this? He'd lost track of time. It was hell being an old man.

Still riding the wave, the boat surged through the first rank of high rises. The buildings flashed by on either side, one of them so close Julius felt as if he could have snatched a takeout menu from one of the windows slipping by.

What city was this even? He didn't recognize it, and he didn't have time to figure it out, because after that first near miss Julius wasn't so lucky the second time.

*   *   *

Isaacs went looking for Okun, to give him the terrible news about the reappearance of the aliens—although he had a sense that Brakish's recovery might be related to it. The contact he'd experienced clearly still affected him, and no one knew what the long-term consequences might be.

He turned and stepped into Brakish's room.

"Oh no," he said. Brakish was gone. The walls—every inch of them—were covered in scrawled alien symbols.

Isaacs spun and ran out of the room.

If Brakish was at all in possession of his faculties, there was only one place he would be going. His lab. And if he was again under control of the aliens, he would be headed the same direction, because the alien-research lab was attached to the prison wing. Isaacs had a terrible feeling in the pit of his stomach, but he had to stay focused on the one good thing.

Brakish was back. Nothing was going to take him away again.

* * *

General Adams saluted as Patricia, her father, and Agent Travis disembarked from the C-130 in the middle of a dust storm.

"Glad to have you back, Mr. President," Adams said. "It's been far too long." Despite his words, his expression spoke volumes as he stared at the haunted, unkempt man who stood before him. When last they'd faced such a situation, a younger Thomas Whitmore had been the strong leader during the War of '96.

"Is David here?" Whitmore asked.

"Not yet. Morrison's tug is ten minutes out."

"As soon as they land have them meet us at the prison," Whitmore said. To Patricia he sounded more focused than he had in years. "We need to interrogate one."

That worried her. What exactly did he have planned? The last contact he'd had with an alien had scarred him for two decades, and he'd never recovered. What would happen if it occurred again?

* * *

Legacy Squadron made reentry just east of the alien ship and shot across the North Atlantic until they reached the New England coast. Around them, the massive landing petals unfolded and drove themselves deep into the Earth's crust.

"All aircraft within the sound of my voice," General Adams said over the open frequency. "We've lost most of Asia and Europe, and the devastation in our capital is beyond imagination."

"My mom is in D.C.," Dylan said.

Adams hadn't heard him. "The rally point for all functioning military forces is Area 51," he went on—then interference cut the signal.

"Rain, take the lead," Dylan said. "I'll meet you there."

The rest of the squadron thundered on west as Dylan's fighter banked to the south. He'd already lost his father, and then his stepfather. He wasn't going to lose his mother, too.

* * *

They heard the aliens before they could see the prison cells. The shrieks and screeching sounded all the way down the hall, and grew in intensity as they got closer.

God, Patricia thought. *What could make them do that?*

It had to be the ship. Somehow, they had to know.

When they reached the monitor station at the entrance to the prison wing, the techs were all staring at their screens, unsure what to do. Patricia was shocked to see Brakish Okun there, too, awake after twenty years. He was wearing nothing but a johnny gown, and he'd forgotten to tie the back.

"Why are they screaming?" she asked, trying to stay focused on what was important.

"They're not screaming," Okun said, his eyes alight with discovery. He seemed completely himself again, and entirely unaware that he wasn't quite decent.

"They're celebrating."

34

Jasmine got to the roof with the new mother and her baby—*who is doing just fine, thank you very much*—just in time to see the last rescue helicopter taking off.

They stared at it receding into the distance, and then they saw one of the vast ship's landing feet plunging down toward the ground. When it punched into the earth, it was as if an earthquake had struck the hospital. A wave of debris crashed against the lower floors and Jasmine was knocked flat. She glanced over at the mother and baby, and saw that they were all right. The mother was exhausted, of course, but she was still running on the adrenaline of the delivery—and panic.

And if she was panicked, she had good reason.

Jasmine scanned the damage to the hospital, and realized there was no way for them to get off the roof. That was it. She had tried, but at long last she was losing hope. She didn't know whether Dylan was dead or alive, and she didn't think she was going to live much longer, once the alien ship decided it was time to start destroying cities again.

She caught the young mother's eye, and saw her silently pleading for Jasmine to say something—*anything* that would give her a reason to believe. She had just given birth, and she was desperate to know that her baby wasn't going to die.

But Jasmine couldn't do it. There was nothing she could say.

* * *

Dylan's fighter screamed over the hospital, where he saw his mother with another woman—carrying a baby?

All right, he thought. This was going to be tricky. He banked over to the White House, where evac choppers were loading up and taking off. As one of the choppers lifted off, Dylan hailed him on an emergency frequency.

"I have bodies on the hospital roof that need immediate evac!"

"Negative," the pilot answered. "We were given orders to—"

"I don't give a shit about your orders!" Dylan brought the fighter around in a tight turn. "Pick up those civilians, or I'll shoot you down myself!"

* * *

As the alien ship's landing leg settled deeper into the ground, it pushed more debris into the bottom floors of the hospital. The entire building started to buckle and the roof tilted. Jasmine and the young mother crouched down and held on for dear life.

"We're gonna die, aren't we?" the young woman said.

"Look at me," Jasmine said. The woman did. "We're not gonna die. Do you hear me? We're *not gonna die*."

A jet screamed overhead, and she winced. Was an attack coming? The hospital wouldn't survive it, and neither would they.

Following the jet came a Marine helicopter. It swung

low, and a Marine leaned out of the open fuselage door, extending his hand.

"Let's go!" Jasmine shouted over the rotor wash. She helped the woman and her baby safely into the chopper. Then something occurred to her. Was that the same jet that had just flown over a minute ago? She looked up, and recognized the decals on its nose.

Dylan. Jasmine smiled in joy and relief. She smiled up at him, and was sure that he had seen her. The Marine got the mother and baby settled and reached back for Jasmine.

He missed her hand by inches.

The entire hospital complex collapsed.

* * *

"Noooooo!" Dylan screamed into his mic as the debris wave plowed the hospital under, and his mother was lost in the churning rubble. He brought the fighter around in a screaming turn. "No, no, no…"

The entire complex was an unrecognizable mass of debris. Fires were already burning inside it. The Marine chopper was hailing him, telling him they had all survivors on board and were withdrawing to Andrews to transfer them. Dylan didn't answer.

He made one more pass over the wreckage, and then he turned the fighter west. As he completed the turn, he took a good long look at the alien ship, and swore to himself he would see the aliens dead. He had tried to save his mother, and couldn't. But he would avenge her.

It was less than a minute later when the landing petal from the alien ship extended hooks to brace the ship's incalculable weight, and one of them obliterated the White House and everyone still in it.

* * *

Patricia stared at the alien prisoners shown on the monitors. General Adams stood with her, Agent Travis and Okun just behind them. All were mesmerized by the creatures.

"Patricia, our chamber contains their telepathy," Adams explained, seeking to reassure her. "Limiting their effect on our minds."

Yet what her father wanted to do would place him on the other side of those screens.

"Sir, you can't send someone in there with one of those things," she said. Whitmore wanted to interrogate one of them, but how could that be done without risking permanent damage, or worse. How dangerous would they be when they were so agitated?

"She's right," Lieutenant Ritter said. "Their biometrics are off the charts."

"So we double the sedative gas," Adams proposed. "We're not going to sit around here and watch the world go down in flames."

Suddenly an alarm went off on the monitor console. Instantly a tech scanned the readouts, hitting a button that stopped the strident sound.

"Sir," he said, sounding as if he couldn't believe his own words, "one of the prison cells is docking with the chamber."

Patricia looked around, and a pang of fear struck her.

"Where's my dad?"

"He went in there," Okun said. He pointed at an open doorway. It led into an isolation chamber where aliens could be brought individually for examination. It could be sealed on both sides.

Led by Patricia, they rushed into the chamber, and discovered that Whitmore had already locked himself inside its docking compartment. He was standing at a control panel, and had brought one of the modular cells over to lock onto the other side. If he opened the mating doorway, he would be alone in there with one of the aliens.

Patricia banged at the thick glass as General Adams demanded answers from the staff.

"Who the hell let him in there?"

"Dad!" Patricia shouted through the glass. "It's too dangerous!"

He looked at her, fully present and committed.

"It's the only way we stand a chance."

She turned to Adams. "We need to get him out of there!"

Adams in turn looked to Ritter, who was working at the console that controlled the isolation chamber's remote arm and locking mechanisms.

"He overrode the system," Ritter said.

Agent Travis stood next to Patricia. "Sir," he said loudly, "please unlock the door."

"Don't worry about me," Whitmore said. "Just get as many answers as you can." There was a flash of the old Tom Whitmore there as he hit a button, triggering the gas system. The thick cloud of sedative gas flooded the room, obscuring their vision, and from the far side Patricia heard the hiss of the cell door opening.

Then there was a commotion behind her. More people entered, and when she looked over she saw David Levinson, followed by three individuals she didn't recognize.

"Whitmore locked himself in there," Adams said.

"Oh no, Tom..." David stood gazing at the window. Patricia knew what would come next. They'd seen it before. Okun had experienced it himself.

At first there was nothing but haze, hanging there for a long, tense moment. Then Whitmore slammed forward into the glass, an alien tentacle wrapped around his neck.

Oh God, Patricia thought. *This will kill him.*

David stepped forward. He was the only one of them with enough presence of mind to try to salvage something from Whitmore's sacrifice.

"Can you hear us?" he said.

"Sheeeee has arriiiived. Sheeeee has arriiiiived," the alien said through Whitmore. Its chokehold on him reduced his voice to a strained rasp.

"Who is 'she'?" David asked, keeping his voice calm.

"Sheeeeeeeee is aaaaaalllll."

"What does 'she' want?" Adams said, perhaps unwittingly echoing what Whitmore himself had asked of an alien twenty years before, when it spoke through Dr. Okun.

"Yoourrrr plannnet," the alien said. "Feeeed and growww. Feeeed and growww."

35

Whitmore started to choke and shiver as the alien kept repeating its message. His eyes were wide and staring.

"That's enough!" Patricia said. They had to do something.

Suddenly, from the back of the room, Okun shouted out. "It's killing him!"

"Get him out of there!" Adams bellowed.

Agent Travis grabbed an alien blaster from one of the prison techs. "Move!" he commanded, and as Whitmore fell out of sight, he opened fire on the glass. The other guards joined in, and their combined fire shattered the barrier, but instead of hiding, the alien came after them. In the blink of an eye it was through the window and into the room, snatching a blaster from one of the techs and spraying fire all around. Everyone dove for cover.

Except Dikembe.

In one smooth series of motions, he leaned out of its firing line, unsheathed his machetes, and severed its tentacles with expert strokes. Then, before it could react, he pivoted and stabbed both blades into its back. The alien shrieked, collapsing and dropping the blaster. Its biomechanical suit split open and the real alien inside slithered out, flailing after the dropped blaster. Dikembe stepped forward and put one of the machetes through its skull...

Just as Jake Morrison walked in.

Patricia rushed to her father's side. He was unconscious, with livid welts on his neck from the tentacle's grip.

"Get a medical team!" she shouted. Then she bent over him. "Dad. Wake up, Dad! Please wake up!"

David stood a little to the side. "Bravest man I've ever seen," he said quietly.

Patricia saw Jake, and his presence enabled her to calm down. He came over to kneel beside her while they waited for the medical team.

Dikembe began cleaning his machetes. Floyd Rosenberg sidled up to him.

"That was intense," the accountant said quietly. "One more notch, huh?"

*   *   *

Samantha Blackwell guided her mom's station wagon carefully through the flooded streets of Austin, Texas. She didn't know exactly what had happened, but she had her brothers, Bobby and Felix, and her little sister, Daisy, in the car, and they were going inland.

Some kind of tidal wave had struck, but on the radio she'd heard people talking about aliens, too. "From what we can tell," a radio announcer said, "the entire east coast of the United States is gone. What took the aliens two days to destroy last time was gone in two minutes..."

She passed an oil tanker that had crushed a line of houses along the street. Ahead there was a drilling platform that must have been torn loose out in the Gulf and dumped here. Samantha was kind of in shock, but she was doing her best. It would have been a lot easier if Daisy wasn't wailing and Ginger wasn't barking so much in the back seat.

"Daisy, stop crying," Sam said, "and can you please shut

that stupid dog up?" She had to concentrate on driving.

"She's scared, okay?" Felix said, cradling the little terrier. He was eleven, four years younger than Sam and four years older than Daisy, who didn't stop crying.

"I want Mommy!" she wailed.

Bobby, who had wanted to drive even though he was only thirteen, tried to calm her down.

"We'll find her, Daisy. Don't worry."

"No we won't," Felix said. "They're both dead."

"That's enough," Sam said, even though she thought he was probably right.

"You shouldn't be driving," Bobby said. "You don't even have your license."

"I don't think anyone is gonna pull us over," Sam shot back. "The radio said to head inland, so that's where we're going." She worked the station wagon around a fishing boat dumped on its side in the street. As they passed it, Bobby called out.

"Stop! There's a man on that boat!"

Sam shook her head. "I'm not stopping. He's probably dead."

"No," Bobby insisted. "He was moving."

"We can't pick up everyone we see. We already picked up that annoying mutt."

"Ginger's not a mutt!" Daisy said, just to be contrary. But it stopped her wailing for a minute.

Felix was still looking out of the window at the boat.

"We have to stop! He's really old. He needs our help."

Fine, Sam thought. She hit the brakes. Bobby and Felix threw open the doors, jumped out, and climbed over boxes and boxes of drenched books that had spilled out of the tilted boat. Bobby poked at the old man while Felix got distracted by the books. He picked one up.

"Help me unbuckle him," Bobby said. "I think he's knocked out."

Felix pocketed the book and went to help his brother. They got the old man unbuckled and he fell to the ground with a heavy thud.

"If he wasn't knocked out," Sam said, "he is now."

* * *

Once Whitmore had been carted off to the hospital wing to be stabilized, Catherine and David headed for the hangar where the tug was parked, still holding the piece of wreckage from Van de Graaff Crater. It was blackened by reentry but seemed otherwise intact—or at least as intact as it had been after its shattering impact on the Moon's surface.

"I don't think it's a coincidence it showed up right before they did," Catherine said.

David nodded. "I think you're right." He was certain that this ship wasn't from the same alien civilization that was attacking them. Judging from Catherine's phrasing, she was too.

"Baby, where are you going?" The voice came from the hangar door. When they turned, David saw Dr. Brakish Okun coming into the hangar and making a beeline for the piece of wreckage, followed closely by Milton Isaacs. David wondered how Isaacs must feel, having the love of his life back right when he couldn't enjoy it because of the new invasion.

"Where did you get this?" Okun asked, marveling at the wreckage. He was still wearing a hospital johnny.

"From the ship we shot down," David said.

"All the answers are in there," Okun said decisively. "We have to cut it open."

"Who is he?" Catherine whispered.

"He used to run this place before the first attack."

The hangar intercom spat static. "Director Levinson,

please report to the command center immediately." David started walking, but paused to look back at Catherine.

"You coming?" he asked. "We need all the brain power we can get."

"Call us as soon as you cut it open," she said to Okun, and then she left with David.

*　*　*

"You heard the lady!" Okun said to the assembled techs, most of whom had been in high school the last time he'd been conscious. "This isn't Madam Tussaud's Wax Museum—people move around here!"

The techs just stared at him, not sure what to do. Isaacs figured he could help, but there were a couple of things to take care of first.

"I'm happy you want to dive right back into work," he said to Brakish, who was glaring around the hangar wondering why nobody was doing anything. He still didn't know exactly how long he'd been in his coma. "But maybe we should get you some pants."

*　*　*

David got to the command center as a technical officer in Area 51's satellite surveillance group made an announcement.

"We have infrared, sir!"

An infrared image of the giant alien ship appeared on a large monitor screen. David was a little taken aback by the number of little red dots in the satellite's field of view. There were thousands of them. Many thousands.

"Are those…?" Catherine began.

David finished for her. "Yes. Aliens." Then as the satellite's view scrolled to the center of the ship, out over the middle of the Atlantic Ocean, a gigantic red mass dominated the view. "Enlarge," David said. The satellite view zeroed in, and they saw the huge red mass was moving. It was alive.

"This must be what the alien meant by 'she is all,'" David said as it dawned on him. Then General Adams got his attention.

"Director Levinson, I have Cheyenne Mountain and the remaining world leaders online."

David followed Adams into the middle of the room. President Lanford appeared on a screen, as did a number of other world leaders—but several of the screens that should have hosted other leaders remained blank, a stark reminder of the losses humanity had already suffered.

"David," the president said. "What can you tell us?"

"Ma'am, we were wrong," he said right away. "They're not like locusts. They're more like bees. Like a hive, and I think we just found their queen. A very *big* queen." He glanced over at General Adams.

"The alien we interrogated kept referring to a 'she,'" Adams said, picking up the briefing. "This is an infrared image we just received." He pulled up the image of the large red mass at the center of the alien ship.

"Christ almighty," the president said.

"Sir," Lieutenant Ritter said from a nearby terminal, "we've just received this from the USS *Alabama*." He tapped in a command and a live video feed appeared, showing a huge plasma beam shooting out from the bottom of the gargantuan alien ship into the Atlantic Ocean. It was wreathed in steam, but the image was clear enough that David was fairly certain what was happening. It mirrored what had happened in the Republic of Umbutu.

"David, is this one of their plasma drills?" the president asked.

"I believe so."

"Are they sucking up our water?" Secretary Tanner asked.

"No. We were finally able to measure the hole under the ship in Africa. It was almost two thousand miles deep. We always assumed they wanted our natural resources, but I think we were wrong."

"So what do they want?" Tanner snapped.

David took a breath.

"Our molten core," he said. "No core means no magnetic fields, no protection from solar radiation. Our atmosphere would evaporate. Basically, the end of life as we know it." There was only shocked silence in the room after that, and it lasted for a long moment. Then President Lanford asked the question on all of their minds.

"How long do we have?"

"Based on the measurements we took in Africa, I'd say less than twelve hours. But we need eyes on the source."

More silence as the finality of the situation sunk in. Tanner was the first one to speak.

"So you're saying we're already finished."

"Not necessarily," David said. "The drilling in Africa stopped when we blew up their mother ship."

"I don't understand," the Russian president said.

"There must have been a 'queen' up there that we didn't know about," David explained. "Assuming that this hive theory holds true, if we blow up this queen, maybe it could work again."

"So what can we do?" Lanford asked.

"We don't have a hell of a lot of options," Adams said. "But if their shield phasing is the same as last time, we can neutralize it. Then we send every fighter we've got and blanket her with cold fusion bombs."

"How do we know this'll work?" Tanner challenged

them. "Your weapons haven't been very effective so far, Levinson."

Funny, David thought. *You sure were eager to use them yesterday.* Catherine stepped up before he could put his foot in his mouth, though.

"This man has done nothing but devote his life to protecting our planet," she said angrily. "*No one* could have prevented this—"

"Catherine," David said. This was a little more than he needed right at the moment, although he appreciated the sentiment.

"Who the hell is she?" Tanner demanded. "This is a classified briefing, General."

General Adams signaled to two nearby soldiers, who escorted Catherine out. David was glad she had stuck up for him, but also glad she had left without causing more trouble with Tanner. He was already in enough trouble. When she was gone, he turned back to the screens.

"Madam President," he said, "I'm afraid this is the only option we have."

The president considered her options, the weight of what was left of the world clearly all on her shoulders. Then she said what David had known she would say.

"Let's do it."

The commander-in-chief had spoken. Adams turned to Ritter.

"Scramble our fighters," he ordered.

36

Whitmore dreamed, and in his dream he saw a vast chamber, its interior a furious collage of images cycling through the entire history of human civilization, from the first marks on clay tablets right up through the steel plates laid as the foundation of Rhea Base. The images blurred faster and faster, too fast for him to follow, but something was watching them, soaking them in, searching…

The images all froze. One of them was slowly drawn out. It was the spherical ship emerging from the wormhole near the Moon.

An inhuman scream echoed through the chamber, and through Whitmore's terrified dreaming mind.

* * *

Patricia and Jake noticed Whitmore's fingers twitching as he lay unconscious in bed. Dr. Isaacs was checking his vital signs and reading through the initial reports of the incident of his contact with the alien prisoner.

"Is he going to be all right?" Patricia asked.

"His exposure was limited," Isaacs said. "He's strong. He'll pull through." He gave them a confident doctorly nod and left.

Patricia turned to Jake. "I thought I'd lost you."

"Why, because the Moon exploded?" Jake joked. "It'll take more than that to keep me away from you."

Patricia laughed through tears. "I guess I should've known better." They kissed, and Patricia felt more certain than ever that as long as Jake was around, there was a chance everything would work out. He had that effect on her, and it was a big reason why she loved him.

"Hey, sorry to interrupt," Charlie said, poking his head in the door. "Jake, they called for an attack. Pre-flight briefing in five!" Then he disappeared again.

It was "all hands on deck," just like the stories of the War of '96, when an alcoholic crop duster had saved a million lives. Even pilots who hadn't completed training were called in, and that meant both Jake and Patricia. She gazed down at her father, so helpless and fragile. There was nothing she could do for him, though.

"We should get suited up," she said.

"Patricia—" he began, but she cut him off.

"Just because I haven't flown in a while doesn't mean I've forgotten how."

"I know that," Jake said. After a pause he added, "You should stay with your father."

"They're going to need every pilot they can get up there," she said. She didn't add that she had always wanted to fly, just as much as he had, and that she didn't need him keeping her out of danger like she was some kind of damsel in distress.

"Please," Jake said. She knew why, and she didn't answer. He kissed her again and added, "I'll come find you after the briefing."

Then he was gone.

Patricia looked down at her father.

She had a decision to make.

* * *

Jake made his way through a group of pilots suiting up for the attack, heading for his locker he's been assigned, but before he got to it, he saw Dylan Hiller.

So he made it back.

A moment later he saw that Dylan was crying, his eyes fixed on an old picture of him and his mother taped to the inside of his locker door.

Oh, man, Jake thought. *Jasmine*. "I'm sorry," he said. What else could you say?

Dylan wiped the tears away. Jake was lousy at dealing with people, but he understood in that moment that this was a situation where he actually *did* have something to say.

"I know I'm probably the last guy you want to hear from," he said slowly, "but I've been where you are. I know how deep it hurts." He thought back, to the fires burning in Los Angeles, seen from high in the mountains twenty years before. "Take that pain and use it," he said. Dylan looked at him for the first time since he'd started talking. "She wouldn't want you to give up now."

A flight officer saw Dylan. "Hiller! Where have you been? General Adams is looking for you. You're leading the attack."

Dylan didn't move. The officer waited, looking impatient.

"Dylan," Jake said. "You have to lead us."

He saw his friend get himself together—just a new set of his jaw, a little straightening of the shoulders.

"See you up there, Lieutenant," Dylan said. Then he followed the officer out of the locker room.

Jake opened up his own locker. Usually there was just his tug coverall in there, but today there was an old helmet. His old fighter pilot helmet. For a minute he couldn't even touch it, because he was about to do the one thing he'd always wanted to do, and the anxiety of that almost got the better of him. But he had to take his own advice. He picked up the helmet, feeling its weight in his hands. They were all going to need to lead, and they all had something to avenge.

He headed into the briefing theater, and found that Charlie had saved him a seat. A final call echoed over the intercom.

"All pilots report to the briefing theater immediately." Jake could feel the other pilots in the room looking at him. Many of them knew the story about him and Dylan, and others had heard of his escapades up on the Moon—Lao's version, anyway.

"Forget them," Charlie said. "They're just jealous of our rugged good looks."

Jake couldn't say it because of the whole man thing, but there was nobody in the world he would rather have had at his side.

*   *   *

They got the old man into the car and kept going west and north.

Eventually they ended up in San Antonio, and Sam figured out how to use a gas pump. Cars were driving in every direction, cutting through fields, turning across the median between the freeway lanes... it was chaos. More than once she almost freaked out. She had never driven before, and this was no way to learn.

In the back seat, Felix crawled over to the old man, who was still conked out, and dug into his pockets for a wallet. Sam caught this in the rearview mirror.

"You saved him so you can mug him?"

Felix took out the old man's driver's license and held it up next to the cover of the book he'd taken from the boat.

"Holy shit, it *is* him! He's David Levinson's dad."

Everybody knew who David Levinson was. He was famous.

"Watch your mouth," Sam said, because she thought that's what her mother would have said. Bobby snatched the book out of his brother's hand, waved it around, and shook the old man's leg.

"Hey, is this really you?" he demanded.

The old man woke up, sat up, and hit his head on the roof.

"Ouch," he said, and he looked around. "Where am I?" He seemed pretty confused, and got more confused when Ginger the dog climbed on him and started licking his face.

"We rescued you," Daisy said proudly.

Felix introduced himself, remembering his manners. He was also a little star struck.

"I'm Felix. This is my brother Bobby, that's my baby sister Daisy—and the mean one driving is our sister Sam."

"It's nice to meet you all," the man said.

"What's your son like?" Bobby asked.

Felix jumped in before Julius could answer.

"Can you get us his autograph?" he asked. "How often do you see him?"

"Well, these days I only see him around Thanksgiving. Although last year he had to cancel."

"You haven't seen him in a year and a half?" Bobby was amazed at this.

"He's a very busy man," Julius said defensively. "What about you? Where are your parents?"

None of them wanted to answer that one.

Eventually Sam spoke up. "Visiting our grandpa in Florida," she said.

"I see." Julius nodded, understanding what she meant. He seemed to be getting his bearings. "Well, the important thing is that you're all safe." He looked out of the car windows and what he saw seemed to confuse him. "Where are we, exactly?"

"New Mexico," Bobby said. "We found you in Austin."

"Wowser. That was some wave."

"So, where should we go, Mr. Levinson?" Felix asked. He still had Julius's book on his lap.

"He's not the boss," Sam said, unwilling to be ordered around by some stranger they'd found in a boat. "We're going where I say we go."

"I don't want to step on anyone's toes," Julius said carefully, "but the safest place to be right now is next to my David."

Maybe so, Sam thought. David Levinson would know what to do. If Julius knew where he was, that would work.

She kept driving.

37

Dylan and General Adams prepared for the briefing. Adams expressed his condolences on Hiller's mother, but he was all business. A lot of people had died. Their job was to keep alive as many of the rest as they could. The monitor behind them showed the logo of the Earth Space Defense program. The camera operator checked all of his feeds and then got their attention.

"You're on in five… four… three… two…"

The image of the two men appeared on the theater's screen, and on many other screens just like it all over the world. General Adams took the podium while Dylan waited to the side, and an inset window displayed a hologram of the satellite's infrared image of the alien queen.

Adams wasn't a man who enjoyed small talk, or public speaking, so he skipped introductory pleasantries and addressed the central concern.

"This red mass at the center of the ship is your target," he said to the gathered pilots. "Analysts have confirmed that the aliens are a hive, controlled by a queen, who has her own protective ship."

The monitor set next to the camera displayed a number of windows, each filled with the serious faces of pilots in different nations. Earth Space Defense was administered out of Area 51, but true to President Whitmore's vision, it was a worldwide endeavor. To fight extraterrestrial threats, humanity had needed to surmount its old rivalries. Today their ability to do that would be put to the test. Many of the screens were blank.

"A majority of Asia, the Middle East, Europe, and parts of Africa have been destroyed. North and South America are the last continents standing. It's now up to you." A map appeared on the big screen, showing the alien ship's location and the destroyed areas. Then it was replaced by a mission plan.

"We'll send a fleet of drones to go in ahead of you and disable their shields. Your mission is to fly cover for the bombers, which will be armed with cold fusion warheads. The blast should penetrate the hull and kill the alien queen," Adams went on, as the screen ran an animation of the mission's path. "Captain Hiller will brief you on the flight plan." He turned. "Captain?"

Dylan stepped to the microphone. He gathered himself, and began.

"We'll all try to converge at the same time, but whoever gets to the center first delivers the payload. We have to expect they're going to come at us with everything they got. Protect the bombers at all cost."

That was the mission part. Now came the inspiration and leadership part. Dylan saw Rain, Jake, and Charlie sitting near each other in the video feed from the Area 51 hangar. Old friends, new partners.

"Our whole lives have built up to this moment," he said. "We've had our fingers on the trigger for a long time. I know some of you thought this day would never come." Dylan knew he hadn't, but now that the time had come, he was ready. More than ready. Pissed off and ready to take it out on some aliens.

"But it's here," he went on, his voice rising a little. All

over the world, pilots leaned forward in their seats, picking up on his intensifying emotion. "Now we've got to step up and remind these assholes Earth's not for the taking, 'cause I guess they didn't get the message the first time."

He paused before going on, as the emotion of the War of '96—all the fear he'd felt as a child seeing the burning cities and the immense, seemingly invincible ships—rose up in him, along with the face of his mother.

"Remember what we're fighting for," he said fiercely. "We all lost someone we love. So let's do it for them."

In a dozen languages, pilots all over the world erupted in cheers and headed out to their fighters. Watching the video feeds, Dylan saw it all happen. General Adams clapped him on the shoulder. Dylan gave him a nod and then he strode away, knowing he'd done his job thus far, and pledging to himself that he would make his dad proud.

*   *   *

In the briefing theater, Charlie spotted Rain. He elbowed Jake. "She's here. I'm gonna go for it."

"The world's facing annihilation, and you're trying to get a date?"

"Exactly," Charlie said. "Emotions are running high. She's probably feeling vulnerable. I know I am."

Jake couldn't help but grin as Charlie ran ahead and met up with the group of pilots who entered the hangar.

"Hey, so after we save the day, maybe you and I could get a bite to eat. I'm thinking a nice steak dinner." She didn't stop walking. "You're not a vegetarian are you?"

Rain climbed into her fighter and then, from the cockpit, she looked at him for the first time since he'd started talking.

"No."

"Is that 'no' to dinner, or 'no' you're not a vegetarian?"

"No to everything," Rain said. Her cockpit canopy closed and Charlie stood watching her for a moment until he had to turn away and walk to his own jet.

"It's happening," he said confidently.

*   *   *

On the other side of the hangar, Jake ran through pre-flight checks when Patricia called his name. She ran up to him and wrapped him up in a tight hug.

"I love you," she said into the side of his neck.

"Look at me," Jake said. "I promise, I'm coming back."

She held his gaze. Jake thought in that moment that no matter what had happened with flight training or tug mishaps or career plans, he was the luckiest man on earth, because when it came right down to it, all that mattered was going to sleep every night knowing he was loved.

"The one on Harrison Street," she said. "With the stone walkway."

It took him a second to switch gears, then it dawned on him. *Sure*, Jake thought. *Now she decides.*

"If it's still there," he said with a smile.

Jake wasn't a big fan of prolonged goodbyes, but the kiss she planted on him almost made him reconsider that position. When she let him go, she was crying.

"Go kick their ass," she said.

Jake climbed into his cockpit. He looked at her as his canopy swung shut and sealed, soaking up as much of her presence as he could, because he didn't know if he'd ever see her again.

*   *   *

On the ground outside the immense hangar doors, Floyd Rosenberg stood next to Dikembe. They were watching the fighters take off, wave after wave lifting at a shallow angle away from the base and then accelerating into a rising curve to the east. Floyd wasn't a sentimental guy, but the sight awed him and made him feel proud to be a small part of the government that had helped make this all possible.

But only a small part. In addition to being proud, Floyd was frustrated. He'd watched other people do heroic stuff, and all he did was schlep around a briefcase and try to make sure that different columns of numbers matched up.

"Everyone's going off to be a hero, and what am I doing? Collecting receipts and consolidating spreadsheets," he complained. God, he wanted to be part of it. Suddenly disgusted with the way he'd spent his life, he slammed his briefcase into a nearby trash can.

Then he turned to Dikembe. "Can you teach me what you did with your machetes earlier? The slicing and dicing?" As he talked, Floyd mimicked the motions as he remembered them.

"No," Dikembe said. He walked away, his body language making it clear that he didn't want company.

"Yeah, well, I taught myself to solve a Rubik's cube when I was seven, so I'll figure something out," Floyd said—to himself because there was no one else around. It didn't matter. He wasn't going to miss this chance.

Leaving the briefcase in the trash where it belonged, he headed back inside to find something heroic to do.

* * *

The crew of the *Alison* was the kind of drunk men got when the world was about to end. Usually McQuaide kept the liquor cabinet locked up until they'd gotten salvage onboard, but what the hell. The cabinet was wide open, and its contents were just about gone. Ana-Lisa poked her head in.

"What are you idiots doing?" she demanded.

All McQuaide could do was shrug.

"The world is going to end," he said. "And worse, we lost the gold. So we thought we'd drink a little."

Boudreaux chuckled at his understatement. Ana-Lisa held up the satellite phone.

"The U.S. government's on the line. They say the aliens are drilling to the Earth's core and they're looking for a ship in the area to monitor their progress. We're the only ones left."

The only ones stupid enough to stick around, McQuaide thought. "Tell them we'll do it for a hundred million dollars," he cracked. They were all laughing when Ana-Lisa relayed this message into the sat-phone. Then a moment later, she looked up, a shocked expression on her face.

"They said it's a deal," she said.

Even drunk, they worked fast.

*   *   *

Thirty minutes later they had the submersible back in action and approaching the point on the seabed where the plasma beam burned toward the Earth's interior. The government had relayed all the information they had about the plasma beam and the depth of the crust and mantle in that area.

The robot craft had its own ground-penetrating radar that could tell how far down the beam had gone, and Boudreaux was doing calculations like a madman while McQuaide hovered over him, telling him to go faster.

Boudreaux looked up. "Working off their calculations," he said, "with the rate of sediment depletion… they will breach the Earth's core in ten and a half hours."

McQuaide thought about this for a moment. Then he went looking for the booze again.

* * *

Okun had tried everything he could think of to pry the piece of wreckage apart, but whatever alloy it was composed of had a truly incredible hardness. They couldn't get enough leverage to break pieces off it and reach the sphere inside. So now they were going to the next step—an industrial-strength diamond cutter.

A tech was handing it to him just as the nebbish accountant—the one who seemed to trail around after Levinson—wandered in, looking as if he was hoping someone would ask him to play.

Sure enough, as Okun hefted the cutter and got a sense of its balance, the accountant—Floyd, that was his name—spoke up.

"Is there anything I can do to help?"

"Yeah," Okun said, not taking his eyes off the piece of wreckage, specifically the spot he thought might be the seam through which he could cut most easily. "Back up."

The blade spun up with a loud shriek and he leaned it into the hull. The whine of its motor rose higher, and the cutter jerked in Okun's hands the minute its blade connected, spinning at fifteen thousand revolutions per minute. Nothing. He pushed on it a little more, sure he was feeling it start to bite, then—

BANG!

The blade shattered into shrapnel that pinged all over that part of the hangar, and barely missed impaling Floyd the accountant.

Man, Okun thought. *This stuff is incredible.* He made

a note to his future self that he needed to figure out its composition, and start a project to reverse-engineer a design for it. "So much for that," he said.

"Now what?" Floyd asked. He looked a little nervous.

Okun turned to the tech who had brought him the diamond cutter. "Do we still have the LXR-73?"

"What's the LXR-73?" Floyd asked. Apparently the tech had no idea either, because he just stared at Okun. People stared at him a lot. He didn't mind. He was who he was, and if they wanted to stare, that was cool. He had more important things to worry about.

If you want something done... Okun thought. He led the group all the way to the back of the hangar, where he'd just put away the LXR-73... well, if by "just" you meant twenty years ago. That was a big thought he didn't have room for at the moment, so he stowed it and paid attention to the matter at hand. He was going to get into that piece of wreckage and get the sphere out if he had to invent a disintegrator ray to do it.

Sitting on the top shelf of a large steel unit on the hangar's back wall was a metal crate almost the size of a coffin. Painted on the crate in capital letters was a warning.

HANDLE WITH EXTREME CAUTION – LASER

"There it is," Okun said gleefully. If abrasion wouldn't do the trick, even at fifteen thousand rpm, then he would just have to go with heat. Plus it had been a while since he'd taken the LXR-73 out for a test drive.

Floyd looked even more unnerved, most likely deterred by the big warning label. Okun had him pegged as the kind of guy who obeyed every warning label he'd ever seen.

"What is that?" Floyd asked. "Some kind of alien laser?"

"No," Okun said with a big grin on his face. "That's an Okun laser."

* * *

Isaacs knew Brakish would be obsessing over the piece of wreckage until he got the sphere out, so he took the chance to show Catherine Marceaux what Brakish had been doing earlier that day. She was an expert, after all, and Isaacs was a great believer in expertise.

So he stood with her in Brakish's hospital room while she gaped at the hundreds of alien symbols drawn on the walls.

"How can his connection be this strong?" she wondered.

"During the first attack, he was exposed to their collective mind. Completely unfiltered."

"It's a miracle it didn't kill him," she said, pulling out a camera. "I need to ask him about this."

"I already have," Isaacs said. "He doesn't know what any of it means. He doesn't even remember drawing them." That's why he had wanted to get Levinson involved, but Levinson had suggested that he talk to Catherine instead. Surely *someone* could make some sense of this.

Her camera started clicking and Isaacs watched her, preoccupied with worry about Brakish. He was back, and seemed exactly the same as he had been before the coma... but how could he ever really know for sure?

38

David and General Adams stood in the middle of the Area 51 command center, watching the big screen that displayed the progress of the drones. Behind them flew the first waves of the hybrid fighters approaching from the west. Other fighter wings, carefully timed, closed in on the enemy from other directions, having taken off from their bases across Europe, Asia, and Africa.

"The drones are approaching the target," a flight officer said.

David watched the tiny specks move across the screen.

"Moment of truth," he said softly. Live video came up from a surveillance chopper hovering over the Potomac estuary south of Washington, D.C. The drones buzzed toward the alien ship from every direction, stopping when its shields activated and using electromagnetic locks to hold themselves in position on the shield perimeter. Hundreds of them repeated this process in a matter of seconds, and as soon as all of them had made contact with the shield, they emitted a simultaneous pulse.

David held his breath.

The shield flared brightly at every point where the drones touched it—then it began to fracture and lose cohesion. The drones, their electronics fried by the release of energy, fell away as the shield began to evaporate.

"Yes!" he shouted, pumping his fist. David had put years into the drone design and testing, and to see it work filled him with elation.

The professional soldiers who filled the command center played it cool, but he knew they felt the same way he did. General Adams, also maintaining his calm, issued an update to the fighters.

"Shields are down. You're clear to engage."

*   *   *

Dylan heard Adams's order just as Legacy Squadron came close enough to see the alien ship, its hull rising into the clouds and extending to the horizon both north and south. Its curvature was barely visible, now that they were getting closer.

"Command, we have visual," he reported, and he activated the combat camera feeds. The closer they got, the more detail he could see, and there was something they hadn't observed before. Near the places where the ship's landing petals had buried themselves in the ground, giant roots were growing out. Already they had covered most of downtown D.C. The Washington Monument stuck up out of a thick tangle, and from the look of it, even that would be covered soon.

"What the hell is that?" Charlie said.

"Looks like it's *growing*," Jake said. It was a new wrinkle—the last ships hadn't done that.

As Legacy Squadron gained altitude to fly over the ship, it sank in how huge it really was. By the time they got close to the top of its hull, they were well into the stratosphere, nearing the atmosphere's upper boundary.

"Where are their fighters?" Charlie wondered. "Why haven't they attacked us yet?"

"Careful what you wish for," Jake said, as the pilots all observed gigantic cannons deploying from the ship's hull.

"You had to jinx us!" he added.

The cannons opened fire, obliterating several of the jets in the first wave.

"Evade, evade!" Dylan ordered. In every direction the human fighters broke formation and took evasive action. As they did, huge hangar doors slid open in the leviathan's hull and hundreds of alien fighter craft shot out. They were nothing like the alien fighters from the War of '96. Dylan and the other pilots had trained extensively in simulators against those craft. These were sleeker, more agile, faster...

And wielded better weaponry. In the first few seconds after their deployment, dozens of the human hybrid jets were down, blown to fragments in midair or sent spiraling down to crash against the gigantic superstructure.

"Jesus, look at their firepower," General Adams said from the command center. Dylan wondered if he knew the comm was open.

He slalomed through the air over the giant ship, dodging other craft, falling wreckage, and fusillades of green energy that seemed to come from every direction. Dylan had always received top marks for accuracy, and he dropped one alien fighter after another—*That one's for my mom! That one too!*—but it didn't seem to make any difference in their numbers. He was drawing attention, too.

Three of the enemy dropped into a formation on his tail. He jinked one way, and then hauled the fighter into a tight Immelmann that put one of the three in his sights. It disappeared in a fireball, but as fast as Dylan could shoot, the moment it took him to lock the target was enough for the other two fighters to be right back on his ass again.

"Son of a bitch," he growled. This was going to be trouble.

He put the fighter through its paces, moving through

tight random curves to try and stay one step ahead of the pursuing pilots. Abruptly a cockpit alarm went off, warning that he was too close to another craft.

No *shit*, he thought, and then he saw something through the canopy.

As he glanced up, Dylan realized it was Jake Morrison, coming right at him. Jake's wing-mounted cannons opened up, the blasts passing what seemed like bare inches over Dylan's head, and both bogeys blipped off of Dylan's radar.

"You can thank me later!" Jake sang out as he shot by.

"I could use a little help, too!" Charlie called out.

Jake rolled his fighter in that direction, but Rain got there before he did, knocking Charlie's pursuer out of the sky.

"I got you covered," she said.

"Okay, now I *have* to take you out," he said. "Or we could also stay in? I make a killer Bolognese."

Dylan could almost hear her rolling her eyes.

"Shut up and focus on staying alive!"

*   *   *

That was going to be a problem for all of them, Jake thought. From the moment the alien fighters had come out, Legacy Squadron was fighting for its life. They weren't able to get above the giant ship and escort the bombers to the central target point, where the fusion warheads were supposed to punch through and kill the queen. The bombers, in fact, were going up in smoke way too fast. The aliens seemed to have noticed the difference between them and the fighters.

"Command, we can't get to the top of the ship. It's too heavily armed! We're dropping like flies here!" He swerved under the barrel of a cannon, strafing the side of the alien ship just on general principles—and then he noticed that its hangar doors were still open. "But we could try to fly inside! Lieutenant Miller and I request permission to enter the enemy ship."

"We do?"

"That's suicide," David Levinson said.

"Morrison's right," Dylan said. They were getting massacred in the air, and that situation was only going to get worse. "It's our only shot."

"We'll trigger the bombs from the command center so we can give you enough time to get out of there," Adams said, agreeing quickly to the plan.

"Jake, follow my lead," Dylan said.

"I'm on your six." Jake shot a pursuing alien practically off the aileron of the nearest bomber, and checked the squadron I.D. decal. "B-7, you're with me." Following Dylan, and with the bomber right behind him, he roared into the alien ship, with dozens of the fighters on his tail.

* * *

Dylan and Jake led the tight formation through the cavernous interior of the alien ship, with a convoy of a half-dozen bombers behind them and then Charlie and Rain forming the caboose.

Behind the first group were dozens of other human fighter–bomber formations, and hundreds—maybe thousands—of alien fighters in hot pursuit. They kept going east, toward the center of the ship, tearing through a series of tunnels each of which was miles wide, and then they burst out into the central dome, so large they could barely see the curve of its walls.

Alien machinery pumped and hummed in the walls, powering the gargantuan plasma drill at the very center of the ship. The top of the drilling mechanism got closer and brighter as they arrowed toward the target. Jake saw that the drill was also pumping magma up out of the Earth's mantle, routing it through a complex network of pipes to God knew where.

"Command, we're approaching the center," he said, and added more quietly, "This is too easy." But they kept flying, and kept climbing, higher and higher to where the alien queen had to be.

* * *

Whitmore woke up screaming. Again. Patricia and Agent Travis jumped up from their chairs in his hospital room.

"Dad!"

"She knows!" Whitmore said. "I saw her, Patty. You have to warn them! Please—she knows they're coming!"

Patricia looked at her father, and she was torn. Were these just more ravings? She didn't think so. Dr. Okun had suffered another attack, and scribbled alien symbols all over his room. Why wouldn't her father, who had also been in contact with the aliens? It made sense that he might suffer an attack when they returned.

If so, wouldn't that mean he was in touch with their thoughts?

She believed in him.

Patricia ran for the command center.

* * *

Almost there, Jake thought. Another few seconds and the bombers could drop their payloads, and they could all do a one-eighty and shoot their way out before the queen met her nuclear end.

A blinding pulse of light washed through the entire interior of the vast dome, covering hundreds of miles in an instant. Jake's engines cut out as if he'd flipped a switch. Which of course he hadn't—but someone had.

"Command, I have engine failure—"

"Goddammit," Charlie called. "Mine too!"

All around them, fighters spiraled down toward the floor, ten miles below. Jake and Charlie saw the other pilots wrestling with their controls, running emergency protocols, talking each other down. That was what pilots did. Your plane stopped working, you tried to fix it—and you kept trying until it fired up again or you augured in.

Augured in. That's what the old test pilots had called a crash.

Other pilots were ejecting, taking their chances on their own. Jake thought he might be about to join them, but he had at least one thing to do first. His fighter was in a flat spin, the g-forces on the edge of causing him to black out. But Jake couldn't let that happen. Not yet. Not until he'd let Adams know what they still had to do.

Blackness closed in around his peripheral vision, but his fingers found the comm switch. He struggled to toggle his comm back open. Panting from the g-forces compressing his lungs and his diaphragm, he tried to talk.

* * *

"It's a trap!" Patricia shouted, bursting into the command center. "You have to get them out of there!" Then she stopped, and her heart sank.

The looks on all their faces told her that they already knew. She heard Jake's voice over the comm, broken up by static.

"We're f-falling... E-everybody is g-going down... I repeat, you have... to trigger... the bombs!"

Silence in the command center. Nobody wanted to issue the order.

Another voice joined Jake's, just as broken up and struggling.

"Don't l-let us d-die for nothing!" Dylan Hiller said.

David looked at Patricia. She looked at Adams.

"Initiate detonation," Adams ordered.

* * *

The bay doors on all the bombers began to open at once, revealing the cold fusion bombs.

Appearing from the shadowed distance, and moving with incredible speed, alien objects zeroed in on each bomb and attached themselves. Lights flickered across their surfaces.

* * *

Jake waited for Charlie to say it—

This is how I die!

But Charlie didn't.

* * *

"Detonation sequence initiated," Lieutenant Ritter said.

Jake's voice crackled over the comm again. "Tell P— love— her!"

"I love you, too," she whispered.

Ritter monitored the countdown.

"Three," he said.

"Two.

"One."

39

Jake was rapidly losing the rest of his vision from the force of his fighter's spin, but when the bombs went off, he was still together enough to notice that he hadn't been vaporized. A hundred tiny stars appeared simultaneously inside the immense dome—but each was contained in a tight sphere, each not much larger than a bomber.

"N—negative impact! The bombs were contained—by an energy shield—" He tried to say more, but he was completely out of breath. The simulators had never been like this.

One of his plane's wings snapped off, and other pieces started to follow.

The bottom of the alien ship was coming up mighty fast. Now maybe it was time to eject.

*　*　*

"The ship's outer doors are closing!" the first flight officer said. In a state of complete shock, everyone in the command center watched the massive hangar doors shut.

"We've lost their signal, sir," Ritter reported.

David kicked a console, angry and frustrated. Patricia stood motionless, unable to process what she'd just heard.

Jake was alive, or had been a moment ago. How many other pilots were trapped inside the alien ship? How would they get them out?

"Something's happening!" one of the staff officers alerted them.

David raced to one of the monitors feeding satellite views of the alien ship from different orbital vantage points. A small opening, neither a hangar bay nor a cannon aperture, was forming at a point on the hull distant from the location of the Legacy Squadron dogfight. An object of some sort—moving too fast to identify or see in any detail—shot up out of the ship. Another satellite picked up its trajectory. As it got to the boundary between atmosphere and space, it exploded, sending an expanding concentric wavefront washing around the Earth.

As the wavefront touched each satellite in low Earth orbit, a tiny flash of light appeared, signaling the satellite's destruction. Much higher up, in geostationary orbit, other satellites blew apart, joining the wreckage of the orbital cannons in a ring of debris.

One by one, the monitors in the command center fizzled out, and a moment later the room went dark. Illuminated only by emergency lights, officers and staff swung into action, trying to recover their surveillance capabilities and get the power working again. In the midst of it all, David sank into a chair, heartsick and defeated.

"She baited us," he said to no one in particular.

Their best shot had been wasted.

*   *   *

Catherine Marceaux took the images from Okun's room straight to the one person on Earth she thought might know enough to help her understand them. In a dark room generally used for interrogations, she sat with Dikembe

Umbutu, displaying the images on a large screen.

"You understand some of their language," she said urgently. "I want you to tell me if any of these symbols mean anything to you."

Dikembe looked doubtful. "We only decoded a handful of their symbols, and even those we can't be sure of."

"Please try," she said.

He focused on the first image she displayed.

"Anything?" Catherine asked.

Dikembe shook his head. She cycled forward to the next image.

"What about this one?"

*   *   *

The interior of Cheyenne Mountain facility was barely controlled chaos, with people swarming in every direction, trying to reestablish contact with the outside world. In the control room, President Lanford waited as long as she could, but finally she lost her patience.

"Someone give me a situation report!"

"We're trying," Tanner said, "but all satellites are down. We're completely blind."

The president didn't reply. Between that and the failure of the bombing run, she thought things had about hit rock bottom.

Then emergency klaxons sounded. "What's that?"

"Proximity alert," a nearby officer responded.

"How close are they?" Lanford demanded.

A huge, echoing boom answered her question as a plasma beam cut through the reinforced concrete wall of the control room, scattering chunks of debris. Everyone dove for cover, and when Lanford stood up again she saw that the rug in the middle of the room was on fire. It bore the presidential seal.

Through the smoke, aliens appeared, walking down a tunnel they had cut from the surface. Lanford had never seen them before—not in person—but she'd watched enough video footage to know that these were twice as big as the ones they'd encountered last time. The aliens hadn't wasted the twenty years since the War of '96 either.

They were headed straight for her.

"Get behind me, Madam President!" Tanner shouted. He grabbed a fallen officer's sidearm and emptied it at the approaching figures, joined a moment later by fire from Secret Service agents. The bullets had no visible effect on the aliens. The nearest of them whipped out a tentacle and put an end to Tanner's unexpected show of bravery.

Even in the middle of the chaos, Lanford was affected by his devotion. She'd always considered him a purely political animal, and now he had defended her with his life.

She didn't have much time to think about it, though, because the next person the aliens grabbed was her.

*   *   *

Somewhere in the middle of nowhere in New Mexico, Sam drove past a mile-long lineup of cars waiting at a gas station.

"Look at the line," she said. "There's like a thousand cars. We'll never get gas here."

"Have a little faith," Julius said.

"Really?" she responded. "You want to talk about faith? My parents are probably dead, and most of my friends—"

"She's only upset because her boyfriend, Kyle, is for sure a goner," Bobby said.

At that, Sam broke down in tears. Shooting a venomous look at Bobby, Julius said, "Pull over, sweetie. Get some air." Sam eased the car to a halt on the left side of the road, which made Julius nervous. She got out and stared at the horizon.

Poor kid, Julius thought. He walked around the car to stand beside her.

"I'm very sorry for everything you're going through," he said quietly. Then he looked back at the other children, and made sure she saw him looking. "But they're still here. And so are you." He wasn't getting through to her. She just stared off into space. "I lost David's mother when he was very young," Julius went on. "I didn't think I could go on, but I knew I had to, for him."

"What's your point?" she said.

One hundred percent teenager, this one, Julius thought.

"You're gonna have to do the same thing for your little brothers and sister, and when it feels impossible, ask for help from the big guy up there." He gestured toward the sky. "You might be surprised by how much he listens."

She went silent, and he figured she was thinking about it. Kindness almost always got through, in his experience, even if expressions of faith didn't. Just then, a gas station attendant came walking along the road.

"We're all out!" he shouted. "Sorry. Pumps are dry!" He didn't even go back to the station, just kept on walking.

"Clearly *he's* taken the day off," Sam said bitterly.

Julius waved this little obstacle away.

"Something will come up," he replied stoically. "Now let me drive, give you a bit of a break."

Sam looked better. More together.

She looked at him and said, "You would've been a good grandpa."

This gave Julius a little pang.

"Maybe one day," he said as Sam handed him the keys.

* * *

Flanked by two Marines, Lieutenant Ritter entered the command center, where General Adams was trying to get reports on the status of the aliens' drilling progress, other nations' military responses... anything. But they were for all intents and purposes cut off from the world. He turned to Ritter and noted immediately that one of the Marines carried the suitcase known colloquially as the football.

"General, Cheyenne Mountain is gone," Ritter said, keeping his professional cool even in the direst of circumstances. "All seventeen members of the presidential line of succession are presumed dead. To the best of our knowledge, you're the highest-ranking officer still alive."

The other Marine held a Bible out at waist height, for General Adams's right hand.

"We need to swear you in, sir," Ritter continued.

David Levinson watched the proceedings with visible cynicism. "I'd say congratulations, but under the circumstances, it seems more appropriate to wish you good luck."

Then he got up and left. Adams placed his hand on the Bible and the Marine began to administer the presidential oath of office.

*   *   *

Whitmore had been right all along, and he'd never wished so hard that he would be wrong. This was even worse than '96. Much worse. They were scattered, isolated, defenseless... and mourning.

His cane clicked along the concrete floor as he searched through the personnel section of Area 51 until he found Patricia. She was in the pilots' locker room, sitting in front of a particular locker.

Joints creaking, Whitmore sat down on the long bench next to her.

"I'm so sorry," he said.

"They never had a chance," she said, her voice dull and almost without inflection. "You were right. We're not gonna beat them this time."

Whitmore just looked at her, his beautiful and intelligent and resourceful daughter, who had survived so much when she was a child and lost her mother in this very research complex. He wished he could say something to comfort her, but he knew anything he said would be a lie.

40

The first thing Jake heard when he started to regain consciousness was screaming.

Human screaming.

Then he registered gunfire, and reflexively grabbed around for a weapon, but he couldn't reach anything. He opened his eyes, his head clearing a little, and he saw that he was hanging from some kind of giant machine, moving slowly through an endless field of otherworldly vegetation. He'd have thought he was dead and in some insane afterlife if he wasn't hearing people screaming.

Or maybe this was hell?

He looked around, swinging in his chute harness, which was caught on a protruding part of the harvester. In the distance he saw alien soldiers massacring the surviving pilots. The wreckage of burning jets and bombers—and a lot of alien fighters, as well—speckled the field as far as the eye could see.

So he was alive, but maybe not for long, if he didn't get moving.

Jake unbuckled the chute harness and fell into the marshy field with a splash. The water was up to his knees, and cold as hell. He got to his feet and looked around, and the first thing he saw was a detachment of alien soldiers headed right for him. They opened fire, shredding the vegetation around him. He lost his balance trying to run, and someone came out of nowhere, tackling him out of the way of a second barrage.

When he got himself clear of the muck again he saw that his rescuer was none other than Dylan Hiller, who had taken a round to the leg while saving Jake. Dylan was tough, however—he took off running.

"Your leg," Jake said, and he ran after him, just catching Dylan's answer.

"I'll live."

They ran until they found a thicket that might provide some decent cover, and ducked out of sight.

"We gotta get the hell out of here," Jake whispered.

"They're closing in on both sides," Dylan said, looking back toward their pursuers. "There's nowhere to run."

The aliens came closer. Jake held as still as he ever had in his life. It wasn't going to work, though. They were on the verge of being discovered when there was a tap from Dylan. He looked over and saw Dylan slipping down under the water.

Good idea, Jake thought. He sucked in a deep gulp of air and did the same, hoping he could hold his breath long enough for the aliens to pass by.

*   *   *

Julius rolled down the main street of some one-horse town in the middle of Nevada at about fifteen miles an hour, ignoring the blaring horns and upraised fingers of passing traffic.

"If we go any slower, we'll be going backwards," Bobby griped.

Julius didn't want to hear it. "We have to conserve our gas."

"Area 51 is still seventy-five miles away, and we're running on fumes," Sam said. She was right, but Julius didn't know what to do about it. They hadn't seen a gas station with working pumps all day.

Up ahead, he saw a school bus on the side of the road, its side painted with the words CAMP JACKRABBIT. A dozen or so kids wearing rabbit ears hung around outside the bus, trying to stay out of the merciless Nevada sun. Julius thought something didn't seem right, so he pulled the car to a stop and powered down the passenger side window.

"Who's in charge here?"

A freckled redheaded boy with a name tag that said "Henry" answered.

"No one. Our driver left us to take a ride to Minnesota."

"He left you? Just like that?" Julius was disgusted. Who would do that to a bunch of kids in rabbit ears?

"He went to go have sex with his girlfriend," another kid said—this one with the name tag "Dennis."

"It's his wife, stupid." That was "Kevin."

Julius had an idea. He got out of the car.

"Where are you going?" Sam asked, but he didn't answer until he'd climbed into the bus and turned the ignition, just to see. The gas gauge went up, up... three-quarters of a tank! Even in a gas-guzzling hog like this, he thought, that had to be enough to make seventy-five miles.

He stuck his head out of the window.

"All aboard!"

"What about our car?"

"We'll get you a new one when you get your license," Julius said. He was impatient to take advantage of this good fortune, and get going to see David. His son would have answers. "Everyone in! We're off to see the wizard!"

*   *   *

In the fields hundreds of feet below Rain Lao's dangling feet, the massacre of the other surviving pilots was over. Alien soldiers filed back into their troop transports. They hadn't seen Rain, but it wouldn't matter soon, because she was snagged on a protruding piece of the ship's interior, with a fatal fall below her and her parachute slowly tearing loose above.

Rrrrriippp.

Her time was running out.

"Just taking in the scenery?" someone said from nearby. Rain looked over and saw, of all people, Charlie. He was perched on a ledge a few meters away.

"It's not going to hold," she said.

"You have to swing yourself to the edge," Charlie said. He scooted along the ledge as far as he could, but he still couldn't reach her. "I'll catch you."

"What if you don't?"

Charlie looked down at the distant ground, then back up to her. "Positive thinking is key in a situation like this."

Well, she thought, *I can't very well just hang here and wait to die.* Rain kicked herself into a series of swings. Each movement brought her a little closer to Charlie's outstretched hands, but each one also tore the chute a little more. Far below, she heard the thrum of the alien transports powering up their engines.

That was another problem. Whether or not she could get to Charlie, they were both dead if the aliens noticed them, and she was hard to miss when she was flailing around like this.

"Almost there," Charlie said. "Just a bit more!"

Rain swung one more time.

Snap!

The parachute tore loose, but Charlie was quicker than gravity, and he caught both of her wrists before she could fall. For a long moment she swayed over the drop, her life literally in his hands. Then he pulled her up and they both ducked back into the shadow of the column that had snagged her chute.

One of the alien transports flew past. They practically held their breath until it was gone into the distance and they were sure they hadn't been spotted.

"Thanks," Rain said. "You saved my life."

"Oh, it's… um…" For the first time she'd ever seen, he wasn't sure what to say.

"I've never seen you so quiet," she said. Maybe she liked him a little. Just a little.

"This is kinda like a date," he said. "We even got to hold hands."

Rain rolled her eyes. "Aaaand he's back."

* * *

President Lanford snapped awake in darkness, sweaty and disoriented. She couldn't tell where she was. Had the aliens pressed their attack on Cheyenne Mountain? Was anyone left? Was she even there still?

"Hello?" she called out. "Is anyone here?"

In the darkness she heard something moving. Feet scraping the ground, or… something larger? She couldn't tell. The room seemed huge, and sounds didn't carry well.

"Show yourself! I can hear you."

Out of the shadows, she saw Tanner slowly lumbering toward her.

"Tanner, thank God!" she said, grateful to see a familiar face and also remembering how brave he'd been when the aliens attacked—

Then she saw it. A giant tentacle, thick as her leg, translucent with strange fluid running through it… wrapped around Tanner's neck. His feet barely touched the ground.

She wasn't in Cheyenne Mountain. She had to be on the alien ship.

"Oh no," Lanford said, backing away from him, and then Tanner spoke.

"Wherrrrre issss it?"

A holographic image appeared. It was a representation of the spherical ship that had come out of the wormhole by the Moon, and it started playing in a constant loop near Tanner.

"We shot it down," Lanford said. "It crashed on the Moon." Why did the aliens care about the ship if it wasn't theirs, as David thought? And if it was, couldn't they find it on their own?

"Not the shiiippp," the alien said through Tanner. "I waaaaant what waaass insiiiddde—"

Something else moved in the darkness, beyond the radius of the faint light falling on Lanford and Tanner, and a moment later a massive alien head descended into view. The alien queen must have been a hundred feet tall, Lanford thought, stunned by the scale and sheer malevolence of what she was seeing.

The infrared image hadn't done her justice. Her head was the size of a house, each eye nearly as big as Lanford herself, the slope of her skull extending back into the darkness. She was horrific, a thing out of human nightmares, predatory and evil—but Lanford could also recognize that she was beautiful, in the way all living things had a certain beauty. That wasn't going to stop her from killing the queen, though. Not for a minute.

"I don't give a shit what you're looking for," she said, right into the creature's monstrous face. "I know I won't live to see it, but we're gonna beat you again, you ugly bitch!"

That was all she had to say, and when she was done saying it, President Elizabeth Lanford stood defiantly in front of the alien queen, preparing to die.

* * *

With Okun fussing over them the entire time, the hangar crew got the LXR-73 mounted on a crane so they could move it across the hangar to where the piece of wreckage still hung in the tug's cargo arms. The laser bumped over a crack in the floor.

"Careful!" he said. "Don't agitate the crystals!"

Floyd was watching the proceedings, wondering if maybe he should be in another state. Okun turned and spoke to him.

"Built it back in '94," he said. "Had to shelve it though after the meltdown in sector G." He gave it an affectionate kick and a frightening noise came out of it, as if it might blow up at any moment.

"What meltdown?" Floyd asked nervously. "Are we sure this thing is safe?"

Okun gave him a big grin. "Not in the slightest." He flicked a pair of welding goggles down over his eyes, and as soon as the laser was in position, he powered it up and started cutting into the wreckage.

Floyd weighed pride against safety, and safety won. He took cover behind a console, waiting for the whole thing to go *blooey*.

* * *

"Stop," Dikembe said. "Go back."

Catherine clicked back. Dikembe stared at two symbols on the display. One was the familiar circle-and-line. Catherine recognized the other from the charts Dikembe had tacked up to the walls in his study—

"What?" she demanded. "What do you see?"

Dikembe waited a moment. "That symbol means 'hunt,'" he said.

At last we're getting somewhere, Catherine thought—but where? "If that's 'hunt' and the circle means 'fear,' then maybe they're being hunted by it."

"Or the opposite," Dikembe said.

Maybe he was right, she thought, and then she remembered something else, from another case. She started digging through her laptop case files until she came up with the one she was after.

"I had one case study in Brazil where my patient didn't describe the circle as fear. He referred to it as 'enemy.' What if the aliens aren't afraid of it?"

What if instead they were at war with it?

*   *   *

When the satellites went down, the crew of the *Alison* had to find a new way to keep in touch with the American government. Ana-Lisa and Jacques thought they remembered a shortwave radio stored down below somewhere. When they found it, they dragged it up into the tech room, where McQuaide and Boudreaux were watching the drill on the monitor. The aliens either hadn't noticed the submersible or didn't care.

"We found a shortwave in the hold," Ana-Lisa announced. "We should be able to communicate with that." The captain nodded as Boudreaux noticed something on the monitor. A sudden upwelling of bright-red sludge, boiling into slag around the plasma beam. Ana-Lisa saw it, too. "What's that?"

"The drill cracking the outer mantle?" Boudreaux offered. "But that shouldn't happen for another—" A thought occurred to him and he grabbed the pad he'd used to do his math before. "Oh, no. No *no no*…"

"What's no no no?" McQuaide wanted to know.

"We didn't compensate for the porousness of the

mesosphere," Boudreaux said, as if either McQuaide or Ana-Lisa would know what that meant. He finished his new round of calculations and sat back. "We don't have seven hours left until the Earth core breach. We have two."

There wasn't enough booze in the world to make McQuaide feel better about that.

*   *   *

The laser did the trick, and didn't even blow up in the process. Floyd stood up as Okun powered down the laser and yelled at the crew member inside the tug.

"Pull!"

The tug's arms engaged and pulled the wreckage apart, releasing the smooth sphere from its battered casing. It hit the floor with an ear-splitting *clang* and then rolled slowly toward Okun. He beamed down at it.

"Hello, gorgeous," he said. "It's time to see what secrets you're hiding." Waving the rest of the team over, he started issuing orders. "Let's run every scan, and find out what we're dealing with here!"

Amazing, Floyd thought. He'd never in his life met someone he considered a bona fide mad scientist, but Dr. Brakish Okun fit the bill perfectly.

41

Not knowing where else to go, David wandered into the fighter hangar and stared out into its emptiness. Without the fighters and their crews, the place felt uncomfortably like a graveyard. A few mechanics and ground crew milled about without purpose—or maybe that was David projecting, because he sure as hell didn't know what his purpose was now.

Everything he'd done had failed.

"Well, Dad," he said, "Earth's gonna be destroyed and in the end it wasn't even global warming."

"David," Tom Whitmore said from behind him.

David turned around. "Ah, President Whitmore! Good to see you up and about, Tom. You gave us a scare."

"It's been a while," Whitmore said.

"Connie's funeral," David said. "I miss her every day. At least she didn't have to see this." Since Whitmore was there, David kept up his confession. He had to get it off his chest. "I had twenty years to get us ready. I threw myself into work, ignored my wife, my father… and we never had a chance, did we?"

"We didn't last time either," Whitmore said. After a pause, he added, "We always knew they were coming back. We've been fighting this war in our heads for a long time. It's worn us down."

That's one way to look at it, David thought. "Maybe we just got lucky last time."

"You think that was luck?" Whitmore said. "David, look how far we've come. For the last twenty years, our planet has stood united. That's unprecedented in human history. That's sacred. That's worth dying for. We convinced an entire generation this was a battle we could win, and they believed us. And now we have to believe in them. We can't let them down."

Despite himself, David was inspired.

He wasn't the only one. A soldier passing by had stopped to listen. Some of the other ground crew personnel, seeing the former president in the room, also started paying attention. Whitmore saw this and turned so he could speak to all of them.

"Look around you," he said. "They're the reason why we all have to fight. Until our last breath. It wasn't luck. It was our resolve. Our will to live. We don't run. We don't lose hope. That's not who we are. We sacrifice for each other, no matter what the cost might be. That's what makes us human. That's what will lead us to victory."

The last time Whitmore had given a speech like that, his audience was a ragtag group of pilots about to fly a suicide mission. This time it was a small gathering of mechanics and soldiers, in a base emptied out of all its combat capability, two thousand miles from an alien ship that in a few hours would destroy the planet—but it didn't matter. Whitmore had stirred them, given them a little hope. They clapped for him, the sound echoing through the hangar, and David couldn't help but smile.

"He always had a way with words," he said to the onlookers.

The hangar loudspeaker popped, breaking up the mood. "Director Levinson to the research hangar."

David turned to Whitmore. "After you."

As they walked out, David noticed that Whitmore had left his cane behind.

* * *

As they got to the end of the corridor leading to the research hangar, Dikembe and Catherine came rushing around the corner, nearly piling into the former president. Catherine looked flushed and excited. He knew that look. She'd found something amid the litter of symbols Okun had drawn all over his walls during his latest fugue.

"David!" she said, the excitement in her voice, as well. "They're *hunting* it."

Together they hurried to the research hangar, where the sphere sat on a worktable while Okun swiped and pounded feverishly at a large computer console. It was a beautiful thing, David thought. Whatever its intended function, its form was... perfect. There were many objects in the world that were pleasant to look at, but this was different. David found himself in the unusual position of being unable to articulate his response to the sphere. It... it got to him.

"You guys have to see this," Okun said. They gathered with him as he went on. "I've run every possible scan, and it's not giving off any kind of signal. I mean *nothing*. It's as though this thing doesn't exist."

David understood what he was getting at. A device created with such advanced technology would be giving off some kind of electromagnetic signal, along some frequency that could be detected. If it wasn't, that was by design.

"Almost like it's trying to hide itself." He, Whitmore, and Catherine were so caught up in Okun's enthusiasm that none of them noticed Floyd Rosenberg approaching the sphere with an oddly captivated expression on his face.

"It's really smooth."

They looked up. Rosenberg had placed both hands on the sphere and was gazing at it as if he was in love with it, David thought, or it had beguiled his mind in some way.

"You're not wearing gloves!" Okun protested. "You'll contaminate it!"

"Remove your hands, Floyd," David said, trying to dial back Okun's response a little.

"That's weird," Floyd said. "I can't." The surface of the sphere shifted, roiled somehow, and Rosenberg's hands disappeared into it. His eyes got wide and fearful. "Okay, I'm trapped now!" he said. "Can someone please do something? It's *swallowing* me!"

They gathered around him, making half-motions like they were thinking of trying to pull him away, but David spoke up before anyone could do something rash.

"Just stay calm, and don't panic."

"This thing is trying to eat me, and you're telling me not to panic?" Floyd was getting pretty worked up, David thought. Approaching a full-blown panic attack.

Then with a quiet *whoosh* accompanied by an almost subsonic hum that rose and faded in a fraction of a second, the sphere released Floyd's hands and rose to hover above the table. It stopped when it had reached a height that put it roughly at eye level with the humans. Then it stayed where it was.

If it was hiding before, David thought, *it certainly isn't anymore.* He motioned to one of Okun's techs. "Get the general," he said.

*   *   *

In her chamber in the alien ship, the queen let out a shriek that echoed through the entire central dome, full of rage and hate. President Elizabeth Lanford watched as the holographic display changed, the sphere replaced by two symbols in the alien language. The massive creature's head swung toward her and lowered. Beyond her, more light spilled into the room as giant mechanical doors slid open, revealing a monstrous suit of mechanical armor.

Lanford's eyes met the alien queen's. She knew what was coming and she had moved beyond the fear of it.

We're not like you, she thought. *You are going to kill me, but that won't matter because any other human can step into my role and lead us. But you... when one of us gets to you, and we will, that's the end for all of your drones and soldiers. All of you.*

And that's why we're going to win.

* * *

Dylan, Jake, and a handful of other surviving pilots gathered at the edge of the field, near the base of one of the columns that reached from the ship's floor to landing platforms hundreds of feet above. Maybe thousands. Jake usually was a good judge of distance, but the strange environment made it difficult.

"We need to get up on those platforms," Dylan said.

"Steal their fighters and bust out of here," Jake agreed. "I like your thinking." Dylan had punched him in the mouth, Dylan had saved his life. They had history now. New history.

"Only problem is, how the hell are we going to open those doors?"

As if on cue, the platforms flooded with alien pilots who swarmed into their fighters and took off in the direction of faint daylight visible in the distance.

"It looks like they're mobilizing for an attack," Dylan said.

Nodding, Jake said, "And I think they just hit the garage clicker for us."

They started to climb.

*   *   *

Ritter and Adams, followed by a security team, came into the research hangar shortly after David put out the call. They all walked in a complete circle around the sphere.

"This thing better not be a Trojan horse, David," Adams said.

"I don't think it's a danger to us," Catherine said, "but it might be to them."

Okun nodded toward Floyd. "He turned it on just by touching it."

The dark line partially encircling the sphere—where the bright blue line had partially encircled the larger spherical ship—began to glow. Then it spoke.

"I activated myself when I detected your biological signature to be different from theirs."

"It speaks!" Okun exulted. "In English!"

"I deconstructed your primitive language using your radio signals after you failed to recognize my attempt to communicate."

"We're primitive?" Okun said, as if it was a new and exciting idea.

"Correct. My kind shed our biological existence for a virtual one thousands of years ago."

"It's a floating super computer," Floyd marveled.

"That is an underestimation of my capacities. I carry the combined intelligence of my entire species." Its voice was evenly modulated and pleasant to hear, David thought. Obviously designed to make itself that way for human hearing. That would be part of the research for a machine like this. *Sorry*, he thought inadvertently. *Not a machine. Being.*

"Far out," Okun said, sounding like the old hippie he was.

"Why are you here?" David asked. He was having a

very hard time not pointing at the sphere and shouting *I was right!* at the top of his lungs. *See? It's not one of theirs!* He wished Tanner were around just so David could rub his warmongering face in his mistake.

On the other hand, none of that mattered now. What mattered was Catherine's idea. If the aliens were hunting this... being... that meant they were afraid of it, too. The human race might well benefit from knowing why.

"Of all the species in all the galaxies they have faced, you are the only ones who ever defeated them. When I intercepted their distress call, I knew they would come to exterminate you," the sphere said. "I came to evacuate as many of you as possible."

David nodded. "Why did they come now? After twenty years?"

"Time is relative in space travel. Twenty years for you was only days for them. I tried to warn you, but you attacked me with the same weapons they used on us."

"They attacked you?" David thought he was starting to understand how the different symbols fit together... and what the aliens were after, but he wanted the sphere to say it.

"Correct," it said. "A harvester ship conquered our planet and sucked out its molten core." As it spoke it projected a hologram to illustrate. The massive vessel latched onto the planet and began to grow the same kinds of vine-like structures that were now enveloping the east coast of the United States. "They use planetary cores to refuel their ships and grow their technology. They have done this to thousands of species. They are Armageddon. The end of everything."

The hologram showed a smaller ship budding from the hull of the harvester, and detaching. It was an exact copy of the mother ship they had destroyed during the War of '96.

So that was just a baby, David thought. *One of probably thousands sent out into the universe to find the next feeding ground*. He'd seen the growth of their technology on the level of individual organisms, but it was another thing to observe it at such a massive scale. The combination of biotechnology and advanced materials science was both intoxicating—because of the possibilities—and terrifying, because of the race that possessed it.

Within the hologram, a swarm of spherical ships rose from the planet and attacked the harvester. A battle unfolded.

"I was the sole survivor," the sphere finished.

"I am so sorry to hear that, Gorgeous," Okun said.

"What is gorgeous?" the sphere asked. "You used that word before."

"Um, I'll tell you later," Okun said.

David wanted to stay on topic. "Do you have a plan?"

Another hologram replaced the first. An Earthlike planet, bristling with defense cannons. "There is a planet where survivors from other fallen worlds work to build weapons to defeat them once and for all," the sphere said. "Your victory was our inspiration, but now that I am activated, the queen will detect my signature and hunt me down."

"She's already on her way," Dikembe said. No one challenged this. They knew the connection Dikembe had, and how he had suffered to achieve it.

Whitmore nodded. "Yes. She's coming."

"What happens when we kill her?" David asked.

"No one has ever killed a harvester queen," the sphere said, "but as a hive, I believe her soldiers will fall. But it is too late now. You must terminate me, or she will acquire the coordinates of the refugee planet... and that will be the end."

That gave David an idea. If the queen wanted the sphere so badly...

"Wait a second," he said. "If we're so sure she's coming here, maybe we can bait her like she baited us."

They all turned to him, and he started to outline a plan.

42

Jake thought they would probably be climbing this column forever. It had plenty of footholds, sure, but it was like miles high, and Dylan was struggling. Jake saw it, and he saw the other pilots seeing it.

"How you doing?" he asked, trying not to make a big deal out of it. Dylan followed suit and tried to play it off, but Jake could see he was hurting.

"Don't let me slow you down."

"Take a minute," Jake said. They needed Dylan. They needed everyone, but maybe especially him. So they stopped on a ledge for a minute. Jake had a lot to say to Dylan, but he didn't know how to start the conversation. How did you clear the air, in the middle of an alien spaceship, with a guy who had just lost his mother? It was a tough situation. He was glad when Dylan saved him the trouble of figuring it out.

"Let's get going," he said, getting back to his feet. They kept climbing.

* * *

David and Okun walked with Adams, laying out for him their plan of attack. It was speculative, depended on lots of variables, and would require the unprecedented coordination of several different kinds of technology that had never before interacted, but they pretty much thought it might work.

"Well, General," David began, and then he corrected himself. "Mr. President. Dr. Okun thinks we can replicate the sphere's RF radiation signal—"

"English, please," Adams said.

Okun decided to explain it himself. "Every computer emits a radioactive signature, whether it's your laptop, your phone, even your watch. The sphere has an RFR that's completely off the charts." He didn't bother trying to explain how it was off the charts, or what charts it was off. Ordinary people usually didn't want to know that stuff, and anyway, David was already picking up where he had left off.

"We think this 'signature' is what their queen detected when we unlocked it," David explained. "If we put the sphere inside the isolation chamber, and pack the decoy transmitter on a tug loaded with cold fusion bombs..."

"We can fly it up her royal ass and... *bon voyage*!" Okun finished in fine style.

"You set off cold fusion bombs, you'll kill everyone from here to Houston!" Adams said. The queen was on her way—they knew that from the sphere. They had to kill her but Adams, even faced with this extreme situation, wasn't ready to detonate cold fusion bombs on American soil. Ten miles in the air over Washington, D.C., that was one thing. Their ship would have absorbed most of the blast.

But in open air, on the ground?

Not a chance.

David, having worked with Adams for years, had figured he might object on these lines.

"Not if we use the shield generators from the base to contain the blast."

"Then what's going to protect us?" Adams shot back.

"Do you have a better idea, sir?" David asked.

General—President—Adams turned to Ritter. "Get every able-bodied person to grab a blaster and get ready to shoot some aliens."

Excellent, David thought. *He's going for it.* It was a good thing, too, because that was the only plan they had. "Now we just need a way to see her coming," he said, and Adams surprised him by coming up with an idea that David thought might solve that problem more easily than he'd thought.

Area 51 was full of old storage hangars attached to the parts of the complex that had existed since 1947 or shortly thereafter. Adams led David to one of those, and they stood back watching as a crew whipped a large tarp off a radar truck from the 1950s. It was perfect, David thought—a tech so old and out of date that the aliens probably wouldn't even think to look for it.

"It was supposed to go to the Smithsonian," Adams said.

David was glad they hadn't gotten around to the donation. He tossed two officers a pair of walkie-talkies.

"Drive it to the highest point you can find that has visual contact with the base," he said. "The higher the better."

*   *   *

Fifteen minutes later a crew had changed the oil, along with the plugs and wires and the distributor cap and rotor. Those old parts were stowed in crates near the truck itself. They found an additive to put in modern gas that let the old engine burn it, and when they turned the key it fired right up.

God bless good old technology, David thought. The officers and their walkie-talkies roared away into the desert, headed for the nearest mountains.

* * *

Whitmore had seen enough. He'd heard enough. He'd listened enough and maybe he'd even talked enough.

But he hadn't done enough.

He was walking between the banks of lockers in the pilots' locker room, seeing each one as a tombstone. Agent Travis was with him, but Whitmore was used to that. Travis was almost an extension of him at this point, like one of those weird parts of the body about whose function you were never certain.

Whitmore flipped open lockers as he walked past them, one by one. They were all empty, row after row... and then he flipped one open and saw a flight suit still hanging inside. He stopped.

On the inside of the locker door was a small vanity mirror. Whitmore saw himself in it, saw the gray in his hair—which he couldn't do anything about. The wrinkles—ditto—and the long gray beard he'd grown over the past years when the alien visions had worsened.

Now that he could do something about, he thought as he saw the shaving kit on the locker shelf.

* * *

Patricia had been angling for a way to get back in the air since Jake had given her the spiel about watching her dad. Now she was glad to have the chance—though she would have traded it away in a picosecond if it meant having Jake back.

Dr. Okun was placing the decoy transmitter inside

the reassembled bit of wreckage from the spherical ship. The wreckage was locked securely in the grip of a tug—the same one, as it happened, Jake had liberated from the Moon Base. David and President Adams took care of the briefing as ordnance handlers loaded cold fusion bombs onto the tug. They watched as Okun got the decoy and the wreckage arranged just the way he liked it.

He was a particular man.

"The idea is to bait her into following us into the salt flats," David explained. "Once she's got it, we'll set off the bombs from inside her ship."

"Let's get it done," Patricia said. She was ready to go. Ready to avenge Jake, to prove herself, now that her father was back. All of it. The whole nine yards.

"Well," he said, "there's a small catch. They took out our satellites, which means someone is gonna have to fly it. Manually."

There was grim silence among the pilots. Everyone knew what David meant. Whoever flew the tug was going on a suicide mission.

"I know we're asking you for the ultimate sacrifice," he continued, "but you're the only pilots we have left. We need a volunteer."

"I'll do it," someone said from behind Adams and David.

*   *   *

The voice was commanding. They turned, and at first David did not recognize Tom Whitmore. He was in a flight suit and had shaved his beard, combed his hair… he was a lot closer to the president David had known in 1996, than the haunted wreck David first heard about in 2015.

"Dad," Patricia said from the group of pilots. "What are you doing?"

"Patty—"

"Sir, he's in no shape to fly," she said to Adams. "This mission is too important. We can't have him compromise it." She sounded desperate.

He's in a tough spot, David thought. It seemed as if Adams didn't necessarily agree with Patricia's assessment. He could also see, however, that the newly minted president was loath to send his predecessor on a suicide mission.

"Patty, please," Tom Whitmore said. "There are a lot of reasons why I'm the best choice for this. You're all going to have to pick up the pieces when this is over. This is my part."

He looked to General—*President* Adams. The man nodded respectfully. Then Whitmore walked away, and Patricia turned to Agent Travis, who appeared to be waiting for her instructions. They had a routine worked out for when Whitmore did something neither of them wanted him to do.

"Travis, under no circumstance is he to get in that ship," Patricia said. "Understood?"

Ordinarily the Secret Service agent would have just nodded, but given the circumstances, he had a question.

"Who's going to replace him?"

"I will," Patricia said.

Judging from Travis's expression, it wasn't at all what he—or David, for that matter—had wanted to hear.

*   *   *

They were almost there. Jake and Dylan led the group of pilots now, and they were very close to the spot where the columns broadened out into the bases of the landing platforms.

"Good thing we're not scared of heights," Jake said.

"I don't know many pilots who are," Dylan observed, and Jake couldn't pass up the chance.

"I've been told I have a real altitude problem."

Dylan just looked at him. "You shouldn't do that joke again."

"You didn't think that worked? It's funny on a few levels," Jake said, and he would have explained, but right then Charlie popped his head over the nearby ledge.

"Jake!"

Hearing his name and suddenly seeing Charlie nearly made Jake jump over the ledge.

"God! That's a hell of a time to scare a guy!" Then as Charlie made his apologies, Jake changed his approach. "It's good to see you," he said.

"Good to see you, too," Charlie replied. He nodded to Dylan and the others.

"I didn't think you made it," Jake said.

Charlie seemed offended. "Why not?"

"No, it's just… you know. You haven't flown a fighter in a while and…" Jake remembered an old saying. So old, in fact, that he had no idea where it came from, but he had always taken it as a guiding principle. *When you're in a hole, stop digging.* "You're alive," he said to Charlie. "That's what counts."

"Enough with the reunion," Rain snapped from a low spot in a nearby ledge, where she was watching more alien fighters take off. "They're gonna hear us."

"More of us made it," Charlie said happily. Jake thought he knew what Charlie meant, but he couldn't believe it.

She didn't actually agree to go out with him, did she?

"You're still talking loud," she told him.

Charlie quieted right down. "Right."

Jake and the rest of the pilots climbed over and scurried toward Rain, keeping themselves as low as possible. Above them was a control station. Only a few alien fighters remained. They needed those fighters.

"So what now?" Charlie asked. "Go in guns blazing?"

"Whatever we do, we gotta move now, or there won't be any fighters left," Dylan pointed out. So Jake figured the time had come for decisive action. He stood up and started walking toward the control station.

"What are you doing?" Charlie said.

"Just get to those fighters, and don't leave me hanging," Jake said, then he snorted back a laugh. When he got away from the ledge and out in the open where the aliens in the control station could see him, he started waving his arms and yelling.

"Excuse me! Over here!" It took a little while, but the aliens finally spotted him. They shrieked in fury. "There you go!" Jake shouted, still waving. "Hi, how are you?"

On the other side of the platform, he saw Charlie, Rain, and Dylan make a mad dash for the fighters. They climbed aboard.

Time for the grand finale, he thought. "I usually don't hold a grudge," he shouted, keeping a smile on his face, "but you killed my parents, so I think I'll make an exception for you!" And with that, he unzipped his flight suit—not easy, but Jake had practice—and let fly in full view of the alien control station.

*   *   *

From the alien fighter Rain and Charlie had chosen, both of them stared in astonishment.

"Is he…?" Rain couldn't bring herself to finish the question.

"Just marking his territory," Charlie said. He settled into the gunner's seat and touched the handles. Holographic targeting screens activated. "We're in business!" he crowed. "Their interface hasn't changed."

*   *   *

Huge doors hissed open at the base of the control station. A platoon of aliens appeared, blazing away at Jake. He sprinted along the flight deck and took cover, thinking maybe he had overplayed his hand, like, fatally.

All of a sudden an alien fighter swooped down and blew the attacking aliens to hell. He looked up and saw Rain piloting, with Charlie shooting. *Perfect.* Maybe this was going to work after all.

One of the aliens, wounded but alive, began crawling toward its weapon. Jake couldn't help himself. He'd heard stories about how Steve Hiller had knocked one of them out with a single punch, out in the desert. He wanted in on that legend, man. So he ran up, took a crow hop to reset his weight, and clocked the alien with the heaviest right hook he had ever delivered.

The alien's head snapped around...

Then it snapped back to peer malevolently at Jake as with one of its tentacles it picked up the weapon it had dropped.

Bad idea, he realized. *Have to work on my boxing technique.* Except if he died, it wouldn't matter. The alien leveled its weapon—and a laser blast from Charlie vaporized its head.

"Now would be a good time to run, Jake!" Charlie offered. Jake ran like hell toward the fighter Dylan had already boarded. He climbed in and headed straight for the gunner's seat, as Dylan watched, surprised.

"You don't want to fly?"

"Hell, no," Jake said. "I want to shoot."

"Any time, gentlemen!" Rain called from her fighter as it circled overhead. The other surviving pilots held formation behind her.

Dylan lifted off and followed the others toward the distant daylight, just as an onslaught of enemy fighters showed up in pursuit.

43

David waited to climb one of the heavy military trucks known to soldiers back in the day as a deuce-and-a-half, referring to their weight of two-and-a-half tons. A crane lowered one of the base's shield generators onto the truck's flatbed.

"David!" Catherine called to him, pulling up in a jeep. Wasn't she from Paris? He didn't even know she had a driver's license.

"Oh, hey," he said, trying to sound casual. Then Catherine completely disarmed him by being sincere.

"I just wanted to wish you good luck."

"You, too," he said, "and thanks for standing up for me back there." It already seemed like ages ago, but the time could still be counted in hours. It had meant a lot to him that she would go to bat for him, even though she clearly still held a grudge about the failure of their brief romance.

"I meant every word," Catherine said, in a way that struck David as especially French. It also made him reconsider. Maybe things hadn't quite failed after all.

"For whatever it's worth," he said after a moment, "you're the only woman I've been with since Connie died, and I regret that I didn't take the time to see what could have been." It felt important to say it out loud, especially if they were all going to die soon.

Catherine smiled up at him. "I don't know what to say."

David smiled back. "That's a first," he said, and with a wink he got onto the truck and drove off into the salt flats, with the old city destroyer looming over the truck as it disappeared into the heat-shimmering distance.

*   *   *

Jake had his fun blasting away at the pursuing alien fighters while Dylan hauled ass to get them out of the ship. The giant tunnel through which they were flying was turning darker. They'd become separated from the rest of the group, and Charlie started shouting over the comm.

"Big closing doors! Big closing doors! Jake, where are you?"

"We're on our way! Rain, how long do we have?"

"Thirty seconds, max," she said over the sound of energy weapons and crashing alien pursuers.

"No, Rain, stop! Stop! Bank left!" Charlie screamed.

"We have to go!" she said.

"We're not leaving anybody else behind. Nobody else dies today! You with me?"

She was. She pulled their fighter around and headed back for Jake and Dylan.

"It's getting dicey up here," Jake commented. He kept firing, but they were far outnumbered.

"Rain, get out of here," Dylan said.

"Respectfully, sir, no way in hell," Charlie replied.

"Lieutenant Miller, that's an order!" Enemy fighters clogged the tunnel behind them, laying down a maze of fire that Dylan was barely able to avoid. They weren't going to make it. Jake decided he might as well do that air-clearing thing he'd been considering a little while back.

"If we don't make it," he said, "I just want you to know I'm really sorry for almost killing you during training."

"If we don't make it out of here, I just want you to know I'm not at all sorry for hitting you in the face," Dylan shot back.

Jake cracked a smile—and then out of nowhere came Rain's fighter, with Charlie blasting away at the aliens.

"Way to go, Charlie!" Jake yelled.

"If we live through this, I'm demoting you both!" Dylan added, but he was grinning as he said it. They gunned their fighters toward the closing doors.

"Fair enough!" Charlie responded. Cannon impacts rocked Jake and Dylan's fighter as they bore down on the closing doors.

"Hold onto your seat, buddy!" Dylan said, and for a moment it was just like old times, hot-dogging fighters through places where fighters weren't meant to go.

Then they were out, rocketing through the closing hangar bay doors less than a second before they clanged shut. Trapped on the inside, pursuing alien fighters smashed themselves to molten wreckage. Sitting in the turret control seat, Jake wiped sweat from his forehead.

"Jake, come in! Jake?" Charlie sounded worried. He and Rain had sprinted far ahead with the rest of the stolen fighters.

"You miss me?" Jake said as Dylan got them closer. He could see Charlie in the other cockpit, lighting up as he confirmed that they'd made it. "I told you, you'd get lonely without me."

Charlie laughed.

"All right, aviators," Dylan said. "Let's turn and burn. Clock's ticking."

They accelerated west as a group, trying to put as much distance as they could between their little formation and the pursuit they all knew would be coming.

*   *   *

"We're up and running, sir," the radio officer called in from a nearby mountaintop when the radar truck was in position and online. "Twelve minutes until Earth's core is breached."

"Good," Adams said. He looked over to the door as Lieutenant Ritter stepped in front of Catherine Marceaux, stopping her from entering the command center.

"I'm sorry, this is a restricted area," Ritter said.

Adams called him off. "Stand down. She can stay." Marceaux knew as much about the aliens' language as anyone else. If she was good enough for Levinson, she was good enough for Adams.

"Thank you, Mr. President," she said as she came to stand next to him. He couldn't get used to hearing that. He'd never had any particular political ambition, and certainly had never imagined being president. He viewed it as a temporary situation until they reestablished contact with Cheyenne Mountain and found out whether or not President Lanford was still alive.

If anyone lived that long, he added mentally as the monstrous radar bogey of the queen's ship appeared on the screen, surrounded by a galaxy of smaller bogeys. It looked like she'd brought every ship she had left, separating her own craft from the main body of the plasma-drilling ship.

"They're coming in fast," he said, and he radioed Levinson. "David, we've got a real shit storm coming our way, and not a lot of time to prepare."

*   *   *

From the lead truck in a convoy speeding across the desert with the shield generators, David answered.

"Give me numbers, Mr. President."

"Twelve minutes, if we're lucky."

"So no time for a lunch break, huh?" David notified the other trucks that it was time to put the plan into action, and see if it was going to work. "Take your positions."

The trucks moved apart and arranged themselves in a picket line across the desert, encircling the spot where they were planning to ambush and trap the alien queen.

*   *   *

Back in the command center Adams hailed a weapons technician who was installing targeting software for the one destroyer cannon on the base they had managed to get functional before the queen arrived.

"What's the status report?"

"We're still configuring it," the tech answered.

"Get it done! Without it we don't stand a chance."

Outside, a crew of technicians climbed over the cannon, rushing to get it ready. Fanned out around them, ground troops readied defensive positions, manning smaller mounted cannons while officers handed out alien blasters to anyone with two hands and two eyes.

Including Floyd Rosenberg, who had dressed for the occasion in a suit of fatigues he'd found in a locker room near the barracks.

"This is way cooler than a machete," he said as he hefted the blaster. With a deafening bang it fired in his hands, destroying a nearby Humvee. Rosenberg flinched away and then raised one hand. God, they were loud! "Sorry! Sorry!" he called to the nearby soldiers, who had taken cover and were now emerging with wary looks on their faces. "My bad. I'll pay for that."

Actually, he really hoped he wouldn't have to, but he had to say something. "That was definitely my fault," he announced to no one in particular, mostly just hoping someone would take a picture of him with the awesome alien blaster.

*   *   *

Adams was making his own preparations. Ritter had found shortwave gear in one of the old sections of the complex, and Adams tuned it to a common frequency for a final speech that he felt obligated to give. He took a microphone from a waiting aide.

"Am I on?"

The aide nodded and Lieutenant Ritter confirmed. "Yes, sir."

He took a deep breath and started to speak.

"What we do in the next twelve minutes will either define the human race, or finish it," he said. "I've been told that people around the world are tuning into this channel on their shortwave radios. To those of you listening: No matter your nationality, color, or creed, I ask that all of you pray for us. No matter what our differences, we are all one people. Whatever happens, succeed or fail, we will face it together, standing as one."

He clicked off. That was all there was to say.

*   *   *

"Damn right."

In the tech room aboard the *Alison*, a hung-over Captain McQuaide nodded at the radio.

*   *   *

Julius roared across the salt flats toward Area 51. They were getting close. They were going to make it. Once he and David were back together, everything would be all right again. He knew it.

Some of the campers had found his book and were quizzing him about the story.

"It says you got to fly on Air Force One," Kevin said, and Julius started to answer.

Dennis interrupted him. "You meet the president?"

Before Julius could answer, Henry butted in.

"My father says that your son never went to space and it's a conspiracy."

"Is that right?" Julius said. *How dare they say that about my David?* "You know what? Your father is a putz!"

Henry looked confused, like he didn't know what a putz was and couldn't decide how offended he should be. Suddenly a high-pitched hum reached all of them, getting louder. It seemed to be coming from the horizon behind them, but when he looked in the rearview mirror, he couldn't see what might be causing it.

"Do you hear that?" Sam asked.

"Yeah," Julius said, still irritated about the conspiracy comment. "Kid's making fun of me."

"No, that sound," she insisted, and at that moment a wave of alien fighter craft screamed overhead.

"Oh, boy," Julius said. *They must be heading for Area 51.* "Hold onto your seats!"

Then the huge shadow of another ship passed over. It was smaller than the city destroyers from the last war, but still maybe a mile in diameter. As it glided overhead, darkness fell inside the bus. They were sitting ducks, Julius thought. If just one of those fighters turned back...

But none of them did. The giant ship and its escort moved on. Julius wished he could tell David, but his phone hadn't survived the tidal wave, and none of the kids' phones were working. Maybe the satellites were down. In any case, they would be at Area 51 soon.

* * *

From the salt flats, David saw the first wave of alien fighters crest the range of mountains to the east.

"They're inbound!" Adams shouted over the radio.

"Yes! I can see that!" David replied. He waved to the team. "We gotta go. Gotta move!"

The alien ships flew over the trucks, hundreds of fighters… and behind them, in the distance but closing fast, David saw the huge shape of what could only be the queen's vessel.

* * *

At Area 51, ground troops held their positions as the fighters closed in. They had visual now.

So many of them, Floyd thought. *How can we fight them all?*

Adams contacted the cannon crew. "They're going to target the cannon first. We won't be able to get too many shots off, so make 'em count." Then the barrage began, the first waves of alien fighters strafing the Area 51 compound and concentrating on the visible defensive positions near the destroyer cannon.

The whole area lit up in fire and thunder, annihilating many of the defenders in the first moments. Blasted around like rag dolls, the bodies of fallen soldiers littered the concrete, but they'd done what was needed—the destroyer cannon was online, and it spun up to fire. Its beam, capable of punching a hole through the Earth's crust, slashed through the ranks of alien fighters, destroying dozens of them at a shot. Wreckage rained from the sky across Area 51.

Inside the command center, Adams watched the queen's ship move closer and closer. They had to wait until just the right moment, when she was close enough to make her move, but not so close that she could detect the real sphere. Adams waited, knowing that every second of hesitation was costing good soldiers their lives.

At the last possible moment, he issued the order.

"Send out the decoy."

*　*　*

Patricia and the rest of the surviving pilots flooded into the hangar, headed toward the remaining fighters. It was time for the last stand, and she was grimly thrilled to be part of it. Then Travis stepped in front of her.

"Patricia."

Whatever it was, she didn't have time for it. "We're wheels up."

"Your dad collapsed," he said.

Oh God, she thought. *Have the aliens struck him again?* What did collapsed mean? She looked over at her fighter, then back at Travis, agonized at the conflict between duty to family and duty to the human race.

"Where is he?" she said.

Agent Travis led her into a side office attached to the hangar. When they were both inside, he shut the door and locked it. Patricia looked around. Her father wasn't anywhere in the room.

"Travis, what are you doing?"

He avoided her look, standing wordless in front of the glass door. Beyond him, in the hangar, Patricia saw her father in his flight suit, climbing aboard the tug. When Travis saw that she'd registered that, he finally spoke.

"I'm sorry."

"Get out of my way," she said, going for the door. He stopped her, and in a different tone, almost pleading, she said, "Don't do this."

"I can't let you go," Travis said. "He asked me, as a

friend. As a father."

"I'm not asking," Patricia said. When he didn't move, she started throwing punches. At first he didn't budge, but he wouldn't retaliate either. She changed her tactics and shoved him to the side enough that she could yank the door open and run out into the hangar.

Too late. The tug carrying the piece of wreckage with the decoy signal had already lifted off.

"Dad!" she screamed uselessly, the sound of the engines drowning out her voice. Frantic, Patricia scanned the hangar. She had to do something.

There was the fighter she'd been assigned, still warmed up but sitting idle. She sprinted toward it. The aliens had taken her mother. They had taken Jake. They were not going to take her father.

*   *   *

In the command center, Adams got notification that the tug and its escorts were in the air.

"The convoy is en route!" he said to the cannon crew. "Give them cover fire now!" The queen was very, very close. If he'd been outside, he would have been able to see her approaching from the east.

The destroyer cannon spun up again and unleashed a blast that tore a path through the alien fighters, clearing a space for the convoy. Flanked by fighter escorts, the tug surged through the space, Thomas Whitmore at the controls. "Here we go, boys," he sang out, cutting into a tight roll just for the sheer joy of flying again. "I'd forgotten how much fun this is!"

He was resolute, clear-headed for the first time in years. This was what he had been born to do. They hadn't finished the job last time, but this time they would.

Or die trying.

44

Okun watched impatiently as technicians finished replacing the isolation chamber's glass shielding. The sphere rested inside, inert. The exact second they sealed the last glass panel, he radioed Adams.

"General, we're back in business."

Adams immediately called Whitmore. "Tom, we're ready on our end. Activate the decoy transmitter on my mark." He counted down to the moment of truth. If the queen didn't bite on this diversion, their last best hope would be gone. "Three... two... one...

"Mark."

He saw on the monitor that Whitmore, still flying over the salt flats toward the ring of trucks with shield generators, had activated the signal. Now they would find out whether it would work.

* * *

Inside the isolation chamber, Okun watched the sphere for a long moment and then decided he couldn't resist. He walked over to it and held his hands close to its surface.

"What are you doing?" Milton asked, sounding alarmed.

"It's isolated, so I'm going to turn it back on."

Even more alarmed, Milton reached out toward Okun.
"Why would you do that?"

Too late. Okun pressed his hands onto the sphere's
surface.

"To see what else this thing knows."

With the same soft *whoosh* and deep thrum as the last
time, the sphere activated and hovered at Okun's eye level.
He could feel it perceiving him, waiting for what he had
to say. Milton stood next to him, frightened but curious—
and loyal, too. Who else would have remained by Okun's
side for twenty years? Brought him orchids? Knitted him
a scarf? No matter what else might be going wrong, no
matter how dire the threats to humankind, Okun knew he
had found the truest love a human being could find.

One of these days he would tell Milton all of that, but
right now there were more pressing things on his mind.

"Excuse me, sorry to bother you," Okun said to the
sphere, "but I had a few questions. If you don't mind."

*   *   *

For a long moment in the command center, Catherine
and Adams watched the queen stay on her path toward
Area 51. They searched for any sign of a change in her
course or speed, any signal that she had detected the
decoy. Nothing.

"Goddammit, she's not taking the bait," Adams said.
He had no idea what to do next.

Then the massive ship shifted. Adams caught his
breath. He didn't dare to believe it—but yes. It had
worked. Catherine saw it, too.

"It's working," she said. "She's following the decoy!"

*   *   *

Out on the salt flats, where he was working on a shield generator to get it powered up and ready, David heard her excited shout over the open frequency.

"We'll be ready!" he shouted back over the sounds of the alien fighters attacking Area 51 a few miles away. More quietly, to himself, he added, "At least we'll try to be."

*　　*　　*

These new alien fighters are something else, Jake thought as he raced toward the front range of the Rocky Mountains. At this pace they were only a few minutes away from Area 51. He couldn't wait to see the look on Patricia's face. They'd made it out of the alien ship, man—that was going to be a great story.

An explosion off his wing rocked the fighter as the pilot flying next to him was blown out of the sky.

"Shit! We got company!" Jake said, seeing a wave of alien ships coming after them.

"We'll lose 'em in the mountains!" Dylan dove low, skimming the tops of pine trees as they ducked into a narrow valley, alien gunships close on their trail. Another of the human-flown fighters disappeared in a fireball, pieces of it raining down into the creek at the bottom of the valley.

Jake returned fire. There were more targets than he knew what to do with. He fired until he started to wonder if the turret barrel would melt, but still there were more alien ships funneling in after them as they swooped and dove through the peaks of the Rockies. The enemy had gotten around them, somehow, and were between them and the other side of the mountains, where Area 51 was. Dylan was going to have to do some fancy flying, Jake thought. He shot down another pursuing gunship and started hollering that they were going the wrong way.

This appeared to give Dylan an idea. He accelerated up and over a saddle between two peaks, cutting back northeast. Jake almost asked him what the hell he was doing, then decided it didn't matter. He'd have to trust Dylan to fly.

All Jake had to do was keep shooting.

*   *   *

"Sir!" one of the shield generator technicians called out, tossing David a pair of binoculars. "You might want to see this!"

The tech pointed, and David looked in that direction. He was astonished twice in a row. Once to see an old-fashioned yellow school bus heading right for the middle of the energy shield... and then, all over again, when he saw that the driver was none other than Julius Levinson.

How had his father, who had been in the Gulf of Mexico the day before, managed to end up driving a school bus full of children across the salt flats? David really wanted to hear that story, but if he was going to, his father would have to survive. If he was inside the shield perimeter, that had a zero percent chance of happening.

"Dad!" he shouted, dropping the binoculars. "Dad! You're driving right into the trap!" Of course his dad couldn't hear him. David ran toward the bus, waving his arms and shouting, trying to make himself unmissable against the monotonous background of the salt flats. He didn't always like being taller than most other people, but it did come in handy when you wanted to get someone's attention. He hoped it would work soon enough.

*   *   *

Watching from the head of the convoy, Whitmore saw the queen's ship angle away from the main armada. Now she was on a course to intercept him. He judged her airspeed, and his own, and realized something.

"We need to slow down, or we'll overshoot the trap!" he said.

They did, but although that put their intercept point right where it needed to be inside the perimeter of shield generators, it created another problem—namely, the queen's escorts could catch them that much sooner. Within a few seconds the air around Whitmore was streaked with energy blasts and the flaming trails of falling fighters.

Patricia was out there, but Whitmore couldn't think of her right now. He had to stay focused and steady. He had to make sure the queen took the hook all the way into her mouth, so when he gave the tip of the rod a little twitch, there would be no way for her to spit it out.

* * *

It turned out Dylan did have an idea, and it was even crazier than Jake might have expected. They arrowed down the face of a mountain, up over another line of peaks, and then through a gap in the foothills.

Ahead of them lay the city of Denver, half crushed under a city destroyer that had fallen in the act of extending its landing petals twenty years ago. Some of them were farther deployed than others, so it sat at an angle, like an awning over the city from Lakewood all the way out to Aurora, and Commerce City down to the Denver Tech Center.

"Rain! Head under the destroyer," Dylan called into the comm. "Let's give 'em a tour of Denver."

"You want to fly under that thing?" Charlie's voice was almost a squeak.

"Why? You scared?" Rain needled him. He shut up. No way was he going to admit to her that, yeah, he was scared. Not when he knew they were so close to having a real date.

He just had to live to see it happen.

The two fighters arced under the wreckage of the city destroyer and the devastated ruins beneath. A lot of people still lived in Denver, but not right under the destroyer because nobody knew how long it would stay balanced as it was—partially on its few landing petals and partially on the tops of Denver's tallest buildings. Millions of tons of alien ship balanced over the city like a cosmic sword of Damocles.

Jake watched the ruins go by. He'd never been there before. Maybe he would come back sometime and be a tourist.

The alien fighters followed them, still hot on their trail, but in the more confined airspace Jake had what the brass liked to call a target-rich environment. He got to work making it target-poor.

*   *   *

"For Christ's sake, Dad," David yelled as he ran across the salt flats flailing his arms around like one of those inflatable dummies he'd seen outside cell-phone stores. "I can't be that hard to see!"

He kept running, and a minute later the bus screeched to a halt. Right after that, Julius piled out, a delighted expression on his face.

"It takes the end of the world to get us together?! Come give me a kiss already!"

"Uh, Dad. Not now," David said, looking at his hand-held monitor to track Whitmore's progress and the queen's course, as well.

"You're a lot taller than I imagined," a teenage girl said.

Julius beamed at David. "You'll be happy to know I made a few acquaintances. Fans, if you can believe it."

"I'm a little busy right now," David said, not looking up from the monitor.

"Always working," his dad griped. "You and I are going to have to talk."

"I said not *now*," David snapped. "Look behind you!"

Julius looked back. So did all the kids. There was the queen's ship, looming over the salt flats, headed right their way.

"Oh," Julius said. "I see."

45

Dylan and Rain raced through the maze-like ruins of downtown Denver, alien gunships in hot pursuit.

"Focus all your firepower on the bottom of every skyscraper in the Mile High City!"

Ooh, Jake thought. *Good idea.* "You hear that, Charlie? Let's blow some shit up!" The two of them blazed away at the lower floors of the tallest buildings, while Dylan and Rain took them through eye-popping turns, staying just ahead of the alien ships. The weaponry tore through concrete and steel, gouging big pieces out of the buildings... and then it started to happen.

Their lower floors undermined, with the incalculable weight of the city destroyer pressing down on them from above, the buildings started to collapse. The gigantic destroyer tipped down.

The fighters' engines ratcheted up to a scream as Dylan and Rain redlined them to get out from under the falling vessel. They made it by scant meters, shooting out into open sky as the destroyer pancaked the deserted ruins below it—and eliminated the last of their pursuit.

"Pretty good idea," Jake said when he'd gotten his heartbeat back under control.

"Not too bad," Dylan agreed. They cut west again, and hoped they would get to Area 51 in time.

*   *   *

As if Whitmore had invoked her, all of a sudden there Patty was, in a fighter of her own, matching his speed.

"You didn't even say goodbye," she said.

He didn't bother to deflect it or beat around the bush. "You wouldn't have let me go."

"You should have let me do this," she said. "You've done enough."

Not quite, he thought.

"You already saved the world once," she continued with tears in her eyes. "You shouldn't have to do it again."

"I'm not saving the world, Patty," Whitmore said. "I'm saving you." He took a long look at his daughter, remembering her as a little girl in the Area 51 hospital a few miles behind them. All grown up now. "It's good to see you flying again. Your place is in the air." He was savoring the moment with her when the tug jerked and its controls stopped responding. Whitmore pulled at them and felt the shudder of some invisible force. The alien fighters veered off.

"I've lost manual control," he said. "She's locked onto me! Patty, go!"

Ahead of them, a hatch slid open in the underbelly of the queen's ship. Patricia held her position—then Whitmore's head snapped back and his eyes lost focus for a moment. Before she could react, he turned to look at her.

"She's in my head," he said, his eyes haunted. "She knows it's a trap!"

The alien fighters that had left them alone when the queen's tractor beam locked on the tug now angled in again, raking the tug with blaster fire. Whitmore got control back as the ship's doors started to close.

"Can you get me to the target, Lieutenant Whitmore?" he asked, with a look through the cockpit window. His voice was rich with confidence and pride.

* * *

Patricia steeled herself for what she knew was coming. There was nothing she could do. She knew what *he* would do, and she knew why, but she couldn't wrap her mind around it. Her mother, Jake, now her father…

But if there was anyone whose life had prepared him for this moment, and the ultimate sacrifice he was about to make, that person was Thomas Whitmore.

"Yes, sir," she said.

Whitmore gunned the tug forward and Patricia kept pace, clearing a path through the swarming alien fighters. Ahead of them the doors kept closing, but the queen had bit hard enough on the hook that they were going to make it.

"It's your time now, Patty," he said as they approached the doors. "I love you."

It was the hardest thing she'd ever had to do, but Patricia peeled away as her father piloted the tug through the closing doors, making it with scant feet to spare.

"I love you, Daddy," she said, not knowing whether he could hear her. Her fingers itched on the firing stud at the end of the jet's control stick—but that would be wasted. Her father's life would be wasted, too, if she didn't get out of there.

She banked away and accelerated out of the shield zone, following the rest of the pilots who had survived this far. The split second she cleared the shield area she heard David yelling.

"Now! Now! Activate!" And then he added, "Dad, get the kids to cover."

Kids? Patricia wondered what kids were doing out there.

Behind her, the shield generators rumbled to life, and the dome spread over the empty desert landscape. Inside it hung the queen's ship... and inside her ship was Thomas Whitmore.

*   *   *

David watched, holding his breath as the queen's ship approached the shield perimeter. The ship hit the shield barrier, and the energy of the interaction crackled out in every direction.

"Come on," David said under his breath. The shield wouldn't last forever. "Do it, Tom. Do it."

*   *   *

Whitmore turned on the tug's lights. All of them. In the darkness he saw two enormous legs moving nearby, straight and hard like those of an insect. Then he saw the rest of the queen as the tug was slowly lifted up so that she and the ex-president were at last face to face.

Two malevolent black eyes rested behind a ridged, pointed snout that fanned back into a dark brown frill. Her claws also looked like those of an insect, and each was far larger than his entire body. Tendrils whipped in the darkness behind her.

She was huge, and yet, somehow, she didn't seem as big as his nightmares.

"Recognize me? You've been in my head too long," Whitmore said.

There was a jolt, and even the queen staggered a little. That was it. The ship must have collided with the shield's perimeter—Levinson had activated it, and it had held.

The rest was up to him. The queen looked away, as if receiving some kind of data from her ship, then back to Whitmore, and he took the chance to rub it in a little.

"That's right," he said, holding up his right hand. In that hand, he held the manual firing control for the fusion bombs. He thought he saw a look of understanding, and felt the wave of her rage in his brain. "On behalf of the planet Earth, happy Fourth of July!"

He hit the trigger.

* * *

The salt flats lit up with a blinding light. The fighters' cockpit windows polarized to save the vision of their pilots, and so too did the exterior windows of Area 51.

David Levinson, who hadn't been at all certain the shields would hold, ducked and covered, just like the boys of his generation had been taught—then looked up just as the roiling force of the explosions dissipated. A moment later the shield did, too.

"Son of a gun did it," David said. Whitmore had sacrificed his life, but the plan had succeeded.

"Do we have confirmation, Levinson?" Adams said from the command center.

For once in his life, Levinson was willing to draw a conclusion before the data was all reported. The dust cloud inside the shield area was beginning to settle, but nothing could have survived that blast.

"I think it's safe to say she's a goner, Mr. President!" He heard cheers from the command center, and then cutting through them came Catherine's voice.

"Sir, if she's dead, then why are her fighters still attacking us?"

* * *

David turned to his father and wrapped him in an emotional embrace. The odds against this reunion were almost beyond calculating. He'd won the lottery surviving two alien invasions with his father still alive. This time in particular, it seemed to him a miracle that Julius had made it through the Gulf tsunami, and then managed to get all the way from Texas to Area 51 just in time... with a bunch of school kids.

"Who are they?" he asked.

"Fans!" Julius answered brightly. "This is Sam, my navigator, her brothers, Felix and Bobby..." Julius introduced the rest of the kids and even the dog while the boy named Henry got out his phone and turned around so he could take a selfie with the queen's destroyed ship in the background.

Then his expression went from smug to confused.

"Excuse me, mister," he said. "Um, is that supposed to happen?"

David turned along with everyone else to see the alien queen, rising out of the churning plume of dust and smoke. She stood upright, two hundred feet tall, partially encased in a dull gray exoskeleton that actually seemed to *merge* with the bony brown carapace of her body. She towered hundreds of feet over the top of them, vaguely resembling a gargantuan praying mantis, the green outline of a shield flickering around her.

Suddenly Catherine's question made sense.

"Shit, she has her own shield," David said. It looked to be damaged, but had held enough for her to survive. Instead of celebrating, then, they had to finish the job—and the first order of business was to get these children out of her way. "Okay, back on the bus, kids. Everyone on the bus!"

They all scrambled back toward the bus. Daisy, the littlest of them, dawdled, looking around. "What about Ginger?"

"Really, the dog?" David sighed. "I guess we have to get the dog." Scanning the area, he saw the tiny terrier barking at the queen. Daisy had already spotted her. She made a mad dash over, scooped up the barking Ginger, and sprinted back to jump on board while David argued with Julius over who should drive.

"Out of the seat, Dad!" David said, shoving his way in front of Julius. "If you drive then we might as well walk!"

"That's what we've been saying all along," Bobby grumbled.

The alien queen, each of her steps yielding a small earthquake, stomped out of the shield perimeter, crushing one of the flatbed trucks. As David got the bus started and moving, one of the campers cried out.

"Sir, it's chasing us."

"Maybe we should play dead, like when a bear attacks you," another of them suggested.

"Does that look like a bear, stupid?" a third kid said.

He heard Catherine's voice then, coming from the monitor he still carried.

"We're detecting movement, David."

Driving like a maniac, with the kids bouncing around in the back, David swerved to avoid one of the queen's legs. She moved incredibly fast, especially compared to a secondhand summer-camp school bus.

"Yup! Lots of movement!" he agreed, stomping on the gas and hoping they could somehow avoid being crushed before they got close enough to Area 51 for Adams to bring the destroyer cannon to bear.

Adams chimed in over the comm. "David, six minutes to Earth's core breach."

The bus roared across the salt flats. Whitmore's sacrifice hadn't been in vain, David thought. The queen was damaged, she was wounded. They just had to find a way to finish her off.

In the next six minutes.

46

The interior of the isolation chamber was filled with a holographic constellation of schematic drawings, star charts, blueprints for machinery beyond human comprehension. It spilled out of the sphere faster than any of them could keep up, but Okun knew what some of it signified, and he knew that with these revelations, humankind stood on the brink of a new golden age.

"Do you have any idea what this means?" he said, to the room at large.

"Not really," Isaacs admitted.

Okun moved from image to image, wanting to touch them, feeling the knowledge start to pour into his head and open up spaces of comprehension he had never imagined he'd be able to find.

"This is going to catapult our civilization forward by thousands of years. Our understanding of space-time, physics, fusion energy, wormholes…"

"Calm down, honey," Isaacs said, and he sounded worried.

"I don't want to calm down!" Okun cried out. This was the greatest thing that could ever have happened to him. Who could be calm at a time like this?

*   *   *

Outside, Area 51 was a war zone. The alien fighters were focused on the destroyer cannon, and with little aerial support, the ground crews couldn't defend it for long. A final salvo from swooping fighters destroyed the turret mount, sending the cannon itself toppling straight into the outside wall of the prison wing.

The impact crushed half of the wing. It shattered the interior walls, and the bay window looking from the prison monitoring station into the cell blocks themselves. Alien prisoners spilled out of their destroyed cells.

"Command!" one of the panicking techs shouted into the comm. "We have a breach!"

"How bad?" Adams asked.

The tech looked into the shattered rubble. It was crawling with aliens. "At least two dozen, sir."

"Under no circumstances can they see the sphere," Adams commanded. "Do whatever it takes!"

One of the prison techs went to a weapons locker while the other shut and locked the doors to the isolation chamber. Inside the chamber, Okun watched the sphere turn itself off and settle to the ground.

"That can't be good," he said.

The two frightened prison techs aimed their blasters toward the broken windows. They couldn't see the aliens anymore, only hear the echoing sound of their shrieks.

"Did you hear that?" the first one said. It sounded to him like they were getting closer, but he couldn't tell from what direction.

"We need backup down here! Now!" the other shouted into the comm.

*   *   *

Patricia kept a constant stream of fire focused on the queen, but her shields were still holding up. The school bus was going to be a flattened wreck in seconds.

"All pilots, target the queen," she said. "Unload everything you've got!" They did so, and their combined power staggered the huge extraterrestrial, starting to overload her shield. It was wearing down under the constant barrage, but she recovered and kept after the bus.

* * *

Inside, all of the kids were staring out of the back windows, watching her get closer and closer. Nothing was stopping her. They were quiet, realizing that this wasn't an adventure anymore. Their lives were actually on the line.

The queen recovered from the latest fighter barrage and gathered herself. Then she leapt into the air, vaulting over the bus.

"That thing just jumped into the air!" Henry shouted.

David couldn't quite hear him. "What did he just say?"

"Something about jumping!" Julius shouted.

David turned to ask Henry to repeat himself just as the queen landed a few yards in front of the bus with an earth-shaking impact. David swerved so hard that for a second he thought the bus was going to tip over—but after going up on two wheels it righted itself, and he kept going.

Overhead, alien fighters arrived to defend the queen, forcing the human fighters to break off their attack and defend themselves. Knowing she was taking her life in her hands with all the hostiles around, Patricia made one last direct run at the towering creature, hitting her with everything the hybrid fighter had. The shield flickered, absorbing the worst of the damage—but then it fizzled and sputtered out.

"Her shields are down!" Patricia shouted. Alien energy

beams crackled past her, but she stayed focused on the primary target. "Open fire!" Banking hard, she hit the queen with another staccato burst of fire, but she'd come in too low. The queen leaped up and, with a swipe of one arm, tore off part of her fighter's tail. Patricia started to spin in a tight descent, unable to see her surroundings through all the smoke from aerial explosions.

Then the ground was coming up fast—she knew that, but she had to time her ejection just right or she would shoot toward the ground, probably get her chute tangled in the plane, and be smeared all over the desert. Not her preferred outcome.

She struggled to get her plane under control, before determining that it wasn't possible, and trying to gauge the pattern of her crazy spin. She thought she had it.

No time to make sure.

She pulled the eject lever, and was blown free of the crashing jet.

*   *   *

Floyd saw Dikembe react to something he heard over the base radio, and when Dikembe took off for the inside of the base, Floyd followed.

"Hey! Where are you going!?"

Dikembe didn't answer. Floyd figured it out soon enough, though, when both of them got to the isolation chamber. It was sealed shut. Dikembe stabbed the intercom button.

"Open the door!"

"Your backup's here!" Floyd added.

Through the window they saw the chamber open from the other side... the side facing the prison monitoring station. Smoke poured through, and within the smoke they saw an alien, dropping the lifeless prison tech it had used to key its entry.

The creature spotted the sphere as Okun and Isaacs turned and froze in terror. Floyd felt the pulse of a telepathic message flash through his brain. It didn't hurt him, but Okun was much more vulnerable to them.

He seized his head and doubled over in agony.

* * *

Out on the salt flats, the queen stopped. Then she turned, breaking off her pursuit of the school bus and lumbering fast toward Area 51.

"She's headed your way!" David called into the radio. What was going on? What had she heard? This wasn't good. If she'd somehow learned of the real sphere…

He hauled the school bus around and headed after her, the roles of cat and mouse suddenly reversed.

"And why are we following her?" Julius demanded, right up next to the driver's seat.

"Stay behind the yellow line, Dad!" David snapped.

* * *

Patricia made it safely to the ground, but was stuck in her ejection seat. Abruptly the queen made a turn straight toward her. Wrestling with the damaged flight harness she kept fighting, even though the alien's immense feet were stomping closer and closer…

She wasn't going to make it.

Then out of nowhere an alien fighter shot into view, peppering the queen with cannon fire and knocking her off balance. The step that would have crushed Patricia to jelly instead smashed down just a few feet away, and then the queen was gone past her.

The alien fighter looped and darted around the queen, blasting away at her damaged shield. Then there was another one, also firing. The shield still flickered, stopping some of their fire but not all of it. Smaller explosions blossomed along her biomechanical suit. Still she kept coming.

How was this possible? Why were the extraterrestrials firing on their own queen? Could they rebel against her? Or had Levinson figured out some way to get control of some of them? Did it have something to do with the sphere?

A lot of questions, and no answers. Patricia wasn't going to get any answers, either, as long as she was trapped in the ejection seat. She returned to working the buckles, looking back and forth between them and the battle.

Suddenly the fighters careened out of control.

* * *

The alien message had momentarily crippled Dikembe as well. When he recovered, he turned to Floyd.

"She's coming."

* * *

Inside the isolation chamber, Okun and Isaacs saw two aliens with blasters come up to the glass. They raised the blasters, and Okun took Isaacs' hand, resigned to his fate.

He was happy, in a way, that at least he had awakened in time that if they were going to die, they could die together.

The aliens opened fire, shattering the glass as Okun and Isaacs dove for cover.

* * *

Outside in the corridor, Floyd couldn't tell exactly what was going on, but knew it was bad. It was time for action. It was time for Floyd Rosenberg to prove he was more than a bean counter, more than an observer while everyone else hogged all the heroic glory.

"Out of the way!" he shouted, and even though Dikembe didn't move Floyd blasted the control panel. The door opened and Floyd unleashed a barrage from the blaster, shooting his way in with barely any idea of what he was shooting at. Blaster fire pocked the walls and blew out computer monitors, filling the room with smoke.

As it started to settle, Floyd looked around. All the aliens in the room were dead. He couldn't believe it! He'd actually cowboyed his way into a rescue, and shot all the bad guys! Dikembe walked up behind him.

"I told you I'd figure it out," Floyd said, maybe a little smugly.

Then he was jerked off balance as an alien tentacle snaked around his legs and pulled him to the side. He screamed, losing his blaster and flailing around, trying to get a grip on the smooth floor—but Dikembe was there, machete blades flashing out to sever the tentacle and then stab the life out of the wounded alien.

After that, it was really quiet for a moment. Dikembe studied him carefully.

"You talk too much," he said.

* * *

Okun poked his head up from behind a research console.

"Baby, we're saved!" he said.

Isaacs' answer was a low agonized groan. Okun rushed over to him and saw that an alien blast had torn though his chest. He knelt beside Isaacs.

"You're gonna be okay," he said firmly.

Isaacs reached up to touch Okun's face. "I love you so much," he said, his voice weak. Shock was already setting in.

"Hey. We'll get you to sick bay and fix you up," Okun

said. It was a bad wound, but the Whitmore Hospital was the best. They could help. He had to believe that.

"It's too late," Isaacs said. "Just… stay with me."

Okun shook his head. "Don't say that." It couldn't be true. He couldn't have just awakened only to have Milton die on him. No.

"It's okay," Isaacs said.

What, Okun thought. What was okay? "Who's gonna water my orchids? Who's gonna comb my hair? Who's gonna remind me to put pants on?"

Isaacs smiled through his agony.

"You always made me laugh," he said, his voice fading. "I'm so happy you're back." Then his eyes fluttered closed and he died in Okun's arms. All Okun could do was watch him go, and think of the twenty years that the aliens had taken from them before they had returned to take Isaacs forever.

"More are coming!" Dikembe called out. He was watching through the broken windows.

Okun jumped up, his face a stony mask. It was the first time Dikembe or Floyd had ever seen him without a smile or a look of boyish wonder.

"Give me that," he said, and he snatched the blaster out of Floyd's hands.

"But, but that's mine—" Floyd protested. Dikembe sheathed his machetes and picked up blasters from the dead aliens. He threw one to Floyd and they fanned out in the isolation chamber, guns trained on the door.

A moment later the aliens poured through the doorway and all three opened fire.

47

Without the destroyer cannon, the ground forces manning the approach to Area 51 did their best, but their small-arms fire couldn't stop the queen. Battered as she was, she reached the complex of buildings and strode directly toward the prison wing. There she started tearing into the roof as the remaining hybrid fighters made firing run after firing run.

Her armor took everything they could throw at it, but she was weakening and appeared to know it. With a gesture she drew all of the alien fighter craft in around her, thousands of them, sending them into tight spins that surrounded her like a moving shield. The base forces fired at it, destroying some of the ships, but there were too many for their fire to penetrate and reach the queen.

"What the hell's happening?" Dylan shouted. The world outside spun past.

"She's using all her fighters as a shield!" Jake called back. That included the ship they were in.

"We gotta get out of this tornado!" Jake could barely hear Dylan's voice over the sound of the vortex.

"Every tornado has an eye, right?" Dylan yelled back. "If we want to get a shot at her, we gotta get up there."

"You're kidding, right?" Charlie said over the comm.

"We have no manual controls left!"

"Does this thing have a fusion drive?" Jake asked.

"Are you *nuts*? It's made for outer space! Down here we'll burn up!"

Aha, Jake thought. "So that's a yes. Just a short burst. I think it's our only chance."

"Yeah," Charlie said. "Our only chance to die."

A burst of interference from the radio was followed by the voice of a command center tech officer.

"Two minutes until Earth's core breach…"

"Dylan, you're ranking officer," Jake said. "It's your call." They were spinning so fast that Jake could barely move from the g-forces, so he almost didn't see Dylan's smile as he spoke.

"You nearly killed me once," Dylan said. "I survived that. Rain, are you in?"

"On three," Rain said, all business.

Dylan reached for the fusion drive switch. "One… two…"

The fusion drives were designed for burns across thousands of miles at accelerations way beyond what a small, light ship could withstand against atmospheric friction. It was entirely possible that when Dylan and Rain hit the switches, their fighters would break apart into little fireballs, quickly lost in the tornado of spinning fighters.

"Three," Dylan said.

"Aaaaaahhhhhhh!" Charlie screamed as the two craft burst straight up through the wall of fighters, tearing a path through the queen's shield, moving so fast that the air seemed to burn and glow outside the cockpit windows. Jake's vision went red from the g-forces, and even over the roar of the destruction around them he could hear the roaring of blood in his ears.

As quickly as they'd flipped the switches on, Dylan and Rain flipped them off again, but in that split second they'd shot two miles into the sky.

"Still alive!" Jake crowed as his vision cleared up and he realized the ships were still in one piece. Mostly. Some little bits were falling off, and there was more smoke than might be considered optimal. But, hey, it had worked!

Dylan was working the joystick. "Our controls are back."

"Yeah," Charlie said, "but our engines are fried." The two fighters slowed, reached the peak of their climb... and began to fall back to Earth.

"So it's a controlled dive," Rain said, which just about summed it up.

* * *

Inside the command center, Adams knew the time had come. They couldn't defend themselves anymore.

"Issue the evacuation order!" He turned to Catherine. "We have to go. Now."

"What about the sphere?" she asked.

The look he gave her said it all. The sphere was lost. Maybe the war was lost, too.

* * *

David pulled the school bus to a halt at the Area 51 gates, watching as the alien queen tore into the building near where the destroyer cannon had fallen against it.

"That's close enough!" Julius said.

"She's going right for it," David said. His mind raced, but he had no idea what they could do to stop her. If she'd survived the fusion bomb...

"Why are they turning into a tornado?" Daisy asked.

"They're protecting her," David said. All of them watched as more and more of the alien fighters were drawn into the protective vortex, spinning around the queen so fast that the attacking human jets couldn't get at her.

If her shields were down, though, the queen was vulnerable, and she'd been damaged by the fusion blast—no question about that. How could they penetrate that wall of fighters? There had to be a way, and if there was, they needed to find it fast, because she would soon have the sphere.

She tore another chunk out of the roof, digging deeper into the prison wing's interior. David knew the isolation chamber was reinforced, but it wouldn't stop her for long. Their time was running out.

*   *   *

Okun was a man of science, a man who loved knowledge, who believed the best about people, and who now was so blindsided by grief that he had become a man possessed.

Milton was dead, after watching over him for twenty years, and Okun would never know anyone else like him. The loss tore a hole in him so wide and deep that the only thing capable of filling it was alien blood. He blasted away at the creatures even though he'd never held a gun in his life, watching each go down and moving on to the next. He exulted in every impact and every wound.

When they were all down, he shot their bodies, until at last he heard Dikembe next to him saying something. Okun stopped firing and heard what he was saying.

"It's over, my friend."

Yes it is, Okun thought. *Everything is over.*

"They're dead!" Rosenberg was riding a wave of adrenaline. "We killed all of them!"

As he spoke, the ceiling of the room tore loose and daylight flooded in, along with a shower of concrete and steel debris. They turned toward the hole in the ceiling as a massive alien claw reached down into the isolation chamber and closed itself around the sphere.

"Except that one," Rosenberg said.

Okun dropped his blaster. He didn't care about anything anymore.

* * *

"My God," David said, looking through a pair of binoculars he'd gotten from one of the campers. "She's got it."

He watched the queen hold the sphere up to her face. She had been hunting it for thousands of years, and now she held it in her hand—the last member of the species that had created her. Her mouth opened in what must have been the gruesome alien equivalent of a triumphant grin.

Then her head jerked up and David saw two of the alien fighters flash upward, tearing themselves free from the wall surrounding her. What was this? A mutiny? In a hive-mind organism? That wasn't possible...

* * *

As they fell out of the sky, Jake spotted the queen. It was harder than he'd expected because of all the smoke and dust coming out of Area 51, drawn skyward by the vortex of fighters around her.

"There she is," he said, pointing.

Dylan worked the joystick to angle the ship's glide toward the queen. "We only get one shot at this," he said. "Make it count."

They lined up their shots, knowing the fate of the human race—of planet Earth itself—rested on their trigger fingers. The queen peered at a little shining metal sphere, almost like a marble...

Oh, Jake thought. *That must be the thing Levinson wanted to get out of the wreckage.*

"You didn't die for nothing, Uncle Jin," Rain said in Chinese. She held her ship steady, diving almost straight down.

"For my mom and dad," Dylan said.

Jake flexed his fingers on the firing controls.

"For our families, Charlie."

"For our families," Charlie echoed.

The queen looked up at them as they fell into the wide upper eye of the tornado. Jake and Charlie knew they would never have a better shot than this one. At almost the same instant they started firing, their two ships strafing the queen down both sides of her armor. Explosions staggered her, and a moment later a much larger one blew out the back of the armor. The queen stumbled and leaned into the vortex as the two rogue fighters fell into it.

This was the tricky part. They had to pull out of the dive and make it through the wall in one piece.

"Keep shooting, Charlie!" Jake called out.

"What do you think I'm doing?"

They shot their way through the wall of the vortex and blasted back out again into the open air above the desert. Now their ships were a real mess, trailing pieces of wreckage and plumes of smoke.

"Mayday, mayday," Jake said, while Dylan tried to keep their final glide as shallow and nonfatal as possible. "We are doing down... Charlie, does this thing have ejection seats?"

"Negati—"

48

"Let me see those!" Julius grabbed the binoculars from David and peered through them. "David, they're shooting at themselves!"

The vortex slowed more, and began to lose cohesion. The two fighters that had broken free were now diving back down, their blasters tearing the queen's armor apart. The gargantuan alien fell to her knees as a fireball blew the back of the armor out. The fighters shrieked overhead and disappeared into twin plumes of smoke, followed shortly by loud twin crashes.

Julius and David and all the children turned back just in time to see the alien queen pitch forward, hitting the tarmac outside the prison wing with a thunderous impact they thought they could feel even this far away.

* * *

The sphere bounced out of her grasp as Adams and Catherine ran out from the command center, the evacuation nearly complete. They saw the queen go down and lose the sphere, and they heard the cheers of the surviving ground troops. For a moment Adams let himself believe that it was over.

Only for a moment, though, because the queen's armor fell away and she struggled out of it, oozing viscous fluid from a number of wounds but focused on one thing and one thing only—the sphere, still rolling across the pavement.

She staggered toward it, crawling with her head low to the ground, reaching out greedily, badly wounded but still dangerous. Looking beyond her, Adams saw a ship coming their way. Bigger than her personal ship, smaller than a city destroyer. She'd called a taxi, and was running like hell to reach it before the human forces could finish her off.

Suddenly, in between her and the ship…

Adams squinted out over the salt flats.

Was that a school bus?

*   *   *

The camp kids cheered when the queen went down, and then they went silent when she climbed out of her destroyed armor. They were *really* quiet as she reached her slimy claw toward the sphere.

"Oh, come on," David said. "Not again."

"Twenty seconds to Earth core breach," a tech said from the command center.

"All right then," David said. He watched the queen trying to get up. "No," he said. "No, you're not." He slammed the bus into gear and stomped on the accelerator.

"Mr. Levinson," Bobby said. "I think you're going the wrong way."

David kept the gas pedal jammed onto the floor and centered the queen in the windshield.

"David!" His father stared at him as if he'd finally lost it—and maybe he had, he mused. "A school bus full of children is not a weapon. David! *David!*"

Ten seconds, David thought. *Maybe less now.*

The queen looked up as the bus roared toward her. She was smaller now that she was out of her biomechanical suit, but still big enough that if she planted a foot on the bus, everyone inside would be crushed. Her head, though…

Five seconds.

The bus hit the sphere, knocking it away from the queen's grasp. Then, a moment later, the vehicle hit the queen's head, exceeding its state-mandated maximum speed of sixty-five miles per hour. Not as fast as David would have wanted to go but, as it turned out, sixty-five miles per hour was more than enough to explode the head like a watermelon dropped off the Empire State Building.

Viscous goo in various shades of green and blue splattered the windshield and bits of the queen slid down the windows. David took a deep breath and let it out in a long sigh. Julius peered through the goo, and behind him the kids stared out as best they could. None of them knew exactly what to say.

The sphere kept rolling for another few yards before coming to a stop in the desert, shining in the late afternoon sun.

* * *

In the tech room of the *Alison*, Ana-Lisa cheered and wrapped Boudreaux up in a big hug as the plasma drill flickered and went out. The submersible rocked in the rush of water collapsing into the space left empty by the plasma beam.

"We're alive!" Ana-Lisa shouted.

McQuaide went one better. "We're rich."

Boudreaux got on the shortwave. "General Adams, the drill is retracting! The core is secure!"

They all heard the cheers from the other end of the connection.

*   *   *

Catherine and President Adams saw the alien queen's gruesome end, and then looked up to see the hundreds of remaining alien fighters tumbling to the ground or colliding in thunderous fireballs. They walked outside, as more and more of the ships crashed, until the skies over Area 51 were clear.

"Not bad," Adams said. "Not bad at all."

Around them, people began to cheer and hug. This time they knew it was real. Humanity had won again.

*   *   *

Patricia had just gotten free of her harness when she saw the two alien fighters take down first the alien rescue ship, and then the queen herself. She stood out in the emptiness of the salt flats watching the mass exodus of alien craft, filled with a fierce pride and joy.

Twice the aliens had attacked.

Twice humanity had banded together to defeat them.

Then her mood changed as the ramp of a nearby crashed fighter creaked open and fell to the ground. Maybe the war wasn't over quite yet, Patricia thought, remembering some of the stories she'd heard about Dikembe Umbutu. She unholstered her sidearm and leveled it at the ramp door of the closest fighter as it opened. She'd seen in the isolation chamber how fast they could move.

"Come and get me!" she shouted, and fired off a round that ricocheted away from the hull near the ramp.

"Whoa, whoa!" a voice called from inside. "Put that gun down, baby!"

Jake! she thought as her eyes went wide.

"Jake!" she cried out as he poked his head into view. She ran to him and gave him the kind of kiss you could only get when you'd just helped save the world.

When they broke the kiss, they saw Dylan watching. He and Jake both smiled.

She did, too.

"We're not even married yet, and you already want to shoot me?" Jake said.

"Shut up and kiss me," she said. He obeyed.

Charlie was standing next to Rain a little way off, both of them watching the reunion.

"We should maybe try that," Charlie said nonchalantly. "Doesn't that look fun?"

After a pause Rain said, "Dinner first."

Charlie couldn't resist a little fist pump. "Yes!"

*   *   *

As the last of the fleeing alien fighters entered the drilling ship's hangars, its plasma beam turned off. The ocean water rushed into the space it had occupied, giving off a roar audible from Western Europe all the way to the east coast of North America.

The ship began to rise, tearing itself free of the roots that it had begun to grow around all of its landing legs, and leaving mile-deep pits in the ground where those legs had anchored. When it had lifted itself clear, the ship retracted the landing petals.

Survivors who had been below its massive body looked up, and could see the sky again.

*   *   *

"Do you think she's dead?" Sam asked as Julius and David got all the kids off the bus.

"You're asking me?" Julius said. David was the expert in this stuff.

Kevin wrinkled his nose. "What's that smell?"

Already the alien queen was beginning to stink. "Imagine after a week in the hot desert sun," Henry said. Felix walked over to her body and reached out toward the immense head.

"Don't touch it!" Bobby ordered his little brother. Who knew what kinds of diseases it might carry? He'd read *The War of the Worlds*.

From Area 51's front gate, Catherine and Adams walked toward the group surrounding David.

"Director Levinson," Adams said. "Well done."

"Thank you, Mr. President," David said. Then he turned his attention to Catherine and started to say something to her. He wasn't even sure what, but she cut him off.

"Don't say anything. You're just going to ruin it."

She has a point, he thought. *Perhaps the situation calls for nonverbal communication.* He was about to kiss her, when his father piped up.

"Who are you? David didn't say anything about a beautiful woman in his life."

"Dad," David said, but Julius kept talking as he interposed himself between David and Catherine.

"I'm Julius. His father."

"*Enchanté*," Catherine said. "I'm Catherine Marceaux. It's nice to meet you."

*　　*　　*

Julius gave her an appraising look.

"Oh, you're French," he said. "Not perfect... but neither is he." Why couldn't David find himself a Jewish girl, Julius wondered. Before he could say it, though, he saw David reading his mind.

"Dad. Would you give us a minute?" David said.

Julius wasn't always good at knowing when to get out of the way, but this time he could pick up the cue.

"I was never here," he said, and he walked off toward the kids, all the while pretending not to notice his David laying a kiss on the French woman. And why not, Julius thought. What was the point of repelling an alien invasion—*again*—if you couldn't get a kiss from a pretty girl afterward?

Sam and her siblings were gathered a little apart from all of the campers, who were still watching the dead queen and daring one another to touch her.

"I've been thinking," Julius said to her. "Maybe you guys should stay with me for a little while."

She looked touched, and then she smiled at him.

"I'd like that," she said. "And you owe me a car."

With an answering grin, Julius looked over at the campers and their examination of the queen's carcass.

"I'll need a bigger boat," he mused. So the situation wasn't all bad.

49

Having finally navigated their way out of the wreckage of the prison wing, Dikembe, Rosenberg, and Okun came running out toward the sphere, still lying a distance from the outstretched hand of the dead queen. Okun put his palms on it.

"Are you okay?"

The sphere rose into the air. "I am," it said. "Thanks to you."

"Ah. This wasn't all for nothing," Okun said.

"You are a remarkable species," the sphere said.

"Not so primitive after all," Okun said, wanting to challenge it a little for looking down its nose—figuratively, of course—at the human race that had done so much to protect it. "You know, a lot of people have sacrificed a lot of things to keep you alive."

There was the briefest of pauses. Then the sphere spoke again.

"Thank you."

Standing nearby, Rosenberg stared at his blaster like a kid with a new toy. *Accountant no more*, he thought. *I'm a battle-hardened veteran of the alien invasion. They'll call this one the War of '16.*

"You think they'll let me keep this?" he asked Dikembe.

Dikembe looked over at him. Floyd looked back, steeling himself. What cruel, dismissive thing would Dikembe hit him with next?

"You have the heart of a warrior," Dikembe said.

This almost brought Floyd to tears. "That's the nicest thing anyone has ever said to me," he said, spreading his arms and still holding the blaster in one hand. "Bring it in for a hug, big man."

Dikembe didn't move.

"No."

Floyd dropped his arms. "Too far," he said. "Now I know the boundaries."

Okun was still talking to the sphere, and judging from the expression on his face, he really liked what he was hearing. Floyd wondered what the next revelation would be.

* * *

Gathered at the edge of the main compound, the survivors looked through the crowd, searching for familiar faces, beginning that sorrowful task of counting the dead.

"You're a hero," Catherine said. "Again." She and David were arm in arm.

Then they heard the familiar sound of alien fighters and spun around. It wasn't aliens coming out of the fighters, however, but five human pilots. Jake and Dylan with Patricia in one, and Charlie following Rain out of the other. Dylan was limping.

"I think they're the real heroes," David said. As the pilots came close, Adams stepped to the front of the crowd.

"Hell of a job," he said, and he snapped them a salute. The entire crowd, military and civilian alike, followed suit. The young pilots, newly minted heroes of Earth, saluted back.

David left Catherine's side and walked up to Jake. "I can't believe you guys made it out," he said.

Jake looked over at Patricia. "I had to keep a promise."

We all had promises to keep, didn't we? David thought.

"I'm sorry about your father," he said to Patricia. He and Tom Whitmore hadn't always seen eye to eye, but they'd grown to respect each other and by the time Whitmore climbed into the tug, David had counted him a friend.

Patricia nodded. The loss was still too fresh for her to really grapple with.

"We're all still here because of him," she said simply. One man's sacrifice had kept billions of others alive.

Suddenly there was motion on the horizon. Visible even from nearly three thousand miles away, the alien ship rose out of Earth's atmosphere, dragging a trail of fiery clouds and debris behind it. For a long moment it remained visible, and then it was gone into deep space.

Dylan couldn't help himself.

"Is that all you got?" he roared at the top of his lungs, channeling his dad. *Family tradition*, he thought. *My dad fought aliens, I fight aliens. My dad talked trash to them, and so do I.*

His shout broke something loose in the crowd, and everyone else there shouted and roared, too. Some of them shook their fists—or raised fingers—at the departing beaten enemy. Others turned to their friends, lovers, and family. They had survived. Relief flooded through them and came out as joyous celebration.

David stood with Patricia, a little aside from the cheering, exultant group. He knew how close it had been, how narrowly humanity had averted extinction. He also knew the aliens would come back.

"I don't know if this planet will survive another attack," he said quietly. He didn't want to interfere with the celebration, but he had to say it to someone. Before Patricia could respond, however, Brakish Okun appeared, the sphere hovering and glowing behind him.

"Director Levinson," he said. "You wouldn't believe what kind of weapons this thing has on its proverbial hard drive. It wants us to lead their galactic resistance." Okun sounded as if he thought this was the greatest idea ever conceived by a sentient mind.

"What do you mean?" David asked. Earth wasn't in any shape to lead a space war.

"Two words," Okun said.

David waited, knowing Okun wouldn't be able to keep it to himself for long... and he was right.

"Interstellar travel."

David nodded. That made sense. The ships had arrived through wormholes, but the humans hadn't yet found any clue as to how the aliens created them, maintained them, operated them...

"Take the fight to them," Adams said. It sounded as if he considered this an excellent idea. David thought he could see his strategist's brain already working at the logistics. This was a little soon, wasn't it? While the fires were still burning, they were already contemplating their counterattack?

Then again, maybe it's not, he mused. Maybe there was no time like the present.

Dylan looked around at the salt flats, the distant mountains, the cheering people...

"I was getting bored of this planet anyway," he said.

Amen, Jake thought. With the help of the sphere's technologies, they would hunt the aliens, would find them wherever they were, and they would make sure that no planet ever had to go through what Earth had just suffered. The aliens had picked a fight with the wrong sentient race.

He took a step up to the sphere.

"When do we leave?" he asked. Then when he saw Patricia looking at him, he added, "After we are married, of course."

Brakish Okun wore a grin, like he always did, but now it had an edge.

"We're gonna kick some serious alien ass," he said.

ABOUT THE AUTHOR

Alex Irvine has published about forty books, including original novels *Buyout, The Narrows,* and *A Scattering of Jades*. His most recent books are *The Division: New York Collapse* and *Batman: Arkham Knight – The Riddler's Gambit*. His other licensed work includes novelizations of *Dawn of the Planet of the Apes, Pacific Rim,* and *Tintin,* plus books related to *Avengers, Transformers, Supernatural,* and *Deus Ex.* He lives in Maine but still roots for the Detroit Tigers.

ACKNOWLEDGEMENTS

Thanks to Dean Devlin and Roland Emmerich, for the first *Independence Day* film (which I watched maybe a dozen times) and for this new one (which I'll probably watch a dozen more); to Greg Keyes, for a slam-bang prequel that gave me more rich backstory to mine; to Steve Saffel and Josh Izzo for keeping the process all on track; to everyone at Titan, just on general principles, because they're all excellent people who love books; and to my wife, Lindsay, and my kids Ian, Emma, Avi, and Violet, for being swell.

INDEPENDENCE DAY: RESURGENCE

OFFICIAL TIMELINE

FIRST CONTACT (Roswell, NM, 7/47): An extraterrestrial craft crash lands near a ranch in Roswell, New Mexico. The U.S. military launches an investigation.

SILENT ZONE (Nevada Desert, 1970s): Dr. Brakish Okun arrives at Area 51 to work with the NSA and CIA on the study of the New Mexico ship.
(*THE COMPLETE INDEPENDENCE DAY OMNIBUS*)

ARRIVAL AND ATTACK (Middle of Atlantic, 7/2/96): A massive alien mother ship enters Earth's orbit, deploying 36 city destroyers to annihilate the world's largest cities. Within 48 hours, 108 cities are reduced to ashes.
(*INDEPENDENCE DAY: THE ORIGINAL MOVIE ADAPTATION*)

EARTH STRIKES BACK (Nevada Desert, 7/4/96): Earth's nations launch a globally coordinated counterattack, destroying the alien mother ship and eliminating the extraterrestrial threat.

WAR IN THE DESERT (Saudi Arabia, 7/4/96): Military pilots in the Saudi Arabian desert witness the destruction

of Jerusalem and engage in a hand-to-hand assault with extraterrestrial crash survivors.
(*THE COMPLETE INDEPENDENCE DAY OMNIBUS*)

TERROR FROM THE DEEP (Atlantic Ocean, 7/5/96): A functioning extraterrestrial craft is discovered beneath the Atlantic Ocean. An investigation—headed by Captain Joshua Adams—is implemented by the U.S. military. (*INDEPENDENCE DAY: DARK FATHOM*)

THE WORLD REBUILDS (11/30/96): Aside from a small pocket of resistance in an isolated area of the African Congo, the alien threat has been neutralized—and the world begins to rise from the ashes. Reconstruction starts as the great cities, monuments, and landmarks of the world are slowly restored to their former glory.

LEADERS UNITE (Royal Palace of Naples, Piazza del Plebiscito, Naples, Italy, 3/17/98): Centuries-old conflicts and political distrust are dissolved to create an unprecedented unity among the nations of the world.

EARTH SPACE DEFENSE FORMED (Geneva, Switzerland, 5/25/98): Following the newly established global peace alliance, the United Nations creates the Earth Space Defense program (ESD) to serve as an early warning system and united global defense unit. In conjunction with this announcement, the ESD launches a worldwide publicity and recruitment campaign.

F-22 ADDS ALIEN TECH (Elmendorf Air Force Base, Anchorage, Alaska, 1/8/99): ESD applies recovered alien shield technology to an F-22 Raptor to understand how they can better integrate other alien technology into future full hybrid fighters. This light experiment will serve as the foundation for the dramatic innovations that the ESD delivers nearly a decade later.

PRESIDENT WHITMORE'S FAREWELL (Washington, D.C., 01/15/01): After two terms in office, President Thomas Whitmore makes his final address to the nation, clearing the way for the newly elected President William Grey.

CONGO GROUND WAR CONTINUES (Democratic Republic of the Congo, Africa, 8/10/01): A faction of aliens continues to hold out in a remote part of the African Congo—the survivors of a stranded city destroyer. The ESD repeatedly offers their support and assistance to the local government, but is met by aggressive refusal. (*INDEPENDENCE DAY: CRUCIBLE*)

U.S. ARMY ADOPTS ALIEN WEAPONRY (El Paso, TX, 10/23/03): Applying new data from recovered alien weaponry, U.S. Army scientists make dramatic advances in applying their findings to military applications.

ALIEN PRISON RUMORS (Area 51, NV, 2/7/05): Rumors of a top-secret alien prison below Area 51 start to gain traction with the general public. ESD officials offer no comment regarding the legitimacy of these reports.

WORLD MOURNS COL. STEVEN HILLER (Area 51, NV, 4/27/07): While he is test-piloting the ESD's first alien–human hybrid fighter, an unknown malfunction causes the untimely death of Col. Hiller. He is survived by his wife, Jasmine, and son, Dylan. (*INDEPENDENCE DAY: CRUCIBLE*)

ESD MOON BASE OPERATIONAL (2/21/09): Monitored from its command center in Beijing, China, the Earth Space

Defense Moon Base opens. Designed with both offensive and defensive weapons capabilities, the Moon Base is the first of several planetary bases designed to monitor our solar system for potential alien threats.

PRESIDENT LANFORD ELECTED (Washington, D.C., 1/20/13): Elizabeth Lanford, the forward-thinking former vice-president under President Lucas Jacobs, is sworn in as the 45th president of the United States, becoming the first woman in history to hold the office.

NEXT GEN HYBRID FIGHTER UNVEILED (Tokyo, Japan, 8/19/14): The next generation of hybrid alien–human vehicles and weapons systems are introduced, after years of research and development from ESD scientists around the world. One of the standouts is the H-8 Global Defender hybrid fighter.

HONORING 20 YEARS OF GLOBAL UNITY (Washington, D.C., 7/4/16): "As we remember the last twenty years, we must also look to the future. The world has rebuilt stronger than we ever imagined and we must promise ourselves, as well as future generations, that we're never caught off-guard again. We must continue to work together to secure the future of the human race—for as long as we stay united, we will survive."

DON'T MISS A SINGLE PART OF THE INDEPENDENCE DAY SAGA

THE NOVELS:

The Complete Independence Day Omnibus
by Dean Devlin & Roland Emmerich, and Steven Molstad

Independence Day: Crucible by Greg Keyes

Independence Day Resurgence by Alex Irvine

BEHIND THE SCENES:

The Art of Independence Day Resurgence

THE GRAPHIC NOVELS:

Independence Day: Dark Fathom
by Victor Gischler and Steve Scott, Rodney Ramos,
Alex Shibao, and Tazio Bettin

Independence Day: The Original Movie Adaptation

TITANBOOKS.COM
TITAN-COMICS.COM

ALSO AVAILABLE FROM TITAN BOOKS

INDEPENDENCE DAY RESURGENCE
BY GREG KEYES

THE OFFICIAL PREQUEL TO THE BLOCKBUSTER FILM!

The invaders were defeated on Independence Day,
but the war left deep scars in the planet and its
people. The roundup of remaining alien soldiers led
to chaotic combat worldwide, and their abandoned
technology led to a new era of military weaponry.
This is the story of the survivors, including war heroes
Steven Hiller and David Levinson, of the rebuilding,
and of the next generation of Earth's defenders.

AVAILABLE NOW!

TITANBOOKS.COM

ALSO AVAILABLE FROM TITAN BOOKS

THE COMPLETE
INDEPENDENCE DAY OMNIBUS
BY DEAN DEVLIN & ROLAND EMMERICH,
AND STEPHEN MOLSTAD

The official novelization of the original blockbuster
that started it all, as a force of unimaginable magnitude
arrives on Earth. Its mission: to eliminate all human
life on the planet. Three complete novels, including:

SILENT ZONE
The official prequel to the original film, revealing
the secrets of Area 51.

WAR IN THE DESERT
Reeling from the enemy onslaught, a few surviving
military pilots face the aliens in fierce hand-to-hand
combat in the Middle East.

AVAILABLE NOW!

TITANBOOKS.COM

ALSO AVAILABLE FROM TITAN BOOKS

THE ART AND MAKING OF INDEPENDENCE DAY RESURGENCE
BY SIMON WARD

The Art and Making of Independence Day Resurgence takes readers from the aftermath of the '96 invasion, through the rebuilding of the planet, and the new, terrifying threat about to hit Earth. This official companion is packed with incredible concept art, costume design, behind-the-scenes photography, and exclusive interviews with cast and crew including Jeff Goldblum and a foreword from director Roland Emmerich.

AVAILABLE NOW!

TITANBOOKS.COM

ALSO AVAILABLE FROM TITAN COMICS

INDEPENDENCE DAY
DARK FATHOM
BY VICTOR GISCHLER AND STEVE SCOTT, RODNEY RAMOS, ALEX SHIBAO, AND TAZIO BETTIN

As our world unites against invaders from beyond the stars, beneath the Atlantic Ocean, another mysterious craft prompts a top-secret investigation by the US military, one which could prove the key to humanity's survival... or its ultimate destruction. The graphic novel collection of the brand new *Independence Day* comic series from Victor Gischler, Steve Scott, Rodney Ramos, Alex Shibao, and Tazio Bettin.

AVAILABLE NOW!

TITAN-COMICS.COM

FOR MORE FANTASTIC FICTION, AUTHOR
EVENTS, EXCLUSIVE EXCERPTS,
COMPETITIONS, LIMITED EDITIONS AND MORE

VISIT OUR WEBSITE
titanbooks.com

LIKE US ON FACEBOOK
facebook.com/titanbooks

FOLLOW US ON TWITTER
@TitanBooks

EMAIL US
readerfeedback@titanemail.com